ABOUT THE AUTHOR

Steven Knight runs his own production company, Knight Whitehall, and has a flourishing TV career as both writer and director. He has devised several game shows for BBC and ITV, including the prime-time interactive show *Talking Telephone Numbers*. He is a successful comedy writer and has written for a string of mainstream and alternative performers, including Ken Dodd, Jim Davidson, Terry Wogan, Chris Tarrant, Philip Schofield, Jonathan Ross and Jasper Carrott. He is the author of two previous novels – *The Movie House*, which was selected for the W. H. Smith fresh talent promotion, and *Alphabet City* – both published by Penguin. He is married with one son and lives in North London.

By the same author

The Movie House
Alphabet City

OUT OF THE BLUE

STEVEN KNIGHT

VIKING

VIKING

Published by the Penguin Group
Penguin Books Ltd, 27 Wrights Lane, London w8 5tz, England
Penguin Books USA Inc., 375 Hudson Street, New York, New York 10014, USA
Penguin Books Australia Ltd, Ringwood, Victoria, Australia
Penguin Books Canada Ltd, 10 Alcorn Avenue, Toronto, Ontario, Canada m4v 3b2
Penguin Books (NZ) Ltd, 182–190 Wairau Road, Auckland 10, New Zealand

Penguin Books Ltd, Registered Offices: Harmondsworth, Middlesex, England

First published 1996
1 3 5 7 9 10 8 6 4 2
First edition

Copyright © Steven Knight, 1996

The moral right of the author has been asserted

Set in 11/13pt Monotype Sabon
Typeset by Datix International Limited, Bungay, Suffolk
Printed in England by Clays Ltd, St Ives plc

A CIP catalogue record for this book is available from the British Library

ISBN 0-670-85711-4

Bastions of wealth
are no defence for the man
who treads the grand altar of justice.
   But ancient violence longs to breed,
new violence comes
no war, no force, no prayer
can hinder the midnight fury stamped
with parent fury moving through the house.

Agamemnon, Aeschylus

CHAPTER ONE

'Peter the painter.'

'Again?'

'My name is Peter. I'm a painter.'

The Cypriot journalist nodded and sucked on his unfiltered cigarette. The Aegean Sea was dark green all around them, and black barren islands jutted out from the surface of the water like the knees and elbows of a giant sleeping on the seabed.

'My name is Thomas,' the journalist said.

Thomas leant over and shook Peter's hand. They had both gone out to the tiny viewing deck at the back of the Flying Dolphin hydrofoil at the same time, and the stillness of the dawn and the beauty of the surroundings made conversation inevitable. Thomas had already explained that he was a journalist for an Athens newspaper. It was the first thing he had said when he had plopped heavily on to the hard wooden bench at the back of the boat, resting his elbow on the flag-pole that stuck out at a forty-five degree angle over the foaming white wake of the engine. He had had a copy of that morning's edition on his lap and he had chuckled at a certain article and then explained why he was laughing. It was because his piece on page six had been badly butchered and didn't make sense any more.

'You are lucky to be a painter,' he said. 'When you paint a picture, no one cuts pieces out of the middle. You paint a horse, no one comes and chops off the horse's head.'

'No, I suppose not.'

'What do you paint?'

'What I see. I'm sorry that is an appalling answer.'

'It is a good answer. It is good enough for me. I know nothing about painting.'

Thomas took a last drag on his fat Greek cigarette and flicked it into the tumult behind the boat, where it disappeared. The sun was rising and the sky was crimson to the east. The air was crimson too, and soft and fragrant. To be on board a boat at dawn in the Aegean, weaving between barren and nameless islands, talking carelessly to a total stranger was a kind of heaven for Peter Callow. It was heaven because it was total freedom. He felt that all his life he had been wearing a heavy armour of clothes that had never properly fitted him and now, at last, he was naked. Even though Thomas looked weary and overheated and sombre, Peter couldn't help but laugh at everything he said. It was as if Thomas were part of the landscape, another enchanting refraction of the light. How delightful it was to be having a conversation of absolutely no significance whatsoever, with someone he would never meet again for the rest of time.

'You see, it is the light,' Thomas said, waving his podgy arm in the air.

'What is?'

'It is the light that brings people like you to my country. There is a certain sort of light here that attracts painters.' Thomas chuckled in the vast chamber of his belly. 'It makes me wonder if you have any light at all in your own country. Maybe it is always dark there.'

Peter laughed as if he were drunk on the light.

'But, of course, I know that it isn't,' Thomas said. 'I know that there is light in London too, and New York for that matter. But you don't care for your own light, so you come to steal ours. You take it home with you on pieces of canvas. It is a kind of theft. It is nothing more than imperialism. What were you before you were a painter?'

The engine revved against a wave. No consequence, no anchors, no purpose other than to drift in this exquisite Aegean light, like a speck of dust.

'I was a designer,' Peter said.

'What did you design?'

'Ships.'

'What sort of ships?'

Peter smiled. This was to be the first test of his anonymity.

The first time he could be other than the man he had always been.

'I really don't remember,' he said.

'Ah, but I do,' Thomas said, getting to his feet. 'I have been an admirer of your work for many years, Mr Callow.'

Peter was unwilling to feel the tug of the anchor, so desperate not to hear the rattle of its chain, the deep, resonant thud as it hit the seabed.

'How do you know my second name?' Peter Callow said.

'I know everything about you,' Thomas said. 'I know that you made a deal with someone in return for your freedom. I know that you sold your soul in order to escape from a life you couldn't live any more.'

Peter Callow got to his feet. Then he froze when Thomas produced a snub-nosed revolver.

'Sit down Mr Callow.'

'Who the hell are you?'

'Not Thomas. Not even a journalist. But then none of us are who we say we are. Isn't that right?'

Peter tried to make a break for the door back into the cabin, but Thomas blocked his path.

'I suppose you could say that I am your past and I have caught up with you. The deal you made has fallen through. Your friend asked me to tell you that he is sorry but he had no choice.'

Thomas pointed the revolver at Peter's head. As the Flying Dolphin sketched its thin white line through the vast greenness of the sea, as the gulls wheeled silently overhead, Peter Callow and Thomas had their short and murderous conversation, over the thumping of the hydrofoil engine. And as the boat turned its nose towards its destination, there was a muffled click, and then Peter Callow's body was dumped into the tumult of spray behind the boat, which foamed red for a few moments. Then what remained of his body, after it had been half-consumed by the engine, floated out into the green vastness, to be carried effortlessly by the gentle currents of the Aegean Sea, and to be washed up in pieces two days later on the island of Skiathos.

CHAPTER TWO

I

That afternoon, in London, Matthew King and his wife Sarah gave a party for their daughter Tanya, who was nine years old. She screamed with delight and excitement when she saw that *everyone* she needed to impress had made it to her 'ball'.

The garden of Matthew's Regency mansion-house looked beautiful in sunlight, like a clearing in a prehistoric forest, with the shadows of leaves waving wildly across the lawn. Beneath the trees, in a spotlight of sunshine, a dozen almost naked eight-year-old children feasted at a table, shouting and pushing torn-up pancakes into their mouths with their fists and sharing big chocolatey grins.

Matthew stood on the patio, narrowing his eyes against the sun, so that the scene looked like footage from a home movie. The colours reminded him of the films he'd seen of himself when he was a child, except this garden was a hundred times larger than any garden he had played in. Huge plane-trees, two acres of velvet lawn, a fountain, a swimming-pool just beginning to settle where a few minutes before it had been boiling with children.

Sarah and her American friend were sitting at an iron garden table, supervising the party through dark glasses, glancing over occasionally to pass some irreverent comment about someone else's child. After a few more glasses of wine they would begin to laugh at each other's children and then, the final irreverence, at their own.

A few yards beyond their table, near a half-pulled sash-window stood a bodyguard with his hands clasped discreetly behind his back, fiddling with worry beads made from turquoise and amber. He wore a dark suit that was an obscenity in the heat, regulation dark glasses and an expression which never changed between sucks of the teeth. His shaded gaze was fixed on one of Tanya's party guests, the daughter of a Jordanian diplomat who rented a modest Gothic palace nearby. Wherever the little girl went she was shadowed by a discreetly armed ex-commando from one of the Druse militias. The bodyguard had refused all offers of food and drink, and his tanned face absorbed the direct glare of the English sun as effortlessly as sandstone. Sarah thought his presence hilarious, but for now she was studiously ignoring him.

'That one there,' Sarah said to her friend, pointing to a blonde girl racing across the lawn, 'that's Marie Crewe's daughter. Her name is Philomena. It gets shortened to Flim and that gets trivialized into Flimsy. That's why I call her Flimsy. And she is, isn't she? Look at her. Like something you'd find in a cobweb. Matthew . . .'

Sarah held out an empty glass and Matthew glared at her before he went inside to fill it with cold white wine. It was Matthew's idea to give the nanny the day off, and Sarah was pressing the point home. When he came back out, Sarah and her friend were laughing. Matthew realized that Sarah was now talking loudly about the Jordanian girl's father, loudly enough for the bodyguard to hear.

'. . . he had his eye scratched out by a peregrine falcon in the desert. Irma gave him cocaine at a dinner party and he sneezed and his fucking eye flew across the table. Irma didn't blink! She said, "Yes, it is *very* strong stuff, Mohammed," . . . apparently in Arabic there is a word for the thing that is one up from embarrassment.'

Shaking with laughter, Sarah and her friend held their wine in their mouths with their hands. Matthew knew that Sarah was now deliberately trying to provoke the bodyguard, to see if she could put some sort of expression on to his features. It was a taunt at Sarah's laziness that she could be so articulate and vicious for no purpose. Once, she'd had ambitions to be a journalist. Now she only indulged her talents at dinner parties and children's birthday parties, making herself feared and popular with the people who feared her most.

Matthew too had once studied and trained for a career, but now he and his wife were like two gleaming electrical appliances with leads but no plugs. Their purpose and their ambition were cut off almost ten years earlier by a bizarre inheritance which meant that neither of them would ever have to work again. They were in their thirties, both handsome and bright, but isolated by their good fortune which had ended their old lives as surely as a paralysing car crash.

For nearly ten years they had been in a kind of restless coma caused by sudden and spectacular wealth. It was a coma which had to be medicated with gin and cocaine and the pointless adrenalin of furious arguments. They expected no one's sympathy except each other's, and that was rarely given.

Out on the lawn, the Jordanian girl and two boys were fighting, and the situation was getting out of hand. Matthew said, 'I'd better go and stop them.' Sarah sighed and shook her head gently at her friend.

'Stop worrying,' she said, 'they're fine.'

'They're picking on the little girl.'

'Who, Natasha? They're just playing with her. Anyway, I think Natasha has brought perfectly adequate protection of her own . . .' Sarah glanced at the bodyguard and giggled. Her friend, who was in awe of Sarah, giggled too.

The Jordanian girl was now pinned to the lawn beneath a jumble of bodies, and the bodyguard had stiffened in an involuntary reflex. Matthew wanted to break up the fight because he knew that if he didn't, the bodyguard might act on impulse, and even draw his gun. Anywhere else the idea of someone pulling a gun at a children's party would have been insane, but Matthew knew that in this part of London, anything was possible.

Their home was in an exclusive and nameless suburb, hidden just north of The Bishops Avenue (not Hampstead, not Highgate, not Finchley, not really *anywhere*), behind a jungle of hedges, high wire fences, guard dogs and the promise of dogs.

Within this privately patrolled compound there were bankers, shipping merchants, swindlers, ivory dealers, minor middle-eastern royalty and their bored American wives, there was even one man who'd started a religion in Singapore and had then closed it down like a redundant factory.

The predominant religion in the compound was Islam, and Sarah found the prickly sobriety of the majority of her neighbours a source of great amusement. They were one of only two English families who could afford to live there, and they existed in a kind of opulent house arrest, behind massive security. The houses were built and furnished with blithe disregard for good taste, because the people here knew that good taste was just a form of consolation for people who couldn't afford vulgarity. Sometimes Matthew would stare out of one of his bedroom windows across the newly gilded Moorish rooftops and imagine that his wealth had transported him to some hot territory in his imagination. It was hard to believe that the two-bedroomed flat where he and Sarah had once struggled to make the rent was just a mile away, hidden by only walls and trees.

They could afford to live anywhere, but Sarah had settled here because she couldn't stand the vindictive literary matriarchy of Hampstead or the sterilized cuteness of London's satellite villages. Matthew lived here because if he had lived in any conventional suburb, there would have been conventional neighbours, and inevitably there would have been questions about how a man like him, middle class, with no aristocratic connections, had come to inherit £25 million from a mother who, until the day she died, lived in squalid retirement on a Greek island, making terrible paintings of bowls of fruit. The truth of how his mother had made her money in the first place wasn't even a secret, it was a mystery, because Matthew didn't know himself.

Matthew squatted down beside Sarah to whisper to her that Natasha's bodyguard was getting twitchy and that he had a real fucking gun underneath his jacket. Ten years in this ghetto hadn't made him feel at ease. Sarah carefully positioned her head to bathe her face in sunlight. Her American friend (the wife of a 'jeweller') began to run her finger around her wine glass, familiar with how easily these exchanges between Matthew and Sarah could degenerate into farcical screaming matches.

Then the squabble on the lawn suddenly resolved itself and the bodyguard relaxed. Matthew saw that their daughter, Tanya, was lifting her skirt and shrieking. One of the boys had begun to kick the air wildly. Three more had linked arms and had begun a chant about the wolf, the wolf. Sarah's friend stretched her legs out to catch more sunlight and hung her arms out to bake. Matthew felt a pointless fury building up inside him, directed at his wife and her best friend, furious that his caution had been made to look idiotic.

Sometimes it made Matthew angry that he alone should carry the burden of their situation, that he alone should always be the one who had to prepare for the calamity which one day must surely come. His garden wall was laced with razor wire, his trees had red eyes studded into the trunks that sent out invisible messages to each other on laser beams, the paths that led to his house were mined with pressure pads, but some day Matthew knew that the sanctity of his beautiful garden would be defiled, because there was no security equipment on earth that could protect against the soft tread of fate.

There was nothing that needed to be done now that the Jordanian girl was being welcomed back into the tribe of children, but Matthew took Sarah's idleness personally. He saw Sarah as an aristocrat of idleness, her skin turning yellow like an old newspaper left to bleach in the sun. These waves of rage at Sarah and at his own indolence swept over him often, and it was taking longer and longer for the feeling of suffocation to pass.

'Darling your shadow's falling over my face,' Sarah said, her eyes closed. She opened them and peered up at him.

'I think they've run out of lemonade,' Matthew said and went back into the kitchen.

Less than a minute later, Tanya's party was over. Fate had made its house call and the second bullet had been fired.

Two detectives, one in a crumpled suit, the other in jeans, T-shirt, and with a gold chain round his neck, sat in Matthew's huge drawing-room. Matthew was pinching tears from his eyes, unable to answer the questions which were being asked. The curtains were closed, but the sun was still shining outside. The detective in jeans took hold of Matthew's arm and squeezed it for a second.

'Mr King,' he said, 'I need you to concentrate. You were saying that you were in the kitchen . . .'

Matthew nodded. A uniformed officer came into the drawing-room and his footsteps echoed on the varnished floorboards. He whispered something to one of the detectives and handed him a small Cellophane bag. Matthew saw through the Cellophane that the bag contained a bullet, three inches long, golden and crushed at the end like a long, thin toffee.

'Mr King? You were saying that you were standing in the kitchen.'

'I went into the kitchen to get some more lemonade. I thought they'd run out of lemonade.'

The uniformed officer left, trying to tread lightly, alarmed at the sound his footsteps made. The whole house – east wing and west, and the hall – was echoing to the heavy tread of policemen, forensic photographers, a priest, a gaunt, coffee-coloured man who had introduced himself with a grin as 'a bullets and bones man', a coroner's assistant, two young doctors who looked like sisters, more uniformed officers. Matthew felt like a guest in his own home. The murder lived here now and it had filled every room with its strange extended family.

'I took the bottle out of the fridge and then I had a cigarette. I was leaning against the fridge and smoking the cigarette and I had my eyes closed . . .'

'And that's when you heard the shot.'

Outside, in the garden, birds were singing sweetly, as if nothing had happened. Matthew wiped his eyes. When the police had arrived half an hour earlier, a female police officer had taken Sarah upstairs and she had been vibrating with terror. Tanya's body was then still lying on the pine table in the kitchen; it was bleeding so much that the tiles on the floor were slippery with blood. Matthew had slipped over twice in the obscene, delirious chaos that had followed in the bullet's wake. He had laid his daughter down on the table gently, but her head had flopped over the edge. He had squeezed her hand, but it was lifeless, like a soft skin glove full of broken crayons.

The other children had watched in silence in the kitchen as his kiss of life turned into a desperate kiss across a huge, unbridgeable divide. There were images all over the house which couldn't be washed away, blood still on his hands and shirt, a stuttering panic in his chest.

'And it was while you were smoking the cigarette that you heard the gunshot, Mr King,' the detective said again.

'Yes.'

Matthew closed his eyes and he could see the whole scene rerunning on his eyelids, as if the brilliance of the sun had made a lasting imprint.

'I had come in for the lemonade and I was smoking a cigarette and then heard what sounded like a branch breaking. In fact, that's what I thought it was. I thought one of the children had climbed one of the trees and had broken a branch. But when I looked, I saw that there was a hole . . . a tiny, round hole with cracks around it in the glass of the patio doors. I ran out into the garden and found my wife and her friend standing there with their mouths open. I thought that they were going to laugh, but they didn't. They didn't make any sound at all. And all the children were standing still, like statues. I thought they were playing that game . . . the one about the wolf, where you have to stand still. But they weren't. Then I saw that my daughter was lying face down on the grass.'

Matthew had walked quickly across the lawn, between the silent statues of children. When he reached Tanya's body he saw that she was lying with her chest in a pool of blood which was growing bigger, until it finally flooded his shoes.

'I told them all to get back into the house,' Matthew heard himself saying. 'I had to scream at them . . .'

Matthew remembered his screams as the howling of a terrific wind which blew life back into the children. They all suddenly became animated again and raced back into the house. Matthew had knelt down and touched Tanya's sunburnt arm, which was still warm. He turned her over and saw a wound the size of a dinner plate in her chest. Like a huge flowering rose, Matthew had thought. For ten years, Matthew's worst fear had always been that when this moment came, it would be his daughter who would pay the bill. Tanya was innocent, and in his aimless prayers he had always asked that she be left out of this, that the Gods of retribution leave her alone. Now he had to consider the possibility that by wishing he had made the opposite happen.

In those first few wild minutes when he had picked up the phone with bloody hands to call the ambulance, he had imagined that perhaps she had fallen on to a knife or had injured herself somehow, but he knew now that it had been a bullet. Someone had fired a bullet that had passed through the length of the house, entering just above the vestibule door, passing through the study and the hall, through the oak-panelled games room, through the wattle and daub wall of the kitchen, through the frame of the patio doors and then out into the garden where it had hit his daughter and then continued on its trajectory through branches, a hedge, a wooden garden fence, as if the business of killing Tanya had been just one minor task to be fulfilled along the way. Her body had hardly deflected it.

'And I saw the bodyguard on the lawn,' Matthew said, spotting a dark figure in his own mental image of that moment. 'He was lying on top of the other little girl. He was protecting *her* . . .'

The two detectives nodded sadly.

'We're pretty sure, Mr King, that the bullet was meant for her. For the Arab girl.'

'But it's my little girl that's dead.'

'She must have run into the line of fire. We're 99 per cent sure that it was the ambassador's daughter they were after.'

'Who were after?'

'We really don't know. We think this one will probably be taken out of our hands. This is specialized territory.'

Before Matthew had been ushered into the drawing-room for questioning, he had heard the bodyguard explaining to someone that the little girl sobbing in his arms was the daughter of the Jordanian ambassador. Straight away all kinds of calls were made, and the house became a venue for professional reunions, clipped and coded conversations, nods of the head. The most important task seemed to be the formulation of a non-committal press release, which could be read out to the growing crowd of reporters who were already gathering at the gate at the end of Matthew's drive.

So far, no one appeared to be entertaining the idea that the murder could be anything to do with Matthew. Except, of course, for Matthew himself.

The two detectives were anxious to leave Matthew alone with his grief now that they had taken his statement. Matthew could hear Tanya among all the other voices in the hall. She was calling out to him in her ordinary voice and Matthew thought that he should go to her and tell her that everything was going to be fine, that all these strangers would leave soon.

'. . . Mr King, would you like some tea or something. Should we call anyone . . .'

Matthew stood up and hurled an onyx table lamp across the room and it jagged on the end of its flex before smashing. He sat down again heavily in his armchair, as if the throwing of the lamp had been some ordinary task which he had forgotten to do and which had to be carried out. The two detectives got to their feet. They looked to be fresh from the beat, unaccustomed to the huge variety of insanity to be found in other people's houses.

The room became warm as the detectives closed the door behind them. It wasn't until he was left alone that Matthew believed that what had happened had really happened and that it couldn't be undone. How flat this world was that time moved from then to now and with no possibility of going back and revising your mistakes. How absurd it was that someone as complex and beautiful as his daughter could be removed completely, all of her, her voice, her temper, her smile, by the flight of three inches of toffee-coloured metal. The house was filled with strange voices, the click and crackle of radios, the panting of sniffer-dogs and the scratching of their claws on the tiled floor of the hallway. Everything in the room had begun to lose its hardness, as if Tanya's death were the unplugging of an enormous freezer. Where before there had been coldness and order, now everything was slowly beginning to thaw and a process of natural decay could begin.

In this new warmth, strange moulds and spores were already beginning to take hold, and old secrets which had been frozen for many years began to drip, drip, drip.

CHAPTER THREE

I

It was a week before Matthew felt ready to speak to the police again and he spent every hour of that week preparing himself. He sat alone in the drawing-room with the curtains closed, trying to piece everything together. He had refused to go to the funeral, in spite of Sarah's pleading, and he hadn't had time to shave or wash. He hadn't slept at all but had discovered that he could live without sleep so long as he kept his mind concentrated.

His task was to find out who had killed Tanya and why. Until that job was completed, he could not allow himself a single absent thought. Nor could he allow himself any feeling of grief. After three days of his intense vigil, Sarah called a doctor, but Matthew had sent her away, flushing the sedatives she left behind down the lavatory.

He decided he couldn't risk the funeral in case the sight of Tanya's tiny coffin burst some membrane and all his resolve would be washed away. He had hardly wept at all and when he did, he cursed himself. There was an iron door somewhere, holding a whole ocean at bay, and he was shoved up against it, pushing with all his might. The doctor had told him that he was suffering from a syndrome called self-referred trauma, and Matthew had told her to stick her self-referred trauma up her cunt. When he finally ventured out into daylight, he was as sleepy and vengeful as an October wasp.

He arrived at Highgate police station unannounced, his wiry, unkempt hair, his week's growth of beard and the look of furious concentration unnerving the desk sergeant. When he explained that he was the father of the girl who had been shot the week before, hasty arrangements were made for an interview. Detective Inspector Joyce led him into an interrogation room which happened to be free.

Matthew was pretty sure that Joyce was the same man who had spoken to him just after the murder, but he couldn't be certain. His memory of that day was still a chaotic, shrieking nightmare of images which he had to keep scaring away like a flock of ravenous birds around carrion. Joyce stared at Matthew with a look of sincere pity.

'You wanted to see me, Mr King.'

'It's about my daughter's murder.'

'Ah, yes.'

Joyce bowed his head and cleared his throat. He was in his mid-fifties, with an air of weariness and a lingering smell of tobacco about him. He obviously had no appetite for this, but he sat down and forced an understanding smile.

'Last time we spoke I didn't make much sense,' Matthew said. 'So maybe I should start from the beginning.'

Joyce nodded.

'You look terrible Mr King. Are you sure you're up to this?'

Matthew pushed his hand through his mass of wiry, black hair.

'I want you to hear what I have to say.'

'Would you like tea or something?'

'No. No tea. No sympathy. OK? Just listen.'

'OK.'

Matthew had tried his theory out on Sarah, but she had sobbed and told him that she needed him to be strong for her not insane like this. She had hit his face and chest with the sides of her fists and for three days they hadn't spoken. For a long time, Tanya had been the only thread that held them together and now that thread was broken. Matthew knew that in losing his daughter he would probably also lose his wife. The only task worthy of his attention now was the search, and he needed Joyce to help him.

He took a deep breath and addressed the ceiling.

'Three weeks ago I got a cassette through the post. The voice said that something bad was going to happen to me or my family.'

Joyce seemed momentarily taken aback as Matthew pulled a torn white envelope from his pocket, his hands shaking.

'Like a fucking idiot I threw the cassette away because I thought it was a joke. But I kept the envelope. I kept it for the stamp. Tanya collects stamps. Collected stamps . . .'

To use the past tense felt almost like killing Tanya all over again, but Matthew could not allow himself the luxury of dwelling on that thought. He needed to keep to a straight line, joining the dots; his mother, the cassette, the envelope, the stamp that completed the diagram. The stamp had the head of a Hellenic warrior, white on red. It was postmarked Skiathos in broken blue ink. Matthew smoothed the creases out of the envelope on the desk. Joyce looked as if he were embarrassed in some way.

'You know, some of the boys in forensics had bets that you were a pop star,' Joyce said with half a chuckle in his voice.

'I'm sorry?'

'They thought you were a pop star. Are you?'

Matthew glared at Joyce and Joyce's attempt at polite conversation died bleeding on the rocks.

'No, Mr Joyce, I'm a technician working on a space project to put monkeys on the moon. Would you like to look at the envelope?'

Joyce took the envelope and peered at it, then placed it back on the desk without registering. High above their heads, the window of the interrogation room was barred and the shadows of the bars fell across the desk and across Matthew's face.

'Mr King,' Joyce said, 'you must understand, we already know why your daughter was shot. We have made an arrest. Perhaps you haven't had a chance to read the papers.'

Matthew fumbled with a cigarette. Joyce hurried to give him a light and used the match to light a cigarette of his own. Sometime in the previous week, Sarah had shown Matthew a newspaper which said that a Jordanian student called Ali Farhouk had been charged with Tanya's murder. The story was that the

student had been aiming at the daughter of the Jordanian ambassador, who'd made his family a target of fundamentalists by
marrying a non-Muslim. They described the murder as a 'tragic
accident'. They described Matthew as a 'reclusive Hampstead
millionaire'.

'I've read the papers,' Matthew said. 'You've got the wrong
man. Tanya's death wasn't an accident. They shot her to get to
me.'

'Who did?'

'I don't know. Someone who knew my mother.'

Their smoke mingled in the strips of sunlight coming from
above. Matthew wished now that he'd shaved and put on a suit.
Anything to make his story more plausible.

'Whoever fired the shot switched off my security system,'
Matthew said. 'I checked it the next day and it was off. Whoever
shot Tanya knew the code. The code was the first four letters of
my mother's maiden name. How would your Jordanian student
know that?'

'Are you sure you wouldn't like tea?'

'My mother lived on the island of Skiathos for the last twenty
years of her life.' Matthew held up the envelope again. 'Look at
the postmark.'

'Mr King, why don't you go home and try to rest.'

'I'm telling you I got a death-threat.'

'And I'm reminding you that an arrest has already been
made.'

'They warned me . . .'

'On a cassette that no one heard but you.'

'I went to the municipal dump to see if I could find it, but they
burn everything.'

'I heard about your visit to the dump, Mr King. If it had been
anyone but you we would have pressed charges for assault.'

Matthew had almost forgotten how angry he had become
with the man who told him that all the rubbish taken to the
dump was incinerated. Joyce forced a smile, but his sympathy
was beginning to drain away. He tapped the table with his
knuckles.

'You know, Mr King, I didn't mention it before, but when we were searching your house for points of entry and exit, we found . . . I think it was roughly two pounds of pure, refined cocaine.'

Matthew looked up at Joyce sharply. The sympathy had all gone now and the sun had stopped striping the desk too.

'Naturally, under the circumstances, we decided not to press charges . . .'

'Circumstances? You call this "circumstances"?'

'What I'm saying is that maybe the cocaine explains your condition.'

'I flushed our entire supply down the lavatory the day after Tanya was shot. Ten thousand pounds' worth, give or take. I used to use it to give my days some kind of variety. I really don't think I need that any more.'

'But you've had your share.'

Joyce was studying Matthew's face like a predator watching prey. Matthew guessed that his professional eye was familiar with the changes brought on by narcotics. A doctor whom Matthew had visited a year before to get help told him that each drug had its own expression which it welded on to the faces of its victims. With heroin it was puzzlement and resignation, with amphetamines it was anger, with cocaine it was fear.

'Yeah, I've had my share,' Matthew mumbled. 'I used to buy it like sugar. It sweetened things. But now I'm clean.'

'For one whole week,' Joyce said with chuckling irony. Matthew despised Joyce for not understanding. He knew that he would never again need to resort to that glow of melancholy delight that cocaine used to give him, that he would never again need it to blunt the blade of the day.

'I'm not who I was,' Matthew said softly, knowing that Joyce couldn't hope to comprehend the enormity of that statement.

'But I'm sure you know that a side effect of persistent cocaine use is paranoia,' Joyce said and pushed the envelope back across the desk. There was no anger in his voice, but Matthew knew that the interview was coming to an end.

'We have some leaflets on rehabilitation in reception. Perhaps you'd like to take some back for your wife.'

Joyce stood up, went to the door and held it open. Matthew tossed his cigarette on to the floor and stepped on it. He'd fucked this up by letting his grief and his anger get the better of him. How could anyone believe what Matthew had come to say? He shouldn't have punched the guy who ran the incinerator at the municipal dump. He shouldn't have hurled the onyx lamp and he shouldn't have waited a week to come here. His grief was a huge engine which would pump inside him anyway. What he needed to do was to hook up the right chains to it, get the belts and pulleys fastened to it so that he could make its energy work for him.

He could fire that engine right now by telling Joyce the truth about his wealth. Once Joyce knew the story, even the bones of it, he might realize that the circumstances of Matthew's life were more bizarre than any coke-fuelled nightmare. He might even realize that the blue-helmeted Hellenic warrior on the Skiathos stamp represented the stepping-off point for a journey into impenetrable darkness.

'You asked me if I was a rock star,' Matthew said, 'and I told you I'm not. I'm not a rocket scientist either. In fact, I'm not "a" anything. There is no indefinite article in front of what I am. And yet, according to my investment bankers, I am now worth something in the region of £30 million.'

Joyce tilted his head, trying hard to hide his curiosity.

'Maybe you don't believe me,' Matthew said, 'but you saw my house with your own eyes, Mr Joyce. Don't you want to know how a man like me comes to be living in a house like that?'

Joyce was still hovering in the doorway. This question had obviously been bothering him for days.

'I don't know . . . maybe you won the National Lottery.'

Matthew smiled.

'Something like that. I mean, I am one of the few people who does know what those poor bastards go through when they win the big prize. Except with me it was different. I won the big prize and I didn't even have to buy a ticket.'

Joyce wiped his mouth with impatience.

'If this is a guessing game, Mr King, I give up.'

'Ten years ago my mother died and left me £25 million in her will,' Matthew said to Joyce, and Joyce finally closed the door. That bald statement of fact always had the same stunning effect, like hitting a fish's head with a rock. Joyce recovered more quickly than most. He dug his hands deep in his pockets and wandered across the interrogation room.

'Lucky you,' he mumbled and raised his head to the barred window.

'Oh, yeah, lucky me.'

'What do you want, sympathy?'

'Not any more.'

'Look, Mr King, this case is closed.'

Matthew got out of his chair and stood at Joyce's shoulder. The sun came out on cue and the bars striped their faces again.

'Should I try to explain to you what it's like to receive that kind of money, out of the blue?'

Joyce fussed with his jacket lapel.

'I don't come from that kind of family,' he said haughtily.

'Neither do I,' Matthew said. 'That is the point. That's why I'm here. No one knows where it came from. My mother was a secretary and a bookkeeper, then a housewife. My father was a civil servant. My mother left home when I was four and became a painter. She went to paint on a Greek island. She spent the last twenty years of her life painting terrible paintings on the island of Skiathos and as far as I've been able to find out, she never sold one of them. So there you have it . . .'

Joyce turned to glance at Matthew over his shoulder, not wanting to be drawn in.

'There you have what?'

'The mystery. I've been trying to find out for nearly ten years where the money came from. I've got a hundred letters from the Greek offshore revenue and taxation office. According to them, she never paid tax because she only earned the equivalent of £2,000 a year as a translator, right up to the day she died. She even drew her British pension from a post office near the harbour. It's been a kind of hobby of mine for ten years, trying to find out, and then I got a cassette telling me that if I didn't stop digging, something bad would happen to me or my family. Well Mr Joyce, I'd say something pretty bad has happened to my family.'

Matthew had to wipe the dew of tears from his eyes and he cursed them. They were the first tears for days and the sight of them horrified him like the sight of fresh blood. It was the word 'family' which had punched a hole in his defences, because now that Tanya was dead, he didn't have a family any more. It was the same feeling he'd had when he was four years old and he woke one morning to a cold and formal explanation from his father that his mother was 'being rather silly' and wouldn't be coming home. She had fled for Skiathos without a word. Matthew had grown up with the feeling that a door had been blown open, exposing him, and there was nothing he could do to close it. Now that same door was open again.

Joyce seemed to be relieved by the sight of Matthew's tears. At last a reaction he could understand. He put his hand on Matthew's shoulder.

'I can't count the times I've seen shock do this to a person,' he said. 'It all seems so unfair, doesn't it?'

The smoke was still rising from Matthew's half-stubbed cigarette. He put his foot on it for a second time and ground it down.

'Yes it does seem very unfair, but I'm not in shock any more. It wasn't really a shock in the first place. She was the only thing I really loved and that's why they took her away from me.'

2

When Matthew arrived back at the gates of his house, a scrum of reporters leapt from the shade of his blue brick wall and began to beat the windows of his silver Mercedes. He drove through them at speed, through the lightning flash of cameras held at arm's length. In the article that Matthew had read about the murder, there was talk of controversy about the way Ali Farhouk was being dealt with. The police had said that he was likely to be deported rather than charged, and there were dark rumours that this was because he was a distant relative of King Hussein. The whiff of favours and corruption had kept the story alive, and the sparks flashed whenever Matthew or Sarah ventured into the outside world.

'How do you feel about your daughter's murderer being let off scot-free, Mr King?' a reporter shouted. Matthew braked hard, leapt from his car, half in and half out of the gates, and grabbed the nearest shirt collar. He swung the body hard against the wall and then turned to the flashing lights, which looked like the shorting out of a huge power cable.

'You people fuck off and leave us alone . . .'

In the blinding light Matthew could see heads bowing and notebooks being produced. He wondered if everything he said would be taken down word for word. There were microphones too. He was breathing hard.

'What happened to my daughter was nothing to do with the Jordanian ambassador,' he yelled. The lightning flashes continued.

'They meant to kill her. It wasn't a mistake. Whoever it was who shot her did it to get to me.'

The flashing became more sporadic. Heads were raised from notebooks.

'It was my fault that she was killed. Ali Farhouk is innocent. It's all my fault . . . Did you hear that? Farhouk didn't kill her.'

Matthew leant back against the blue brick wall. The reporter he had grabbed scuttled from his clutches. Where before there had been yelling and electricity, there were now just a dozen faces, slightly astonished.

'. . . My fault . . .' Matthew said again, and the microphones were lowered. He guessed that this look of fleeting pity was something he would soon have to get used to. He climbed back into his silver Mercedes and the automatic electric gates crashed into his bumper before he pulled away.

The inside of the house was silent. Normally there would have been a nanny and one or two house cleaners and sometimes the gardener drinking tea in the kitchen. Matthew wasn't sure if Sarah had fired them or just given them some time off. He found her sitting on the patio at the white iron table and they didn't speak for a long time. Since the murder, Sarah had been like a viper milked of its venom. In mourning she had reverted to how she used to be when she and Matthew had first met. Without cosmetics, gin and boredom, she was almost vulnerable.

'Are they still out there?' she said softly.

'Yes,' Matthew said. 'They've managed to fuck up the gates. I'll call the police and see if they can move them on.' Matthew smiled and wiped his face, feeling his thick growth of beard. 'Except, I'm not sure the police would listen to me. They think I'm insane.'

They both looked across the long velvet lawn which was already beginning to lose its lustre and its outline after a week without attention. There was a bruise in the centre of it where Tanya had fallen, and Matthew and Sarah couldn't help but stare at it. There were still shreds of police tape fluttering in the trees.

'Do *you* think I'm insane?' Matthew said.

Sarah didn't answer. She was the only other person in the world who knew the full story of the inheritance and so she was the only other person in the world who might take him seriously. Matthew waited a long time for Sarah to answer.

'I take it then that you do think I'm insane,' Matthew said.

'You still think it's something to do with us.'

Matthew knew that Sarah had at least considered the possibility herself. She had only believed the newspaper reports because she wanted them to be true.

'Don't you understand,' she said softly, 'how much harder this would be if her death was meant. If this was our fault.'

'The cassette was posted in Skiathos,' Matthew said. 'The police don't understand what that means, but you and I do. That's why I have to go there. I'm flying out tomorrow. You can come with me or I can go alone. I know, and I think you know, that what happened to Tanya has got something to do with my mother.'

For ten years, all mention of Matthew's mother had been taboo. For Sarah, her evil influence was only a recent phenomenon, whereas Matthew had lived with it all his life.

It wasn't until Matthew was ten that his father finally answered Matthew's questions about his mother in any kind of detail. Up until then, whenever Matthew asked about her, he would repeat that she was 'being rather silly', or if his mood was better, he would say that 'she had gone away to rest'. Matthew had wondered how much 'rest' she could possibly need, but the situation had slowly become normal, like a broken bone setting out of shape. When Matthew's father did finally let slip that she was living on Skiathos, the island became a place that Matthew visited often in his dreams. He found a map on the island in a school textbook, traced it and coloured in the island and the blue sea around it. He learnt the strange names of the villages off by heart and in his childhood fevers, it was an island of vivid lagoons and deep moist caves, with a mountain that grew higher and higher until his fever abated.

All through his childhood, Matthew had thought up reasons to forgive his mother for leaving and made up all kinds of fantastic excuses for the fact that she never even wrote or called. His father simply said that she had had a 'breakdown', and visibly shivered at the idiocy of it, the terrible ignominy.

Life with his father had been chilly and emotionless, and he still remembered his father's occasional cold embraces, their poignant Christmases alone. His father was tall and as he grew older he developed a pronounced stoop, like a very slow and gradual bow to the circumstances of his fate. He had a bureaucrat's complexion, with skin as white and dry as garlic paper. He also had an apparent reluctance ever to leave the swivel chair which he occupied when he worked at his desk, sometimes long into the night. Matthew would watch him at work with morbid curiosity, watching the leaves of white paper fluttering from one pile to the other, following a brief and cursory inspection, sometimes with the addition of a full stop or a comma. On the days when his father travelled to his office in Holborn, all the paper-work would be locked inside a roller bureau, the key hidden even from the housekeeper.

One evening, when his father had been in the kitchen and the papers and files were spread out across the desk, Matthew climbed up into the swivel chair and knelt over the desk. He began to pick up the pieces of paper from one pile and pass them to the other, the way his father did. There was a full ash-tray, the heat of an anglepoise lamp, a pool of orange light. Some of the sheets of paper were bigger than others and had diagrams on them that looked like funny-shaped sailing boats. Some had inked-in black tubes with arrows pointing to the tip and the stern. Matthew had just begun to improve one of the diagrams with a pencil when he felt a sharp blow to the back of his head. It was the only time his father had ever struck him, and the pain of the blow burnt the whole scene into his memory like a vivid frame of film.

It wasn't until he was much older that Matthew found out his father worked for the Ministry of Defence, and that some of his paperwork was considered confidential up to ministerial level.

Matthew always told his schoolfriends that his mother was dead, and he was sure that his father told the same lie to col-leagues and acquaintances. Sometimes, Matthew was convinced that his mother really was dead, and if that was so, then Skia-thos must be the land of the dead, the island where spirits go to paint and rest. The pain of those memories was like bitter stom-ach acid which he even now had to keep swallowing down.

Matthew didn't hear from his mother until after his father had died. A few months after his father's funeral, on his eight-eenth birthday, Matthew received a birthday card in a spidery hand, which said simply, 'Happy birthday, all my love, Mother'. Six months later she sent him another card and a small water-colour of a bowl of fruit which she had painted. It was one of the ugliest pieces of work Matthew had ever seen, but he put it up on his wall anyway, even though its crooked construction and vivid colours chilled him slightly. A year after that, she finally wrote a short and formal letter inviting Matthew to stay with her in her villa.

By then Matthew was at university and he was already sharing a flat with Sarah. They travelled together to Skiathos, and Matthew's reunion with his mother turned into the most nightmarish three days of his life. He and Sarah fled her village without even packing their belongings. Matthew had travelled with the intention of finding out once and for all why it was that his mother had abandoned him. He left sincerely believing that the reason she had left was because she was the closest he had ever come to a truly evil human being.

Within a year she was dead too, and a letter arrived from a firm of lawyers in Athens concerning her estate. At first, Matthew and Sarah had assumed that the figure mentioned was a mistake, that it was meant to be drachmae not pounds sterling. But then the cheque came with its ludicrous parade of noughts, and the nightmare began.

A wasp buzzed around Sarah's face and she flicked back her hair. He studied her as she waved away the wasp that was trying to get to the sweet wine on her lips. Her beauty had dried and hardened over the years. She had spent too many hours in the sun, lying half-asleep with her eyes closed in Marrakesh, Malaya, Portugal, but the smile around her eyes and the softness of her lips had survived the baking and the glazing. Matthew had met her when she was eighteen, and then she had been as bony and ungainly as a colt. These days she was more elegant, as if she had grown into her body. And Sarah had also somehow managed to expand into her wealth, whereas Matthew had always huddled inside it.

'If you go away, I'm going away too,' Sarah said, 'I'm thinking of going to Gibraltar.'

'Gibraltar? Why Gibraltar?'

'Saul is working there.'

'Saul?'

'The architect.'

Sarah blinked hard and then wiped her eyes with the back of her hand and hissed 'shit' to herself. Matthew realized that she was crying and that she had been crying for some time before he'd sat down.

'Saul invited you?'

'Just for a week or two.'

'He invited you to stay?'

'It would just be a holiday.'

A year earlier Matthew had received a call from an American architect called Saul Hoffman. He said that he had taken a year's sabbatical from his practice in Seattle to study Regency design and building methods in England. He had made the point that as far as he could find out from drawings at the RIBA library, Matthew and Sarah's house was the only Regency house in the country which had arched brick cellars similar to those found in medieval butteries. He had seemed extremely anxious to find out if their cellar was in fact part of the foundations of an earlier fifteenth-century building or whether it was a Regency copy. It was the most important thing in the world, it seemed, to establish once and for all if Matthew's cellar was original, an accidental copy or some kind of architectural conceit.

The house, with its elegant brickwork, had attracted the attention of architectural students before. Matthew usually answered inquiries curtly, saying that the place was a private home not a national monument. But Saul Hoffman had the good fortune to catch Matthew at the snow-capped peak of a cocaine expedition, and he had found Saul's squeaky American enthusiasm strangely endearing. Two days later, Saul was installed in the cellar, tapping at the crumbling butter-coloured mortar with a bronze hammer.

Saul had turned up in the flesh during a trough in Matthew's mood, and Matthew had been stunned to discover that the earnest, thin-voiced academic he'd spoken to on the phone looked more like a US marine. He was 6′ 2″, with blond hair cut into a glistening crew cut and the tight, hewn body of a man with too many mirrors in his life. Matthew regretted his invitation immediately, but Saul had breezed into the drawing-room, his little bag of tools and scroll of drawings tucked under his meaty arms, just throbbing with anticipation.

Saul Hoffman's research took eighteen days. Matthew counted every one of them, each tiny tap from the cellar meant another tick of the clock to the day when he would leave. By day seven, it was obvious that this intrusion didn't bother Sarah in the way it bothered Matthew. It seemed that suddenly, Sarah, wrapped around her gin for so many years, had all this time been hiding a passionate interest in Regency and medieval architecture.

He lost her to the cellar by day ten. She wore jeans and a head scarf to clamber into the damp darkness of the cellar ('Hey, I think it really is a darned buttery!') and emerged rarely, blinking in the light, to cast a chilling look of contempt in Matthew's direction.

Matthew found it all bitterly hilarious. He took to tapping out notes on the Steinway piano in the drawing-room with one finger, to drown out the noise of the tapping from below. When Sarah hurried by with a little cellophane bag of mortar, he would try hard to pretend that he was trying hard not to laugh. By this time, open jealousy was forbidden between Matthew and Sarah, since jealousy would be evidence of love, love gone septic. To admit that he was jealous of this absurd over-developed American would have been to lose a round in their endless bout. It may even have ended up being a knockout.

So Matthew tapped on his piano, while Saul tapped away at his foundations, waiting for this ludicrous interlude to be over. When the tapping from below stopped for any length of time, Matthew would fill the cellar in his imagination with erotic images of Sarah and Saul together, making frantic love in the chilly darkness, their breath visible with every groan. Matthew would realize that he had been hitting the same black note over and over again, for ten minutes at a time, as a soundtrack to his grim fantasies.

Matthew never once asked if Sarah was having an affair with Saul, but in his bones he knew that she was. Matthew had had affairs too; brief, complicated arrangements characterized by soulless sex and meetings cancelled through boredom or regret. He knew that he was in no position to confront her, and that if he did and Sarah chose to leave, then Tanya would be dragged in to the grotesque mess they'd made of their lives. The fact that Tanya had always been protected from their unhappiness, the fact that they were absolute in their love for her, had been the only decent thing in either of their lives.

'You mean you'd stay in his house?' Matthew said calmly. Sarah pressed each eye in turn with the back of her hand to staunch the tears, to push them back in.

'You must have known about him,' she said softly. Matthew nodded. The bullet had burst through everything, and suddenly everything that had not been said was being said out loud. It was as if the game was over, the final whistle had been blown, and now the analysis could begin because nothing could now affect the result.

'Did you carry on seeing him after he finished in the house?'

Sarah nodded her head. When the game was in full swing Matthew would have roared with laughter at this point, in order to defend his position, and then he would have begun a vicious assault on Saul's character, the way he looked, his silly obsessions. But now, Matthew had nothing to defend. Tanya was gone.

'He was in London for nine months after he left the house,' Sarah said. 'We used to meet on Sundays. Then he went to Gibraltar. He's renovating a Moorish church.'

'I thought the Moors were Muslims,' Matthew said, as if he were unconcerned.

'It must be a mosque then. I don't know. I just know that he's invited me to stay.'

'It all sounds absolutely crushingly boring,' Matthew said, an echo of former times.

'It no longer matters what you think,' Sarah said, as if it were a simple statement of fact. 'We're both free now aren't we?'

'I suppose we are.'

'He's good to me.'

'And I'm not?'

'As a matter of fact, no, you're not. Saul has been a good

friend to me. I need one. If you want to know the truth, he's invited me there to stay. For good. To live there for ever.'

Matthew and Sarah looked at each other like two battleworn soldiers staring across a smoking battlefield. The absurd truth was that Matthew still loved her. They were no longer welded together by the heat of passion, but he felt that they had both been chosen for the same ordeal, that their fates were intertwined. Their quarrelling and their rivalry had become addictive, as bad relationships often are.

'And what have you told him?' Matthew said.

'That I'm thinking about it . . .'

'Because Tanya has gone,' Matthew said.

He wasn't sure, but he believed this was the first time he had said Tanya's name in Sarah's presence since the murder. And it was the first time he had said out loud that she had 'gone'. He couldn't say dead yet, but he could say out loud that she had gone somewhere with the inference that she would never return. Maybe deep down he still believed that spirits went to live in Skiathos to paint and rest. Maybe that was why he had booked the flight. Matthew still couldn't be sure of his own motives, since the grinding sobriety of life without cocaine was new to him. He felt that he was driving fast on wheel rims.

'He asked me to live with him months ago,' Sarah said. 'But what happened made me realize . . .'

Before Sarah could say what it was that she had realized, Matthew said, 'So fucking go.' The wasp had returned and it buzzed around Matthew's face, making his anger look foolish as he tried to swat it. 'You go if you want to go.'

'It's in your hair.'

Matthew grabbed the insect from his hair and it struggled to freedom from between his fingers without stinging. He wouldn't have noticed if it had stung him.

'So you're going to leave straight away,' Matthew said, incredulously.

Sarah put on her sunglasses to hide her tears and stared across the lawn.

'Don't you understand how it would hurt me if I thought someone meant to kill her?' she said softly.

'I know. You told me.'

'But you don't listen. I don't want you to find out. Don't you see? If you're right, I don't want to know.'

Matthew's resolve failed him momentarily.

'If I cancel Skiathos, will you cancel Gibraltar?' he said.

Sarah shook her head. She seemed to have made up her mind that second.

'I'm going to Gibraltar,' she said.

'To hold Saul's little hammer.'

'He is passionate about it,' Sarah said, not even annoyed by Matthew's sarcasm. 'He *does* things. He does things out there in the world. I need to do things again too. If I stay here I'll rot. We both will, Matty.'

Sarah wiped her cheeks which were now wet with tears. Matthew tried to speak, but found he had to swallow his heart back into his chest. Finally he said, 'Do you love him?'

'I don't know.'

'Do you love me?'

'Not like this. Christ, Matthew, look at us. Look what has become of us.'

Matthew and Sarah were both weeping and trying to hide their tears from each other. The lawn stretched off into the shadows and the ghost of their daughter playing beneath the trees was as tangible as the songs of the birds. The fountain dribbled sparkling water into the sunlight and doves were cooing as if this were the perfect summer day. They both cried for a long time before Matthew stood up and went back into his empty house, where there were no clattering footsteps, no curtains being worn as a princess's robes, no fever to be soothed, no cut knee to be bathed, no screams to be shushed, no elaborate preparations being made for the perfect summer ball.

CHAPTER FOUR

I

The taxi drove with its headlights on full beam to illuminate the winding mountain road that led from the airport to the Skiathos Palace Hotel. The road had been dynamited from the mountainside recently, and the mountains still seemed angry at the intrusion. Everywhere there were rock falls, dangerous overhangs, underwater streams, newly exposed and gurgling into the beam of the headlights like fresh blood.

Matthew sat in the front seat and had his window open so that he could breathe in the vapour of fresh pine which smelt like neat gin. To the left was the darkness of sheer rock, to the right an endless expanse of moonlit ocean. The moonlight and the silence created an intimacy between Matthew and the driver.

'This road is new,' Matthew said. 'I was here ten years ago and we had to take a track right through the middle of the island.'

The driver curled the taxi around a snake bend in the road, a drop of a hundred feet into the ocean just a car's width away.

'They had a Canadian company,' the driver said, 'they used Semtex. We had to have the military here to protect it from the Arabs.'

The driver gestured out to sea, as if 'the Arabs' were waiting somewhere out there, moored in the deep ocean.

'They blew up my house,' he said and he turned to Matthew and grinned.

'Who, the Arabs?' Matthew said.

The driver laughed.

'No, no, the Canadian company. To build the road. They paid good money for just a little pile of stones.'

Matthew wondered if maybe his mother's villa had been dynamited too. If it had, then that would be a fitting end to it. It was hard to get one's bearings in the sea light, but he was sure that the villa his mother had lived in was somewhere higher up the mountain. Ten years ago, when Matthew and Sarah had taken a taxi from the airport, the driver had spent three hours trying to find the place. It had been strange, that first time, to see Skiathos for real after visiting it so often in his imagination, and even now, in the darkness, the grey luminescence of Skiathos mountain made him feel feverish.

For Matthew this island would always be a brightly coloured drawing in a vast, blue-crayon sea, and his mother would always live there on the mountain top, somewhere out in the darkness.

'You know a place near here called the Chapel of St Elena?' Matthew said. The driver braked.

'You want to go there?'

'No. My mother used to live there. Did they put the road through there too?'

The driver shook his head.

'To get up to St Elena you still need a donkey. And a good reason.'

They continued on the coast road for ten kilometres. Matthew could see the lights of cruisers and oil tankers on the horizon, and the lights of Skopelos just across the thin sleeve of ocean. When the taxi slowed to take a bend, he could hear the trilling of cicadas, like faulty wiring tangled up in the pine and sage brush. After six kilometres, the new road joined the old road which Matthew and Sarah had taken ten years earlier and Matthew began to recognize some of the landmarks. He checked his watch. It was about this time that Matthew would normally put Tanya to bed and read her a story.

There was a story she liked best about a mouse and a carpenter. She had heard that story a thousand times, but she never grew tired of it. Sometimes Matthew tried to change it a little, or skip the middle part, but she would sit upright in bed, even if she was half asleep, and demand that he go back to the part where the changes began and do it right. Tanya said that if the story wasn't told properly from the start to the finish, then it wasn't the real story and anything might happen, and the mouse or the carpenter might get hurt.

Matthew grinned and nodded his head at the dark smudges of sage and pine, wiping his eyes with his sleeve.

'Are you OK?' the driver said.

'Yeah. I'm fine. It's hot, isn't it.'

'Yeah. This is a hot island.'

The journey from London had been exhausting. It was now eight days since Matthew had flushed the last of his cocaine down the lavatory and since then, he had had to find new sources of energy. He had felt that his veins were filled with water instead of blood, and his body shook at the slightest exertion. If it hadn't been for the terrifying power of his grief, he would have curled up into a ball or driven the three miles to his dealer's exquisite tudor mansion to regenerate his will to live. But since Tanya's death, the pain of withdrawal was just a tiny detail. Indeed, his physical weakness only served to sharpen his mind. His craving was a single voice drowned out by the roar of the engine.

'You recognize this road?' the driver said. 'This is the old donkey road.'

'Yeah, I remember it,' Matthew said. 'It looks just the same.'

'You here for a holiday?'

'No. Business.'

The driver glanced at Matthew and then hooked his wrists over the steering wheel. Matthew knew that when all the tourists left, this island was a community no bigger than a small village. Around ten kilometres by five, it had a local population of no more than two thousand. Everyone knew everyone who stayed for the winter.

'Tell me something,' Matthew said, 'do you know someone called Rook?'

'Who?'

'Rook. Like in the bird.'

The driver thought for a while.

'Sure. I've heard of him. He owns some bars . . .'

'So he's still alive.'

'Is there any reason he should be dead?'

'He was pretty old last time I saw him. And fat too.'

The driver grinned.

'I'm pretty fat, but I'm still alive.'

The driver laughed and his belly shook. The beams of his headlights kept disappearing into an infinite blackness of sky and ocean as they descended the corkscrew mountain road.

'Is Rook a friend of yours?' the driver said suddenly.

'No. He was a friend of my mother's, ten years ago.'

'I ask because a lot of people don't like him.'

Matthew smiled.

'I know, I'm one of them.'

'Have you got business with Mr Rook?'

'Yes, I have.'

The driver shrugged and pursed his lips as if that was Matthew's funeral.

'He's a hard man to meet,' the driver said. 'He doesn't like visitors.'

'Then I'll have to find a way.'

There was half a kilometre of dark road before the driver said, 'Are you some kind of policeman?'

'No, I'm just interested in justice,' Matthew said.

After that they drove on in silence until they reached the palm-tree avenue that led up to the Skiathos Palace Hotel. Matthew gave the driver the fare on his digital clock, and then doubled it.

'Hey, what's this for?' the driver said.

'That's for the information. Give me your card, maybe we can speak again and you can introduce me to some of those people who don't like Mr Rook.'

The Skiathos Palace Hotel sits on a shelf of rock above a sandy bay called Koukounaries. From the sea it looks like a grounded liner, and looking from the mountain up above there is a pool bathed in blue light, a wide lawn and open-air restaurant where traditional Greek dancers skip for tourists, a hundred chalet rooms with views across the Aegean. People on Skiathos say it is the best hotel in the whole of the Mediterranean lagoon.

A Skiathos Palace bellboy in a starched white uniform with a red sash around his waist pushed a trolley with Matthew's luggage.

'It's a big suite for one man,' the bellboy said with a laugh. He spoke English with a Greek-American accent.

'But I guess it was the only room free, is that right?'

'No, I just wanted the biggest room,' Matthew said.

Matthew handed the bellboy a thousand drachmae as he pushed open the door to the suite.

'Do you live on the island?' Matthew said.

The bellboy skipped into the room and pushed open the shutters. The view of the Aegean was spectacular, with a full moon laying a flat silver pontoon bridge across the sea that looked hard enough to walk on. When the bellboy pushed open the wooden shutters, the bridge stretched all the way to his face turning it to blue steel. He switched on the lights and the bridge vanished.

'I was born here, spent some time in California . . .'

'But you know the island pretty well?'

'Guess so.'

'Good, because there are some things I need.'

The bellboy was already going through his welcome routine on automatic. Flicking on the TV set, opening the mini-bar, fastening the shutters on their latches.

'You name it, Mr King . . .'

Matthew took some more bills from his pocket and handed them to the bellboy. His eyes widened with wonder.

'I need some heroin,' Matthew said.

The bellboy held the notes as if they were delivering a mild electric shock to his hand.

'Say again, sir?'

'Heroin. Opiates.'

Matthew guessed he'd handed the bellboy the equivalent of £500. He clasped the bellboy's fingers around the cash.

'It's OK, I don't want to buy it from you. I just want you to introduce me to someone who knows where I can get some. That money is just for information. And, of course, for you keeping this to yourself.'

The bellboy hesitated before he put the money in his pocket.

'Sure, I'll ask around,' he said, and swallowed hard before backing towards the door. Matthew put his finger to his lips as the bellboy glanced up at him one last time.

After the bellboy had gone, Matthew went out on to the balcony. The soft, mellow air of the islands was just as he remembered it from the time he came here with Sarah. The smell of pine and nightshade was overpowering. To the left of the balcony there was a steep wooded slope that led down to the beach, where the water was licking salt from outcrops of black rock. It was the same bay that he and Sarah had swum in when they had stayed with his mother, and the cave they had used as their own private sanctuary was just visible, a dark mouth gulping in moonlight. On the wooded slope a nightingale was singing and its voice was echoing all across the bay.

'This was a mistake,' Matthew said out loud to himself, then shrugged his shoulders.

He laid his suitcase on its side on the bed and began to unpack. Beneath his clothes he had £20,000 in sterling, banded into £500 lots. There was also £3,000 in drachmae. He piled the clothes on the bed and then stuffed the money into the safe which was only just big enough to take it.

Matthew lay down on the bed, listening to the sound of waves in the darkness, knowing that no matter how restful the evening was, he wouldn't be able to sleep. The engine of his grief was still pumping, ringing bells at certain times, reminding him that this was her bedtime or the time she normally woke and asked for water, occasionally spewing out an image of her face, replaying the story of the mouse and the carpenter who became such good friends. But it was OK for the engine to do all these things because he had it under control now and it had helped him plan this whole thing.

On a small island like this, Matthew knew that anyone who needed heroin would in the end be referred to Rook. Ten years earlier, when Matthew and Sarah had first met him, he went out of his way to impress on them that he was the only source of pure opiates in the whole of the Sporades chain of islands. Matthew would get to him posing as a buyer, then he would find out exactly how much he knew about Tanya's murder.

Rook was a monster in Matthew's imagination, and in Sarah's too. It was Rook, as much as Matthew's mother, who had made their stay on this island a living hell. He had been introduced by Matthew's mother as her only friend, a fat, jolly Englishman with the manners of a diplomat and the warmth of a favourite uncle. Matthew and Sarah had found out too late that Rook and his mother were twin demons, exiled on this fragrant island together by some force which knew that they were too dangerous and damaged to be allowed to mingle with the rest of humanity.

Even before Tanya had been shot, when the cassette first arrived with its Skiathos postmark, Matthew's mind had turned to Rook. There was no rational reason why Rook should be involved, but Matthew had already abandoned the arbitrary strictures of rationality. With Rook it was a feeling, a kind of nausea that had to be a symptom of a larger illness.

If it turned out that Rook was somehow implicated, Matthew would pay someone to kill him. The engine had made that decision for him. Matthew had contacted his broker at Touche Ross and had freed up £5 million in an untraceable checking account, which Matthew planned to use in his search for the truth. If it cost more than that, he would pay it. He would also use it to pay for the deaths of everyone involved, whoever they were, no matter how casual their involvement.

For almost ten years Matthew had been waiting for some kind of vengeance to be played out on him for his good fortune. Now that vengeance was done and he himself had become the avenger. Matthew wasn't sure how much of his outlandish scheme was the result of grief and how much of withdrawal symptoms from cocaine, but he did know for sure that no matter how implausible it might all seem in his own mind, the vastness of his wealth meant that he could make almost anything come true. It had taken Matthew nearly ten years to realize the power that he had at his disposal and at last he had become the kind of man who could harness that power. As he had said to Mr Joyce, he was not who he was.

He spent the rest of the night smoking cigarettes on the balcony listening to the nightingale sing and trying to recall everything that his mother and Mr Rook had said on his first visit to the island, searching for the tiniest clue.

CHAPTER FIVE

I

'It is possible to disapprove of someone morally and yet still hold them dear to your heart,' Matthew's mother had said, as Matthew and Sarah sat at her scrubbed pine table, sipping English lime cordial. She had already said without expression that she preferred to be called Mathilda, rather than Mother or Mum, which she said she hated.

She had also pronounced that she had no intention of letting Matthew and Sarah share a room since they weren't married, and that any sin which they committed under her roof would leave a 'breath of curse' on the whole house. Sarah and Matthew stared dumbly at the table as she spoke, her voice trilling like the song of a thrush. Neither of them knew yet if this was going to be funny or tragic. Sarah snorted into her lime cordial and Matthew knew that Sarah had decided that it was going to be funny.

'Besides,' Mathilda said, her chin raised and her eyes fixed on a corner of the ceiling, 'this is a holy place. You cannot do such a thing in a holy place. Sarah, you need an ashtray.'

She was almost six foot tall, bony and grey-skinned with dark slanting eyes like Matthew's, but cut more deeply into her face. Her hair was a shock of white, and her face had the look of sick skin dried hard on to bone. Matthew had been expecting someone younger and more beautiful. In the photographs which his father had shown him, she was auburn-haired, with a faintly sneering kind of beauty and a distracted gaze. In his memory, she was the smell of lavender and a huge grin, like a crescent moon above him. Now only her eyes were recognizable – the Greek sun had aged her quickly.

The drive to the villa in the mountains had been exhausting, taking the taxi through ugly, tangled scrubland and bare rock. Only the rocky coastline and the blue-green of the ocean had been how Matthew had always imagined them.

The villa itself consisted of a living-room and kitchen in between two shuttered bedrooms. The garden was overgrown and patrolled by yellow-eyed goats. The well in front of the house was choked with weeds, and the roof was shedding tiles into the sage brush. Matthew had had no idea what to expect, but the squalor and the overpowering smell of stale water in the house had shocked him. There was no sign of any painting in progress, no easels or canvasses. Matthew's and Mathilda's reunion had been cold and formal, with the briefest of embraces, followed by a strict instruction about shoes in the house.

Mathilda padded across the cool, grey and scarlet tiles barefoot to swot a mosquito with a Union Jack dishcloth and to fetch a large earthenware bowl for Sarah's ash.

'I don't mind smoking during the day,' she said, 'but I can't have it in the house at night. At night I keep all the doors and windows closed because the mosquitoes here are wild. Mountain mosquitoes will bite anything, and they particularly enjoy English blood. I think it's because it isn't flavoured with garlic. Sarah, put your cigarette out, I'll show you to your room.'

Sarah stubbed her cigarette out and Mathilda lifted the ashtray and balanced it in her palm as if it were filled with scalding water, before tipping the contents into the plastic bag she used as a bin. She then murmured, 'Come, come,' under her breath and Sarah stood to attention. Sarah gave Matthew a look of wild conspiracy, as she dutifully followed Mathilda through the arched doorway into the living-room.

Left alone, Matthew signed and wiped the sweat from his face. He had been as nervous as hell for weeks and now the moment he had been dreading and hoping for had passed just like any other moment. He had given himself strict and silent instructions in the taxi from the airport not to allow tears. He was twenty-three years old, and without a mother he felt that he had grown up more quickly than most people. He didn't want Sarah to know that this was the reunion he had longed for ever since his mother left him, but now he was no longer sure that he had ever really wanted to put skin and bone on to his dreams.

In the event, tears would have been absurd. The woman who led him into the villa had destroyed a lifetime of imagining with just one cold, dry glance in Matthew's direction.

The inside of the house was almost bare of furniture, and the white walls seemed to breathe damp and coolness into the kitchen. The stove had a Perspex belly for wood, and there were two crucifixes hanging on the kitchen wall, one above the door, the other above the sink. When Matthew looked back over his mental image of the villa, as he often did, there was no clue that his mother was anything other than a pauper. Mathilda came back into the kitchen and pulled up a chair at the table.

'I've told her to stay in her room until I have had the chance to talk to you.'

'Oh. Is that OK with her?'

Mathilda waved her bony, grey hand in the air.

'I must get to know you again, Matthew. I must get to know you as well as I can in the time we have. Do you attend church?'

'No, I'm afraid I don't.'

Mathilda lifted her chin and breathed deeply.

'Then that is good. The church in England is no good any more. It is a car without an engine. Those people don't believe any more.'

Matthew nodded his head and glanced at Mathilda's uplifted face. He decided there and then that his father's theory about his mother having had some kind of breakdown was probably correct. Her face, her clothes, the wilderness which had encroached from the mountain on the garden and the house all pointed to it. Matthew could even take some comfort from that. If she hadn't cracked up, she would have stayed. It didn't even matter any more, but he was almost relieved that there was no need to rationalize what she had done because she herself had lost her rationality.

'Sarah is very pretty,' Mathilda said. 'Do you have relations with her?'

'If you mean sex, then yes.'

'Ah. Will you be able to limit your desire while you are here in my house?'

Matthew had to look at his feet, then he looked her in the eye.

'Limit my desire?'

'I mean refrain from sex.'

'I know what you mean. It's just such a bizarre thing to say.'

'They are the rules of the house.'

Matthew shook his head gently.

'Is that all you have to say to me?'

'There are clean towels in each of your rooms.'

'Yeah. Great. Clean towels. Jesus Christ.'

His mother said nothing. When he looked up at her again she was peering up at the ceiling, as if listening to silent music. Matthew thought that he was going to laugh out loud. Far from being portentous or moving, this reunion had already become absurd.

'Christ, aren't you even going to apologize?' Matthew said at last. Mathilda glanced at him quickly, then looked away.

'I will show you to your room. I've told you about the towels, haven't I. Matthew, it is *so* nice to have you here at last.'

Mathilda stood up and gestured towards a room at the opposite side of the house to where Sarah's room was. There was an empty bird cage in the living-room, more crucifixes, a bilious smell of stale incense to go with the smell of stale water.

2

That night they had dinner outside in the wilderness of the garden. The crockery was all cracked and defiantly English. Matthew had already decided that he wanted to get the hell out of there and pretend that the whole stilted reunion had never happened. Sarah had whispered to him, while Mathilda was fetching the plates, that he should give her a chance because she'd been alone for a long time and probably had trouble letting her feelings show.

'Just like you,' Sarah had said, teasing him.

Mathilda brought a paraffin lamp from the kitchen and lit it beside the table. She blew out the match and then stood up, her knees clicking loudly. She glanced down at Sarah's bikini top as she drifted by, shining blue in the light of the lamp. She came back to the table with a black shawl around her shoulders. She also had one in her arms and she handed it to Sarah.

'Your father was a very courageous man,' she said suddenly. 'I keep a photograph here, Matthew, of the time he was in the army.'

She handed Matthew a black and white photo of his father. Matthew saw a familiar half-smile, transposed on to a young man's face. His father was wearing a military uniform. Behind him there was a grey sand-dune.

'You can see from that that he was a major,' Mathilda said. 'That was taken in the Palestine. Nineteen . . . forty-seven, I think.'

Matthew angled the photo against the blue light of the lamp to look more closely. There were mosquitoes crawling over the bulb of the lamp and the garden seemed to be alive with insects, the whole mountain wheezing with their dry chirruping. Matthew went to hand Sarah the photograph, but Mathilda quickly stood up, snatched it out of Matthew's hand and put it into the pocket of her shirt.

'He was such a terror,' Mathilda said. 'During the war we thought he would be shot for some of the things he got up to. But I think they saw the steel in him. They saw that he was a rebel and even the army needs rebels sometimes.'

Matthew spooned some tomatoes and cheese on to a plate and handed it to Sarah. They had only known each other for a year and a half, and lived together for less than a year, but Matthew had already learnt how to sense Sarah's moods from vibrations in the air. The shawl, the rudeness, were beginning to annoy her and she would say something soon. Matthew took a long time serving her food to impress upon her that he was angry with Mathilda too.

'And he was always getting up to pranks. Before he was made

major, I mean. In the war, during an air raid, he was caught stealing apples . . .'

Mathilda launched into a long and inconsequential story about how Matthew's father had been arrested in an orchard near to his barracks in Oxford, and how he had spent the night in the cells. She then treated them both to a series of accounts of the practical jokes that Matthew's father had played on his comrades, none of them worthy of retelling. Matthew and Sarah ate in sullen silence. Sarah shook off her shawl and stroked the bites on her arm.

'But he was a different man by the time you came into the world,' Mathilda said.

'Yes, yes, he was,' Matthew said. 'Thank God.'

Matthew's memory of his father was of a man with no sense of fun and very little wit. The stories that Mathilda told seemed to bear no relation to the man he remembered.

'Matthew, did you pack any cream for bites?' Sarah said softly.

Matthew was about to stand up to fetch the cream, but Mathilda raised her hand.

'Did I ever tell you Matthew, about the crescent moon. The badge he brought back from Palestine.'

Matthew hovered above his seat.

'It was the highest honour the Arabs could bestow upon an infidel. He won it fighting with the Jebel Druse in the Golan Heights.'

'It's OK, I'll get it,' Sarah said and she stomped off into the house. These unspoken rivalries, these moments bursting with tension, so reminded Matthew of life at home before his father died. It was as if his mother had the same capacity for creating discomfort as his father. Matthew sat down, sighed, stroked the sweat from his forehead.

'Mathilda.'

'Yes, my dear.'

'You talk about Dad like he was some kind of hero.'

'So he was.'

Matthew laughed and shook his head.

'What is it, Matthew?'

'So why did you leave him?'

Mathilda cleared her throat and explained to Matthew that his father had been under tremendous pressure during his time in the army and that the pressure could not be imagined by anyone who hadn't heard the stories of the things he had been through. She said that his experiences had changed him and that in the end she had found him intolerable to live with. She was about to continue when Sarah returned to the table.

'Would you mind leaving us alone,' Mathilda said sharply. 'We are discussing family business. And when you return perhaps you could cover yourself up.'

Sarah turned on her heels and walked off into the darkness of the garden, disappearing into the shadows of the olive trees. Matthew pushed his plate away.

'What is the matter with you?' Matthew said as he stood up and walked off in pursuit.

He found Sarah standing by the set of rusted gates, which separated the garden from the scrubland of the mountain. Sarah was rolling a joint, taking great care with the pinch of grass she had tipped from a matchbox. Matthew took her arm and kissed her, and she shook him off.

'Why don't we go and sleep on the beach,' Matthew said. 'This was a bad idea. She's obviously insane.'

Sarah licked the cigarette paper, took out a match and lit the joint. She took a deep drag and the thick white smoke hung in the moonlight.

'She's your mother,' Sarah said. 'Give it a while. We're not here for my benefit. I can handle her.'

The whole mountainside was stretched out before them, the pine forest shimmering blue in the hazy reflections from the sea. Matthew took the joint off her and smoked.

They could both hear Mathilda stacking plates in the garden. Up here, every sound echoed all the way across the mountain. Matthew turned and saw her silhouette against the lights of the house. Matthew kissed Sarah and she blew smoke into his mouth. Then he heard footsteps on the path beyond the gate. He opened his eyes, coughing on the smoke Sarah had blown into

him, and saw a huge white shape suddenly appear in a patch of
moonlight on the mountain path. They both turned and saw a
fat man in a white suit, breathing hard, his hands on his knees.
Sarah quickly licked her fingers and pinched the glowing end of
the joint. The fat man straightened up and peered into the darkness where Sarah and Matthew were embracing.

'Mathilda?' the fat man said.

Matthew stepped out into the moonlight.

'No. Mathilda's in the house.'

'Who the hell are you?'

'I'm her son, Matthew.'

'Son? Oh God.'

The fat man spoke in hoarse, piping tones that didn't fit with
his huge size. He seemed to be on the point of passing out. He
wiped his forehead and Matthew could see that he was glistening with sweat.

'I walk all the way up the mountain for a fuck,' the fat man
said, 'and she's got bloody visitors. She might have told me. The
name's Rook, by the way.'

Rook pushed his stubby hand through the ironwork of the
gate and he and Matthew shook. Sarah stepped out into the
moonlight to take a closer look and Rook smiled at her.

'And who might this be?'

'This is Sarah.'

'Well, Sarah, pleased to meet you. And you, Matthew. I suppose I might as well go back to my house and play with myself
then if she's got bloody visitors.'

He smiled a wicked smile and winked at Sarah.

'For God's sake don't tell her you saw me,' he said, 'I don't
think I quite fit with the image she wants to portray.'

Rook turned on his heels and began to waddle back down the
mountain path, humming to himself as he walked. Matthew
and Sarah were open-mouthed.

'Did he say what I think he said?' Sarah said.

'He said he'd walked all the way up the mountain for a fuck.'

They both shrieked with laughter, the warmth of the grass
made the huge white cloud disappearing into the blackness seem

like the funniest sight they had ever seen. Sarah turned in the direction of the house, where Mathilda was still clearing the table.

'That hypocritical old bitch,' she said with great purpose.

'Sarah, don't say anything.'

Sarah took the joint out of her pocket and relit it. Matthew waited while she smoked it down to her fingers, as dangerous, Matthew thought, as a loaded gun.

3

The next time Matthew set eyes on Mr Rook was on the last night of his stay at Mathilda's villa. It was the last night of a lot of things. Matthew's life had been destroyed even before he received the inheritance, and the process of destruction began with Mr Rook. Years later, Matthew would come to think of this as the evil evening.

Sarah and Matthew had spent the day swimming in the bay and retreating into the cool of the cave to fuck. The sand inside the cave was cold and it made their skin tingle. A night spent in separate rooms had inflamed them both and they fucked hard to hurt Mathilda, as if she were a thin film between them that had to be torn to pieces with their nails and teeth.

They walked back up the mountain along the goat track as the sun was setting over the island of Skopelos. They stopped often to turn around and review the golden majesty of the sun as it bled red and scarlet into the water. The soft island air was filled with the buzzing of insects, the throb of life, as if the whole living mountain were taking its energy direct from the last rays of the sun, preparing for night.

When they walked up the path through Mathilda's orchard, Mr Rook was already sitting at the table, which was set for four. The moment they stepped into the orchard, the glory of the mountain view paled, and the air seemed to turn appreciably colder. When Rook saw them walking down the path, he quickly put down his glass of white wine and beckoned them over like a conspirator.

'In the name of God,' he hissed, looking round at the villa where Mathilda was preparing food, 'don't let on that you saw me last night. And don't tell her what I said. I was a bit . . .'

He waved his chubby, ringed finger around his temple to denote something only he understood. His eyes twinkled in the dying light and he waved Matthew and Sarah into their seats. Then he poured two huge glasses of white wine as he called out, 'Mathilda dear. They're back from the sea and hungry.'

Mathilda darted out of the doorway and hurried to the table. She introduced Matthew to Rook and Rook to Matthew. Sarah didn't exist.

'Ah, Matthew. And how has your day been?' she said sweetly after her partial introduction.

'We had a marvellous time,' Matthew said, looking at Sarah.

'Then you must be hungry.'

Mathilda trotted back into the villa, leaving a huge smile on Mr Rook's podgy face.

'Oh dear,' he said gravely. 'Something of a cold front around this side of the table.'

He leant forward in his chair and patted Sarah's bare knee. Sarah was wearing a short white skirt over her bathing costume. He winked at her.

'Women beware women,' he whispered.

'You noticed,' Sarah said.

Mr Rook chuckled into his chest.

'My dear, Mathilda has been alone too long. When you spend too many years alone you begin to imagine that other people are either angels or devils. Nothing in between. And I think in this case Matthew is the angel and you are the devil.'

Mr Rook took a large swig of wine.

'Has she said that?' Sarah asked. Mr Rook patted her knee again.

'Never you mind about her,' he said and he raised his glass for a toast. 'I have a plan to get her drunk so she falls asleep, then we three can have a jolly time without her. Here's to that. Let's drink to a sleeping Mathilda.'

Matthew and Sarah smiled at each other as they raised their glasses. They had both decided that Mr Rook was exactly what they needed to get them through another evening with Mathilda. As they drank their toast, Mathilda arrived with a tray of teacups, a pot, a jug of milk.

'Oh God, Mathilda, tea?' Mr Rook exclaimed. 'Tea? On a night like this?'

Mathilda hovered over the table, the cups rattling in their saucers.

'I thought it might remind us of home,' she said timidly.

'These children are on holiday, for God's sake, they don't want to be reminded of home. Tea? Go on, take it back.'

Mathilda hesitated and Matthew thought that she was about to burst into tears. Instead she turned on her heels and hurried back into the villa. Mr Rook stretched out in his chair, his huge belly straining against his stained cotton shirt. Matthew and Sarah were amazed at how Mr Rook's presence had changed Mathilda from a cruel schoolmistress into a contrite schoolgirl. She even walked more quickly, as if overeager to please.

'So, Matthew,' Rook said, his hands behind his head, 'I must say, you do have your father's eyes. If I hadn't known, I would have guessed straight away.'

'You knew my father?'

'We worked together many years ago. That's how I know Mathilda.'

Matthew knew that before returning to England to work for the civil service, his father had been in the army for fifteen years.

He had always thought it rather odd that a man as diffident and shy as his father could have ever cut it in the military.

'Oh yes, your father and I were pretty thick after the war,' Rook was saying. 'I would tell you some stories, but I'm afraid that it might make your pretty wife blush.'

'We're not married,' Sarah said and Rook lowered his head and growled.

'All the better,' he said. 'Ammunition. Wonderful ammunition.'

He rubbed his hands together, as Mathilda returned to the table, this time with a large loaf of Greek bread and a bowl of tomatoes. She laid them delicately on the table.

'I was just talking to the lovely Sarah here about the sanctity of marriage,' Rook said and his eyes twinkled wickedly. Mathilda bent down and fumbled with some matches as she lit the paraffin lamp. The lamp began to hiss. The last of the sunlight was replaced by a milky blue light.

'We all agreed around the table that it is a load of humbug,' Rook continued. 'What do you think, Mathilda?'

Mathilda gave him a look of wild embarrassment as she trotted back to the kitchen. Rook leant back in his chair to watch her disappear into the shadows. In the light of the paraffin lamp, his features looked more sickly, as if there was another, thinner face emerging from the layers of flesh.

'She's not a bad old girl really,' he said, then swooped forward to grab his wine and drain his glass. He banged it on the table.

'More wine, Mathilda!' he yelled and his voice echoed around the mountain. Mathilda returned with wine and cheese. She laid the wine in front of Mr Rook and then smoothed her dress on her lap as she sat down.

'Shall we start?' she said, like a demure little bird.

'So we shall,' said Mr Rook, and he began to help himself to food. Mathilda poured herself a little wine, but Mr Rook took up the bottle and filled her glass, winking at Sarah as he did it with no attempt to hide his face from Mathilda. Mathilda accepted the full glass with a little whimper. Matthew and Sarah began to eat. As the night wore on, the humming of the insects and the singing of a nightingale across the bay was drowned out by Mr Rook's endless supply of stories from a life which had been spent, so it seemed, living in every city and every principality in the whole world.

'Of course, Manila is the finest of cities,' Rook said, adding another drop of wine to Mathilda's glass even though it was already full to the brim. 'Finest cafés, finest restaurants, finest prostitutes . . .'

Mathilda cleared her throat. Matthew and Sarah giggled. They had already drunk a bottle of wine each. Mathilda had been keeping pace, reluctantly. Rook had drunk more than all of them put together.

'It has to be said, Mathilda,' Rook said, 'there are degrees of competence in every field. Some whores are better at it than others. The worst are the English, *naturalmente*, the best are in Manila. No, I lie. The worst are Turkish. Old, with beards. I never could understand the Turks. I mean, everybody knows that men prefer young to old. Every man. Every man wants a young little thing, not a worn-out old poker of a woman . . .'

Rook slurped a tomato slice into his mouth and wiped oil from his lips. Matthew couldn't make out Mathilda's features too well in the half-light, but he was sure that she would be offended and that Rook was deliberately offending her. Perhaps he was more drunk than he looked. Sarah was grinning at Rook and glancing occasionally at Mathilda.

'I mean, take little Sarah here,' Rook said. 'Beautiful legs, tight little arse . . . '

He leant forward and clutched her knee. Sarah shifted in her seat. There was a pause filled with the buzz of insects, the sweet song of the nightingale. Matthew decided he should change the direction of the conversation for Sarah's and Mathilda's sake.

'So how come you worked with my father?' he said, helping himself to more wine. For the first time in a long time, Rook said nothing. Mathilda emerged briefly from her inebriation for long enough to give Rook an ice-cold stare.

'Oh, that was a long time ago,' Rook said and waved his hand. 'I won't bore you with it.'

'I'd like to know,' Matthew said.

Mathilda reached for her wine and knocked her glass over. Rook patted the wet tablecloth with his napkin.

'I mean, was he a hero? My father? He never struck me as being very brave.'

Rook sat back in his chair and stared at Matthew without expression. It was as if his eyes had died in his head. In the half-light, it looked like sheer hatred and contempt, switched on and then off again in the space of a few seconds. He looked at Matthew for longer than was polite or comfortable.

'Let me top you up, Sarah,' he said at last, and filled Sarah's glass with wine.

By midnight, Mathilda's head was rocking on to her chest. Rook was telling Matthew and Sarah once more about the prostitutes in the Far East, saying that they were a delicacy to be savoured even more richly than fried sea slug. Matthew and Sarah were both giggling, but by now they had detached themselves from Rook and were sharing their own private joke at his expense. His stories had become more and more obscene and ludicrous as the night wore on, and as Mathilda lost consciousness.

Finally, Rook waved his hand under Mathilda's face to check that she was asleep. When he was sure that she was, he turned to Matthew and Sarah like a magician about to perform his final and most spectacular trick. He lowered his voice.

'But more glorious even than the whores of Manila,' he whispered, 'is the opium of Manila.'

He slowly reached into the top pocket of his jacket and pulled out a large joint, twisted at the end. It was the size of a good cigar. He ran it under his nostrils and sniffed.

Sarah gasped. Matthew swayed in his seat to get a better focus.

'Do you indulge?' Rook said, glancing at Mathilda, who was now unconscious.

'Jesus, yeah,' Sarah exclaimed. Up until that moment, neither Sarah nor Matthew had ever smoked opium or even come across it. They had smoked grass since they had been at College. Matthew felt an unease which Sarah didn't appear to share. She was more drunk than Matthew had ever seen her.

'I knew it,' Rook said. 'I knew that you two were seekers after the finer things in life and this thin white penis of delight is the finest thing on God's earth. Prepare to meet thy maker.'

Matthew watched queasily as Rook lit a match and then lit the twisted end of the joint. The paper glowed for a few seconds and then pure white smoke began to curl up from the tip. Rook blew on the glowing end and wafted it under Mathilda's nose. The smoke curled up around her face and she coughed in her sleep before breathing deeply and sighing.

'Sleep well, my dear,' Rook said like a stage villain, then he put the joint to his lips with great reverence. He took a drag and seemed to be sucking half the mountain into his chest. Matthew found himself inhaling at the same time, holding his breath until finally Rook blew out the grey smoke, stripped of all its narcotic purity.

He passed the joint to Sarah and she dragged hard and coughed. Sarah was still young enough in those days to believe that it was grown-up not to cough, and she spluttered into her chest. Then she took another deep drag and passed it to Matthew.

The smoke tasted of rich spices and felt cold in his throat and lungs. The heaviness of the smoke took him by surprise and it felt as if the smoke were turning to warm oil inside his body. The oil spread through his arms and legs, taking all the strength from his muscles and replacing it with warmth.

As the joint was passed around the circle of three, the cicadas stopped singing, the nightingale fled, the crescent moon began to sweat in the darkness. Suddenly, it felt like the three of them were alone in a cramped warm place, with the dead body of Mathilda. Rook began to talk again, but Matthew couldn't make out what it was that Rook was saying. Then Matthew's ears popped and everything became clear.

'. . . they do sometimes is to squat before you, these girls, and they suck the anxiety from your body. Suck with their honey lips. It feels like a big fat bee sting somewhere in the foundations of your body. An exquisite bee sting of an orgasm . . .'

Matthew saw Rook take Sarah's hand and pull her gently

towards him. Sarah had her head down and her salty blonde hair was hanging over her face. When he took her hand she shuddered and looked around with bewildered eyes.

'If I may borrow you for a moment, my dear, I would like to demonstrate.'

Sarah resisted like a child being woken from a deep sleep, but Rook pulled her gently on to his lap. Matthew leapt to his feet and the world span around. As he stood he kicked the paraffin lamp over and the table was consumed by darkness, apart from the thin light of the moon.

'I would like to demonstrate a particular movement which these girls have perfected . . .'

He pushed Sarah to her feet so that she was bending over the table, her hair falling into the greasy salad bowl. Matthew had managed to get around the table on trembling legs and grab Rook around the throat.

'You get your fucking hands off her,' he slobbered and pushed Rook back in his chair. Rook looked up at Matthew with glassy, dead eyes.

'Oh come along, Matthew. I thought you were your father's son . . .'

Matthew grabbed Sarah around the shoulders and pulled her away. She was only half-conscious. As he dragged her to her feet an empty bottle of wine fell from the table and smashed at Mathilda's feet. Matthew was sure that he saw her eyes open, and it looked to him like the curtains of hell blowing open for just half a second. He was suddenly sure that Mathilda had only been pretending to be asleep, and that now she was having a little peek at how her plan was developing. It might have been the effect of the opium that made Matthew think that, but in the past ten years, he had become more and more convinced.

'You filthy fucking bastard,' Matthew yelled at Rook's face. 'You get your fucking hands off her . . .'

The idea of going back into the villa was now too terrifying. Matthew wanted to breathe the cool sea air and let the beauty of the mountain wash away the spicy poison of the joint.

He dragged Sarah into the orchard and laid her down on the grass.

He supported himself on one elbow and stroked her cheek.

'Are you O K, baby?'

Sarah opened her eyes and smiled.

'O K, baby,' she said.

'That fucking dirty bastard,' Matthew slobbered and Sarah closed her eyes. She began to breathe deeply. The rhythm of her breathing made Matthew's eyes heavy. His elbow gave way and his head fell on to the grass, which smelt of the same spice as the opium. Matthew put his head to one side and threw up. After that, he fell into a deep chamber of nightmares.

5

When he awoke, the first light of dawn was in the sky. His head hurt as if an axe had been put through it. He had been woken by what had been, in his nightmare, the grunting of a goat. When he opened his eyes he saw in the half-light a large white shape pulsating in the darkness beneath an olive tree a few yards away. When he focused he saw that it was Mr Rook. Beneath him, on bended knees, was Sarah, her skirt lifted up her back, her arms pinned behind her head. Matthew saw this vision of hell from the horizontal and heard deep sickening grunts. He sat upright and heard Sarah curse and then say 'please' in her ordinary voice. What had haunted Matthew for ten years was the slowness of Rook's movements, the ordinariness of Sarah's voice, the fact that the sound of Rook's pleasure was louder than Sarah's pain.

The next thing Matthew knew, he had stumbled across the orchard and kicked Rook in the side of the head. Rook clung on for a few more seconds before a second kick sent him sprawling into the grass. Sarah fell forward, sobbing, as Matthew dived on to Rook's enormous belly and dug his hand deep into his crotch and squeezed. Rook rolled over and managed to push Matthew away for long enough to get to his feet. Rook waddled across the lawn between the olive trees as fast as his short legs would carry him. Matthew raced after him and grabbed him around the neck. Rook twisted Matthew's hand and then shook himself free. By the time Matthew reached the gate, Rook had fired the engine of his moped and had set off down the goat track, his huge white body balanced precariously on his tiny moped. A comical sight. A hoot. Mr Rook the irascible old rascal making off down the mountainside.

When Matthew got back to Sarah, she was lying on her back staring up at the sky with a look of frozen horror. Matthew was sobbing and cursing as he pulled her bikini bottom back up her legs and smoothed her short, white skirt down over her thighs. He lay across her body to protect her from all evil, his lips twisted in a prayer that it hadn't really happened, that it had all been a nightmare. The sound of his prayer summoned Mathilda who came tiptoeing out of the villa, holding a small paraffin lamp in front of her.

'What on earth is the matter with the silly girl,' Mathilda said, and Matthew knew, he just knew in his own heart, that Mathilda knew exactly what had happened and that she had planned the whole thing. He knew because he knew her face as well as he knew his own.

'He raped me,' Sarah said, looking up at the steel-grey sky.

Mathilda frowned down on her and then shook her head confidentially at Matthew.

'If she will wear next to nothing . . .'

Matthew wanted to yell so loud it would shatter the moon, but he found that his voice wouldn't function. He could only stare up at her grey, contorted face.

'She's been behaving like a whore, Matthew. You must know that. Mr Rook is a gentleman with those who deserve to be treated in a gentlemanly way . . .'

Mathilda put her bony hands to her mouth and gave a little hiccup of either shock or contempt and then trotted back to the villa and bolted the door. When Matthew realized that Sarah could neither move nor speak, other than to repeat what she had said, he ran back to the villa, smashed a window with his fist, unlocked it and crawled inside to grab their passports and money. He then dragged Sarah down to the harbour, where they caught the next hydrofoil to Athens.

Eight and a half months later, Tanya was born.

Matthew and Sarah never discussed the obvious, horrendous possibility. They both chose to believe that she was the product of their afternoons spent in the cool of the cave at Koukounaries, rather than the rape. But for years, Matthew had studied Tanya's face when she was playing or laughing, trying to catch a glimpse of the ghost of Mr Rook in her features. By the time she was five or six he was sure that she was his child, but there had still been evenings when she tiptoed into their room in the dark, when he woke with a start and was sure he saw the face of the jolly, gentlemanly Mr Rook smiling up at him.

Matthew knew that he had loved Tanya all the more because of his persistent uncertainty. If she was indeed Rook's child, then she was a monster from hell. He had to love her intensely to prove that it wasn't true. The more he loved her, the more proof there was that she wasn't Rook's monstrous ghost. She had grown up to be pretty in an angular kind of way, and sometimes her eyes reminded Matthew of his own mother's, and even the sight of her expressions reborn in his daughter's face gave him some comfort.

It shouldn't have made any difference that she was pretty, but it did. It made the injustice of her death seem all the more profound in Matthew's mind, and it made the venom of his vengeance all the more toxic. For years he had been fighting against Rook in his thoughts, banishing him from his daughter's ancestry. Now it seemed that it was possible that Rook had been instrumental in destroying her, as if he had somehow known he had lost the battle for her and wanted to kill her as one last desperate throw of the dice.

The mystery of who Tanya's father really was had been buried with her body. There would now be no way of knowing for sure. Part of Matthew's desire to confront Rook was driven by a desire to tell him to his face that Tanya had belonged to him and to no one else. He wanted to stare into those eyes one more time and know for sure that this creature and his own daughter could not have been related. As for what would happen after that, Matthew couldn't guess. He suspected that one way or another, Mr Rook would not survive their meeting.

CHAPTER SIX

I

Skiathos police station was a dark tiled corridor with a single cell at the end of it, little different to the many small tourist *pensions* that climbed the foot of the mountain around Skiathos harbour.

Matthew walked from the fish market up through narrow bleached-chalk streets which were already blistering in the morning heat. Polite and silent tourists in shorts and sandals drifted from shop front to shop front, looking vaguely for something to see or do, while the smaller islanders, walnut-skinned and heavily dressed, weaved in between them going about their separate business. It seemed that the islanders had no social intercourse with their northern visitors. These migratory creatures flocked to the island in summer to bask in the warmer air, eat the fish, oil themselves on the rocks. To engage a tourist in conversation would have been seen by the islanders as a madness akin to talking to the birds.

When Matthew approached the reception desk of the police station, he was immediately handed a leaflet and a map by the languid, brown-eyed policeman who presided over a small wooden desk, a TV, a single upright filing cabinet and a full ashtray. There was also a fax machine that looked to be just out of its box.

'Do you speak English?' Matthew said, wiping sweat from his face.

'Sure,' said the policeman. 'Are you lost?'

'No. I'm not lost, I need some information.'

'Shoot.'

A middle-aged woman in voluminous shorts and a floral shirt

poked her head around the open door of the police station and squinted into the darkness, looking for icons, tapestries, statues, an explanatory plaque, anything to fill a few minutes. When she saw the policeman and the bars of the cell she ducked back out into the sunlight. The policeman gave the woman a formal 'Welcome to Skiathos' smile before she disappeared, then gave the same smile to Matthew.

'I was wondering,' Matthew said, 'if there was such a thing as a land register for the island. A register of ownership.'

The policeman's smile lasted for a long time, as he tried to find any of the words Matthew had used in his own mental register of the things that tourists normally said. He drew a blank. Matthew guessed that the policeman could direct him to any restaurant, shrine or church on the island. He could tell him where to buy sun cream, sardine oil, insulin, cockroach powder, leather knapsacks, goatskin gloves. It wasn't going to be easy to conduct ordinary human business on a tourist island like this. Matthew was stepping across the divide. He was a talking bird.

'Such thing as a what?' the policeman said, still smiling.

'A register of ownership. You see, I want to find out who owns a particular villa. It used to belong to someone called Mathilda King, and I was wondering who owned it now. It's up near Koukounaries bay.'

The policeman's eyes lit up and he turned Matthew's map of the island around on the reception desk.

'Koukounaries bay is here. See. You can take a bus or take a taxi. It will cost you . . .'

'No, no, I know where it is. But I need to find out about a particular villa.'

'You want to rent a villa?'

'No, I just want to know who owns it.'

The policeman laid his hands flat on the desk and smiled. Matthew smiled back. He had known that the police station would be a long shot, but he had already run out of other options and it was only 11 a.m. At dawn he'd tiptoed from his hotel suite to the beach and swam alone in the clear water of

Koukounaries bay in the morning chill. Then he had walked five kilometres up the mountain, following a thistle-choked goat track up to Mathilda's villa. He and Sarah had walked up the same track, with Matthew clutching one end of a beach towel and Sarah hanging on to the other as he dragged her up the mountain in the merciless inland heat. When he got to the villa, he found that it was deserted.

Three earthenware pots were still standing guard by the door, but now they had been overrun by wild sage and rosemary. The small orchard was chest high in bamboo and rice grass, and the stepping-stone path to the front door had been reclaimed totally by the wilderness. The brown-tiled roof had sagged and shed half its tiles, and the shutters on the windows had broken free of their fastenings. The silence of this dereliction unnerved him. It was as if no living thing had stepped inside the garden for ten years; even the cicadas had stopped singing. There was a strong smell of septic tanks and nettles coming from the fountain, and the padlock and chain on the gate had rusted and corroded in the salt air.

Matthew had his own picture of the villa which he had carried around inside his head for ten years. In his mind the villa was bathed in moonlight, the white walls shining like bone, Mathilda was standing in the light of the doorway, and somewhere in the shadows of the orchard Mr Rook was doing his evil work. To see the villa in ruins was like peering at the face of an old enemy in death; toothless, sunken, yellowed with age. There was a wooden notice in Greek writing hanging from the gate, and Matthew copied the writing on to the back of his hand.

As he transcribed the curls and twists of the lettering, his hand shook and sweat poured down his body beneath his loose cotton shirt. The urge to run like hell back down the mountain was so strong that he began to back away from the gate even before he had finished. He put his pen back into his shirt pocket and turned down the thistle-choked path again, without once looking back. For the first hundred yards, he felt as if the spirit of the mountain was at his heels, or that Mathilda herself was bounding over the iron gate, furious that her peace had finally been disturbed.

'You want to know who owns it,' the policeman said, repeating Matthew's words without understanding. Matthew wiped his brow.

'I thought maybe there might be a register. I don't know, a register of deeds.'

There was a silent impasse in which the policeman retrieved his stubby cigarette from the ashtray. The air inside the police station smelt of sulphur and smoke. Outside Matthew could hear the weary clip-clop of a donkey's hooves and someone honked a guttural greeting in Greek as they walked by the open door. The policeman waved into the sunlight.

'OK, OK,' Matthew said, 'is there a town hall, an *ayuntami-ento*, a local government office?'

Matthew might just as well have been counting to ten. He looked at the palm of his hand and saw the Greek lettering he had copied down from the villa was beginning to smudge with sweat. He held it up for the policeman to see.

'You see this,' Matthew said. The policeman's eyes widened with puzzlement. 'Can you tell me what this says?'

'Says? Your hand?'

Matthew pointed to the smudged lettering.

'What does this mean? It was written on a sign at the villa . . .'

The policeman backed away from Matthew's hand.

'Can you read it?'

'Ah, read. Sure.'

The policeman took hold of Matthew's hand gently and studied the lettering. It took him a few seconds to work it out and then he waved his hand at Matthew.

'It means go away. Don't come.'

'Keep out.'

'Sure. Keep out.'

'OK, thanks.'

Matthew was trying to think of another approach when a skinny, good-looking islander in a two-tone suit bustled in through the door. He barked something in Greek and the policeman stood to attention. They started to talk first, as if they were resuming a conversation that was already half-way through. The policeman whistled through his teeth with amazement at whatever he was being told. The skinny guy grabbed his own wrist and held it up in the air. The policeman whistled again. Suddenly, Matthew no longer existed, another seagull on a rock. The policeman lifted the hatch of the reception desk and the skinny islander ducked underneath it and hurried to the filing cabinet.

'Excuse me,' Matthew said to his back. 'Do you work here?'

The skinny guy turned around.

'Me?'

'Yes.'

The desk officer raised his eyebrows at Matthew's apparent impropriety.

'That is Inspector Konstantinou,' the policeman said with great reverence.

'Does he speak English?'

Inspector Konstantinou gave Matthew a look of mild disdain and then turned back to searching through his files.

'Yeah, I speak English,' he said. 'Do you speak Greek?'

Konstantinou lifted a file from the cabinet and laid it on the desk, lighting a cigarette with one hand while he did it. The cigarette dangled from his lips as he hurriedly leafed through the file.

'Then I wonder if you can help me,' Matthew said to the top of his head. Konstantinou ignored him. The desk officer put his hand on Matthew's hand.

'The inspector is busy,' he whispered.

'I can see that. I just wanted to ask him if there is such a thing as a land register, a register of ownership . . .'

Konstantinou barked an order in Greek and waved his hand. The policeman quickly handed him a pen. Konstantinou made a note on the file. He underlined something then looked up at Matthew.

'Are you lost my friend?' Konstantinou said.

'No, I'm not lost. I was asking about a land register. I'm trying to find out who owns a villa up near Koukounaries and you see, in-spector, it is rather urgent.'

Matthew wasn't sure of the exact exchange rate, but he knew for sure that the wad of notes he had produced from his pocket was roughly equivalent to £200. He had laid the notes on the reception desk. Konstantinou held his cigarette an inch from his face, as if he'd been turned to stone by the sight of the money. After a few seconds he came back to life.

'You want to exchange some money, my friend?'

'No, I want information.'

'So, go to the tourist information.'

The desk officer drummed his fingers a few inches from the wad of notes.

'It's not tourist information I want. I'm not a tourist. I'm here on business.'

Konstantinou asked a pointed question in Greek, which the desk officer couldn't answer. Konstantinou stroked his clean-shaven chin in exasperation. He had fine delicate features, and a high quiff of thick black hair.

'Listen to me,' he said softly to Matthew. 'Twenty minutes ago a Norwegian woman found a hand on the beach. Yesterday it was an Australian with a foot. Tomorrow my money is on an American with a dick. We've got somebody coming to this island bit by bit. Do you understand?'

'A hand?' Matthew said.

'Yeah, a severed left hand. So now I've got to call every Flying Dolphin booking office on the islands to see who boarded a boat but didn't get off again. It's the engines. Someone falls into the engine, they get cut up into a hundred pieces. And it's me who has to put the pieces back together.'

Konstantinou pushed the wad of notes back across the reception desk towards Matthew, glaring at the desk officer as he did it.

'So you see, we're pretty busy. You keep your money in your pocket, OK? In this office we don't accept gifts.'

Matthew took the money back, folded it slowly and put it in his top pocket. He looked at the desk officer who was wiping his mouth hungrily at the sight of the wad of notes.

'In that case,' Matthew said, 'I'll come back later when you're not so busy.'

'You do that.'

'I'll bring a translator. Is there a good translator on the island?'

Konstantinou's English was excellent and Matthew knew that suggesting a translator would irritate him. The inspector stubbed out his cigarette angrily.

'You don't need a translator in this office.'

'Maybe not. But it's technical information I need.'

'I don't accept gifts. And I don't need a translator for technical information. What is it you want to know?'

Matthew explained that he'd visited a derelict villa that morning near Koukounaries and that he wanted to find out who owned the land. Konstantinou nodded quickly as Matthew spoke, then finally shook his head.

'I understand what you're saying, but I can't help you,' he said firmly and went back to his desk and closed his file.

'So who can? I just need to see the documentation on it.'

Konstantinou smiled as he put the file back into the cabinet and slammed the drawer closed.

'Where are you from?' he said.

'London.'

'I knew it. I lived in London for ten years. You know Finchley?'

Matthew nodded.

'Well, my friend, you're not in London now. If you want documentation, you're in the wrong place. Maybe in ten years we'll have this island organized. If it were up to me it would take five. Until then, you're out of luck.'

A motorbike choked and spluttered into silence on the cobbled street outside. A big-bellied policeman in reflector sunglasses stepped into the station and began to speak gravely in Greek. From the way he slapped his thigh, Matthew guessed that someone had found a leg. Konstantinou covered his eyes with his hands as he listened. Matthew waited a few moments and then realized that he had become invisible again, and he stepped

back out into the white-hot streets without anyone saying
farewell.

2

He took a taxi back to the Skiathos Palace Hotel and slept
through the afternoon. Only the tourists defied all reason and
stayed out in the murderous midday heat. The islanders and
their cats all found some shade and stayed there until their little
piece of the planet became habitable again.

Matthew lay on the bed with the shutters closed and the air-
conditioning on full, so that his room felt damp and earthy. He
could hear the seagulls and the bathers shrieking down below in
the bay. A little after three, there was a knock at the door.

'Mr King,' the bellboy said, 'can I disturb you a moment.'

Matthew led him into the darkness of his room. The bellboy
seemed nervous and in a hurry to get out.

Matthew offered him a beer, but he shook his head.

'There is a guy who runs a beach bar, just down in the bay, a
German guy called Lot. He said he knows someone. He said he
can take you to him.'

Matthew found the key to the safe and unlocked it. He
handed the bellboy a handful of notes. He wasn't sure how
much, but from the look on the boy's face, he guessed it must
have been a month's salary. The bellboy seemed momentarily
ashamed of himself as he took the money, then hurried to the
door. He hovered in the doorway, not sure how to say what he
had to say.

'This guy, Lot,' he said at last, 'I think . . . I guess he'll want
money too.'

'I'm sure he will,' Matthew said with a smile. 'If he takes me
to Mr Rook, I'll see that they both get what they deserve.'

After the bellboy had gone, Matthew stuffed some more notes
into his pocket from his safe, dressed and went down to the bay.

The beach bar at Koukounaries bay was no more than a small roof made of rush matting, with a bar made from planks and driftwood. The speckled shade of the roof covered an area big enough to accommodate a dozen whicker tables, all looking out on to the sparkling green ocean.

Lot and his wife cooked sardines, crabs, yellow mackerel and mullet on a charcoal griddle supported by washed-up timber. Lot's wife said that all the fish was caught by her husband, who went out to fish very early in the morning in his motor launch. That was why he had to sleep in the afternoon, and that was why she was doing all the work. She carried five plates of fish at a time to impatient bathers, who always asked for one more thing when their food was delivered. Another beer, more lemonade, white wine, napkins, always something to send Lot's wife scurrying back to the bar with a half-heard apology. Matthew had already waited an hour and a half for Lot to appear, and the sun was beginning to lose some of its intensity. Most of the bathers were back in the sea. It seemed they only came back on to land to eat and breed.

'So, do you know my husband?' Lot's wife said, sipping her first beer of the day at Matthew's table.

'No, no, I just want to speak to him.'

Lot's wife had been on edge ever since Matthew had asked to see her husband. She had been trying to pump Matthew for information about his business in her own apologetic way. Every time she spoke about Lot she seemed to be trying to make excuses for him, even though no accusation had been made.

'Some days he sleeps longer than others,' she said with an almost perfect English accent. She was German, but Matthew had heard her conversing freely with tourists in Italian, English, Greek and Spanish. 'It depends on how long he was out fishing. Some days it's six hours.'

Matthew nodded. He already felt sorry for Lot's wife and had sketched out a life history. An educated middle-class German who had fallen in love with the island and with the wrong man, working herself to a skeleton to support him. She had the unmistakable air of a dominated woman, a woman who justified her husband to strangers for reasons she herself had forgotten. When Lot finally emerged, bleary, unkempt, spreading around the middle, Matthew knew that he was right. He sat down heavily beside his wife and took a few minutes to adjust to wakefulness.

Matthew guessed from the look in his eyes that his vices were beer and dope, and maybe a little cocaine if it washed up on the shore.

'So, you're the guy from the hotel?' Lot said and put his hand on his wife's bony knee. 'Baby, fetch me a beer.'

Lot's wife hurried to the bar.

'I'm looking for opium,' Matthew said.

Lot narrowed his eyes and looked out to sea. A Flying Dolphin cruiser was skimming across the surface of the sea like a giant long-legged insect.

'Sure,' Lot said, then he pointed out to sea. 'You see that big bastard? That fucking Dolphin? They scare away all the fucking fish from this bay. The engines scare the fish. The only thing I get now is the mullet. The rest I have to buy in. I should get compensation. They're ruining my livelihood. But if you complain these fucking Greeks just go . . .'

Lot shrugged his shoulders and then belched loudly.

'Fuck them,' he said under his breath. Lot's wife arrived with a cold can of beer, which he opened with a flourish.

'So, where?' Matthew said. Lot took a swig of beer.

'The hotel boy said you were pretty anxious.'

Matthew nodded and took out a roll of notes. He'd put aside around £200 for Lot. He wished now that he'd decided on half that amount, but what the hell did it matter. He placed the notes on the table. Lot's wife looked at the money and asked a question in German, and Lot patted her knee with a vicious grin and shushed her.

'Like I said, those Dolphins are killing my business. I've got bills like you have never seen.'

Matthew took some more notes and laid them on the table. The Dolphin had disappeared. A family of bathers were packing their things on the beach.

'That's a lot of money just for an address,' Matthew said.

Lot swept the money from the table and stuffed it into his pocket. Lot's wife watched the money disappear as though it were pearls being thrown into a bottomless ocean.

'Not just an address,' Lot said. 'A taxi service too. We can take a ride on my motorbike. Baby, you clear up the mats. I've got to take this guy to see Mr Rook.'

CHAPTER SEVEN

'I take the red line,' Lot shouted above the throaty roar of his motorbike's engine. Even at this speed his delivery was precise, his accent impeccable. 'The red line is the fastest line, cutting the bends straight. It is also the most dangerous.'

Matthew held on to Lot's body in a terrified embrace. As the sun had set and his bar had emptied, Lot and his wife had put up the storm shutters and Matthew had helped them clear the tables. Lot's wife had smiled weakly at him, as if he were a vision of mercy. Then Lot explained that he'd 'fucked around' with the engine of his motorbike himself to give it more 'fuckin' hell'. Matthew hadn't known what Lot had meant until the bike leapt on to the dirt track that led up the mountain from the beach bar like a frightened stallion. He had immediately yelled, 'Fucking hell!' and Lot had turned and grinned. Now his straggly blond hair whipped around in the backdraught from the bike's break-neck speed.

The mountain road climbed higher, like a thin cord wrapped around the rock, and Lot took the machine to within inches of the two-hundred-feet drop to straighten out the bends.

'Slow down!' Matthew shouted, as the bike splashed into a patch of gravel and then roared back on to the road.

'I'm in a hurry,' Lot shouted.

Lot drove without lights, and the twilight had thickened into darkness by the time they were on their descent. The air smelt clean and fresh, but Lot needed a shower and the smell of his sweat was choking, even on the top of the mountain.

The sound of the bike's engine rang out across the mountain and Matthew dared himself to peek over the precipice into the ocean below. They banked into a bend and almost collided with a tiny donkey carrying a mountain of straw on its back. The chestnut-skinned farm-hand waved his stick at them as they roared past.

'I can roll now,' Lot said and suddenly cut the engine. The only sound Matthew could hear was the wind in his ears. They began to accelerate down the unlit road, the silence even more terrifying than the roar of the engine.

'You feel it? You feel the mountain pushing us down? That's energy. That's the universe.'

'I want to get off.'

'On the way up you got petrol and cogs. But on the way down it's the power of the universe. You feel it?'

Lot was speaking quietly but was still audible now that the descent was unpowered.

'I can go twice as fast without the engine. I just have to control the energy. Make the right turns.'

The bends and kinks in the mountain road got tighter and closer together, until Lot was moving his body like a slalom skier. Twice Matthew thought that he had lost his balance and put his foot out instinctively to break his fall. Lot yelled at him.

'Don't do that! You'll kill us both!'

In total darkness they reached the lower slopes of the mountain. Matthew was gripping Lot so tightly that he could feel pinches of skin between his fingers. And beneath the skin, hard bone. The bike began to slow down and Matthew loosened his grip.

'You shit yourself?' Lot said.

'No.'

'Good. You're OK. Most people shit themselves.'

They pulled up near a bay where several yachts were moored. There was also a jetty where three island fishermen were mending nets by the light of a spirit lamp. Lot climbed off the bike and Matthew stumbled to his feet.

'Where are we?' Matthew said.

'Come.'

Lot headed towards a small shack which was in darkness, its doors locked and the windows shuttered. Above the door there was a hand-painted sign which said 'Costa Rica'.

'I think it's closed,' Matthew said.

'Sure it's closed,' Lot said, reaching for a bunch of keys in the pocket of his shorts. 'I've got to open it.'

He unlocked the door and pushed it open. As he entered the bar, he turned on a light which flickered for a long time before it bathed the room in a hesitant yellow light. The light-bulb buzzed and the air smelt strongly of beer and fish.

'In the day, my wife runs the beach bar,' Lot said, collecting six dirty glasses from the bar with one hand, 'and at night I run this place. I bet you thought I was a lazy bastard sitting there watching her work. But I have to work till after three.'

He walked through some swing doors into the kitchen and a light came on. Matthew could see the stainless steel furnishings through round windows, and a mountain of dirty pots in a sink. The tiled floor was sticky with spilt beer. Lot came back out with a bottle of ouzo and a bottle of whisky, offering both. Matthew took the whisky, Lot took the ouzo. He poured two-shot glasses, handed one to Matthew and then drank the other down.

'The guy you're going to meet is called Rook,' he said, 'I told him that you weren't buying for your own personal use. That's right, isn't it?'

Matthew said that was right. Lot drank down another glass of ouzo.

'So who for?'

'I'll tell Rook when I see him.'

'Do you use speedboats or the Dolphins for transportation?'

'Speed boats.'

'Let me guess. You used to get your stuff in Turkey, but you got pissed off with the guy in Antalya. What's that guy's name . . .?'

Matthew smiled and poured himself another glass of whisky.

'You want names? What are you, a policeman?'

Lot grinned.

'I was going to ask you the same question.'

Lot and Matthew smiled at each other for a few moments, then Lot slapped his belly.

'Nah, you're OK. I can tell. I can smell fish too. Underneath

73

the ocean I can smell shoals with my nose. It drives these Greeks insane the way I do it.'

Lot laughed and went back behind the bar. He began to take bottles of American beer out of a crate and stuff them in an ancient-looking fridge. Then he began to chop the mould off lemons before slicing them and putting them into a beer glass.

'So Mr Rook owns this place,' Matthew said.

'I franchise this place from him. He owns all the land round here. The guys on the jetty want to cut his liver out and give it to the gulls. One day I think they'll do it.'

Matthew took a seat at the bar. Lot handed him a warm beer.

'What time will he be here?' Matthew asked.

'Today's rent day. He'll be here after eleven. He comes out at night. Like those lizards. What are they called . . .'

Matthew took some drachmae from his pocket and placed them on the bar. Lot pushed them back, but Matthew insisted.

'Money's tight, isn't it, Lot?'

'Always.'

'So take the money. Maybe if you help me you can make some more money too. Enough for a new bike, a bar of your own.'

Lot put his hands on his hips and stared at Matthew. He chuckled.

'Help you do what?'

'I don't know yet,' Matthew said.

The three fishermen who had been out on the jetty walked into the bar and rubbed their hands. They greeted Lot shyly and Lot spoke to them in Greek. They sat down and picked up the three glasses of beer with hands that could have been carved from ebony. They nodded at Matthew and then began the business of getting drunk. Matthew drank moderately, knowing that he might have to wait a long time and that if he mixed alcohol with his murderous thoughts, his entire plan could explode before it was primed.

At 1 a.m. a car pulled up outside the bar. Matthew saw the headlights shining through the window, then there was darkness. Lot glanced at Matthew and nodded his head. He swept his hair from his face and straightened some beer mats. The three fishermen, who were now drunk but quiet, all stood up and left the bar, putting their denim caps back on their heads with resolution. Shortly after they left, Mr Rook came in.

He seemed to be half the weight he had been the last time Matthew had seen him. He was wearing knee-length shorts and his legs were varnished brown. The ghost of fat still hung on his frame and he moved awkwardly. His face was drawn and hollow, but the red-rimmed eyes were the same. As he walked into the bar, he greeted Lot in German. Matthew clinked his beer glass with his finger nail. Lot hesitated then opened the till and took out a sheaf of notes. He handed them to Mr Rook, who folded them and pushed them into the back pocket of his shorts. He turned and was about to leave. Lot grabbed his arm and nodded in Matthew's direction. Rook turned.

'Mr Rook,' Matthew said.

'Yes?'

Matthew stood up from his bar stool to face him. He tried to keep the murder out of his eyes.

'You don't remember me, do you?' Matthew said.

Rook glanced at Lot for clues and then shook his head. Not only had Rook lost a lot of weight, he had also shed some of the gravity of his presence. He seemed to be visibly fading away.

'My name is Matthew King. We met ten years ago.'

Rook spent a few moments thinking and then it was as if a switch had been flicked and a hundred mechanisms had been activated. A look of panic swept across Lot's face and he was about to lift the hatch of the bar, but Matthew held it down. Rook began to piece Matthew's face together in the flickering light.

'Matthew?' he breathed.

'You remember.'

'But of course.'

'Everything?'

'Matthew, my dear boy . . .'

Lot looked suddenly relieved and Rook turned to him with a look of insincere delight.

'Lot, get us some drinks. Matthew King . . . goodness . . .'

Lot reached into the fridge for two beers, opened them and poured them.

'Please, Matthew, dear boy . . . won't you take a seat?' Rook said.

'Thank you, Mr Rook, that's very kind.'

Lot brought the beers to the table and Rook felt his bottle with his hand.

'Cold ones, Lot, for Christ's sake . . .'

'Sorry, Mr Rook.'

Lot skipped back behind the bar. Matthew was already disappointed at the way Lot's breezy irreverence had deserted him in Rook's presence. Rook was trying hard to maintain the smile on his face.

'Matthew, what on earth brings you back here? Is your wife . . .'

'You mean Sarah? No, she isn't here. It's just me. I'm on my own this time.'

'Goodness.'

Lot hurried to the table with two glasses of cold beer.

'Thank you, Lot,' Matthew said. 'You can go home now.'

Lot hesitated then smiled, as if this were a joke.

'Send him home, Mr Rook. What I have to say to you is private.'

Matthew stared into Rook's eyes as he spoke. Ten years' worth of fury held at bay with a smile which Matthew knew would be ugly and menacing no matter how hard he tried to soften it. For ten years this moment had been part of a private drama re-enacted in his head once or twice a day. Sarah and he had agreed that they would bury the memory of what had happened. They had decided with great sobriety that they couldn't allow Rook and his memory to dominate their lives, that to do so would be like a second violation. But the horror of it all had never gone away, and when the inheritance came, Matthew had thought that, in some perverse way, his mother was trying to make it up to them.

Lot stood his ground. Matthew wanted to push him to the door.

'Tell him to go home, Mr Rook,' Matthew said again.

Rook blinked slowly and nodded. Lot headed for the door.

'I'll be in touch,' Matthew said, and he rubbed his thumb and forefinger together, signifying money. Matthew was already becoming intoxicated by the power at his fingertips. It was like crossing the top of the mountain on Lot's motorbike. For almost ten years he had been climbing with the weight of the money dragging him down. Now he was on the downslope, and it was the power of the universe at his back.

'So what is it that is so private?' Rook said.

'Someone killed my daughter,' Matthew said, and he swigged his beer without taking his eyes off Rook. Rook seemed genuinely puzzled.

'How awful. Do you have any idea who on earth . . .'

'I have no intention of answering any questions, Mr Rook. I am only going to ask them. And I want you to answer truthfully.'

Rook shifted uneasily in his seat. He seemed to be dealing with some pain that hit him intermittently.

'Why should I?' he gasped.

'Because if you don't, I will pay one of those fishermen out there, or Lot, or someone, to kill you. I have set aside £1 million for your death. I have worked the whole thing out and given everything a priority.'

Mr Rook looked astonished for a few seconds and then recovered his composure. He nodded at his beer glass.

'I should call the police.'

'Call them. I know about your business. Heroin in speed boats.'

Mr Rook chuckled.

'You are obviously insane.'

'Yes. But also rich. Money and insanity are a lethal combination, Mr Rook.'

Mr Rook nodded again, as if he knew this to be true.

'So why are you talking to me?'

'Where did my mother get her money?'

'I have no idea.'

'Why does someone want to stop me from finding out?'

'How the hell should I know?'

'OK, the first question again. Where did my mother get £25 million?'

'I've told you, I don't know.'

Earlier, Matthew had slipped the knife which Lot used to slice the lemons into his pocket. It only had a three-inch blade, but it was sharp as a needle. Now Matthew held it up to the light.

CHAPTER EIGHT

I

Matthew had Rook on the floor, the knife at his chest. It was like handling the skeleton of the man he'd grappled with in the garden ten years before, as if Rook had died that day and had been decomposing ever since. He had very little strength and Matthew easily pushed his arms back and pinned them to the floor.

'For God's sake, Matthew . . .'

'How does it feel, Mr Rook?'

'I'm a sick man . . .'

After ten years this fantasy had flesh and bone. Matthew only wished now that Sarah still loved him, that they were still the same as they had been then. Maybe this would break the curse, if he were just to pierce that flesh and bone with the blade of the knife, puncture him.

'I'll ask you again, where did she get her money?'

Rook spluttered and his face turned scarlet. Matthew decided that Rook was genuinely sick. He couldn't bear the idea that Rook might have died before he could get to him.

'Where?'

'I swear to you, Matthew, I was as shocked as anyone when I heard about the will. I used to lend her money, for Christ's sake. I didn't know she was . . .'

Rook began to choke. Matthew loosened his grip.

'Why would someone want to kill my daughter?'

The engine pumped out an image of Tanya, which made Matthew tighten his grip again. He had never had such energy. His arms were mighty pistons.

'How the hell should I know. For God's sake get off my chest . . .'

Matthew sat on Rook's bony frame for a few more seconds, then climbed off. Rook clutched his chest. His shirt had torn open and Matthew could see a long fresh scar down the length of his breastbone.

'I've just had a fucking triple bypass,' he breathed.

Matthew hauled Rook into a chair and pushed his head back.

'I ought to open you up myself,' Matthew said, pointing the knife at his chest.

'What the hell have you got against me?'

Matthew stared into his eyes. Rook read what was written there.

'Oh, for God's sake, Matthew, I was as high as a . . .'

Matthew slapped his face.

'It was a long time ago . . .' Rook said, trying to sound contrite through his pain.

'Not for me, it wasn't. It was yesterday for me, and for Sarah.'

Rook was breathing hard. Matthew's anger hit him in waves as the engine slipped down a gear. He swept the two beer bottles off the table. Rook finally got his breath back.

'I've changed,' Rook said softly. 'Intimations of mortality and all that. I was a wicked man for a long, long time. I'm sorry about what I did to your wife.'

Matthew looked around the bar. The greasy walls, the wind moaning through the broken window-pane. This wasn't the setting he'd imagined for this scene. He'd always pictured it happening in Mathilda's garden, with Sarah looking on, and Mathilda too. And in his dreams, Rook was as fat as he had been then. Rook reached into his pocket. Matthew was about to brandish the knife, but he took out a bottle of pills and poured two into his hand. He tossed them into his mouth, pushed his head back and swallowed.

'Odd, isn't it? All my life I risk jail to get my supply, and now the doctors are giving them to me like sweets. Do you think I could have a glass of water, Matthew?'

Matthew put his knee on Rook's lap and the knife to his

throat. Suddenly Rook summoned enough strength to push Matthew off.

'You don't frighten me with that thing, Matthew,' Rook said. 'I'm dying anyway. These pills are just a way to ease me into oblivion.'

Matthew pulled up a chair and sat face to face with Rook.

'So, before you go, tell me what you know.'

2

'You have a brother,' Rook said, dragging deeply on one of Matthew's cigarettes. Rook had explained that smoking even one cigarette was tantamount to suicide but that the struggle for life was really no longer worth the candle. His face had turned the colour of bone.

'That is to say, you have a half-brother. My son.'

Matthew had placed the lemon knife on one of the greasy bar tables, so that Rook could see it out of the corner of his eye, a vicious prompt. Matthew only had to glance at it to set Rook talking.

'Your father and I . . . we were good friends. I often visited him and your mother. Then your mother and I had an affair and things got out of hand. Your father was on a tour of duty in Aden, clearing up the mess the wogs were making. Forgive me, could you pass the ashtray.'

Matthew simply stared at Rook, who chuckled and flicked his ash on the floor.

'You've got a point. Not exactly the Ritz, my little empire, is it.'

Matthew reached out for the knife. The shock of what Rook was saying was making him reel, but the engine inside was keeping him steady, pumping a pure antidote to adrenalin into his system like a second heart.

'Your mother fell pregnant and your father knew it couldn't be his. It wasn't so easy to have an abortion in those days and they agreed that she'd have the baby and have it adopted. Which is what they did. It destroyed both of them. You may not believe it, Matthew, but once upon a time your mother and father were such . . . fun.'

Matthew recalled a jolly day at Regent's Park Zoo when his father had made Matthew shriek with laughter with his impressions of the noises all the animals made, or are supposed to make. He remembered his father lifting him on to a warm white statue in the park and saluting him with a huge grin. That day had been like a brief ray of sunlight through thick cloud.

'Your father left the army and went into the Civil Service. You asked me once if he was a hero. Well, he really was a hero of the finest sort. I, on the other hand . . .'

Rook's eyes were beginning to fill with tears. He could hardly draw on his cigarette.

'You have his eyes you know. It's almost like looking at him. The way he'd looked at me when he found out what I had done while he was away doing fine work. He never forgave me and I realize now that I never forgave myself. I don't believe in God, but I believe there are rules. That's what makes life so difficult. There are rules, but there is no referee. What are we supposed to do?'

'When was this?' Matthew said, not troubled by Rook's tears at all.

'My son was born in '60. He was adopted by the British ambassador to Nigeria. Your father arranged it all. He wanted to keep it within the service. He was very senior you know. Quite the James Bond . . .'

'So is this why my mother left?'

It was the hardest question to ask without breaking, but Matthew rode it like a surfer on a wave.

'Your father wanted to have a child of his own quickly after the adoption. Sort of marking his territory. You were born and I suppose you were a constant reminder of the other one. Forgive me, Matthew, but you said you wanted the truth. Your mother told me that she hated you from the moment you were born . . .'

Matthew nodded his head. After a second's pause, Rook continued.

'The idiots at the hospital had let her hold the first one for ten hours. She knew exactly how long. Ten hours she held him and then they took him away. For some reason, when you were born she blamed you. She stuck it for four years and then she fled. She came to stay with me here on Skiathos and I sorted a villa out for her. Not much of a place, but I had very little to offer her. I suppose we were in love with each other. That was the point. But there was all this past coming between us. That was why she made me walk up the mountain every night. She would never let me live with her. She made me walk up this ugly mountain every evening to prove to God that she wasn't a wicked woman. I did her penance for her.'

There was a long silence while Matthew twisted the knife round and round in his hand. Outside the fishermen were dragging their boats across the dark shale, ready for another night's fishing.

'Did my mother leave this other son anything in her will?'

'She left him the villa. As far as I know, that was all she had to leave at the time. Then I was told about the money. The monstrosity. I swear to you on all that I hold holy, which isn't much, that I knew nothing about the money until she died. But Matthew, if you're looking for someone who has a grievance against you, then I would say it would have to be your half-brother. If he is any son of mine, he would be mightily aggrieved at the injustice.'

Outside the boats splashed into the water. Matthew used the knife to dig a groove into the soft wood of the greasy table.

'Do you know what his name was, this half-brother of mine?'

'Your mother called him Peter. I have no idea if the people who adopted him kept the name. But they were called Callow. So the man you are looking for is probably called Peter Callow.'

CHAPTER NINE

I

Matthew stared at himself in the mirror as another handful of wiry black hair fell from his face. The barber sang arias as he cut Matthew's face out of its jungle undergrowth. The barber was fat and laughed a lot and his belly felt warm against Matthew's shoulder. The barber's shop was hidden in a dog-leg of a side street, on the hot, dry land of islander territory, away from the streams of tourists. The shop had three faded photographs of sharp-looking Greek men from the 1950s in the window. The single shelf above the barber's chair had a lone bottle of Portugal water and a photograph of a woman in a bikini to distract the customer.

After the barber had cut Matthew's hair short, he began to trim the excess of his beard and moustache. When the growth was down to a manageable size, the barber began to lather a badger-hair shaving brush, his aria trembling in his throat as he whipped the cream into suds.

'So what, are you getting married?' the barber said as he began to daub the suds on to Matthew's chin.

'No, just changing the way I look,' Matthew said. 'I want to look more like what I am.'

The barber peered at Matthew's reflection.

'So, what are you?'

'I don't know. I'll find out when you've finished.'

The barber shrugged and continued to lather Matthew's beard. Matthew had decided that every change should lead to another. He had woken that morning and realized that he had been hiding behind his wiry tangle of hair for too long, like Ben Gunn stranded for ten years on a deserted island. During the night he had decided that when he had finished in Skiathos, he had business in Athens, London, maybe Nigeria. Nigeria might lead back to London or Paris or Buenos Aires. Matthew had the whole world laid before him and he knew that his final destination would be Gibraltar. To finish his business and get to Gibraltar in one piece, he would need to look like a man who should be taken seriously.

The barber was half-way through his work with the razor when the bell on the barber's shop door tinkled and Inspector Konstantinou walked in. He strolled up to Matthew with a look of weary irritation, his hands pushed deep into the trouser pockets of his suit.

'I've been looking for you all over the fucking island,' Konstantinou said. The barber stepped away from Matthew's chin and sheathed his razor. Konstantinou clutched the barber's shoulder, pursed his lips and nodded that he should continue his work. The barber opened his razor again and his hand shook a little. Konstantinou was obviously well known on the island.

'For me?' Matthew said. 'Why?'

Matthew thought that maybe Rook had filed a complaint, though that was unlikely. He could see Konstantinou in the mirror, picking up a magazine and flicking through the pages.

'Yesterday you were in my office asking about a villa,' Konstantinou said at last. 'You said it was a villa up by Koukounaries bay. Is this the place?'

Konstantinou held open the magazine at a particular page. The magazine was some sort of property guide to the island. Matthew studied the photograph of an ivy-covered villa reflected in the mirror and shook his head.

'OK, what about this?' Konstantinou said, flicking to another page.

'No. Inspector what are you getting at?'

'This one maybe?'

Another photo which Konstantinou turned to at random. He seemed to be taking all of his anger out on the pages of the magazine.

'No. The villa I was asking about is . . .'

'Koukounaries bay,' Konstantinou said. 'The old chapel of St Elena. Half-way up the mountain. Am I right?'

Matthew threw the white sheet off his chest and stood up. The barber stood on tiptoes to dab cream from his face.

'That's right. Do you know who owns it?'

'Yeah, I know who owns it. The guy was coming here to Skiathos to retire. He was going to sit up there and paint. His sister told me he was a terrible painter, but he was going to paint up there anyway.'

Konstantinou grabbed Matthew by the collar and pushed him up against the window of the barber's shop. The barber stepped back and almost fell into his own chair. The bottle of Portugal water rocked and toppled and then smashed into a fragrant puddle.

'Except now, the guy is in pieces in a refrigerator. We've got the hand, the foot, the leg, the jacket. In the jacket we find the guy's name and address. So tell me. What do you know about a guy called Peter Callow.'

2

The sleepy desk sergeant was reading a two-day-old copy of the *Guardian*, leaning against a desk with his ankles crossed. He looked to be a natural product of the island, fattened on fish oil and goat's milk, seasoned in the sun, too hot for strong opinions. As he read, he picked his solid, ivory-white teeth with a steel paper-clip. Inspector Konstantinou sat opposite Matthew and peered up at his subordinate with a kind of weary fascination.

'He only reads four words of English,' Konstantinou whispered. 'So why is he staring at it?'

The desk sergeant's pretence obviously irritated Konstantinou in a way which Matthew could never hope to understand. After his arrest in the barber's shop, Matthew had suggested that Konstantinou send out for the paper to add credence to his story. Matthew had told him everything, beginning with the inheritance, his daughter's murder, his trip to see Rook and his discovery that he had a half-brother called Peter Callow. A half-brother who was now being pieced together in a fish-packing plant that doubled as the morgue, on the other side of the island.

Konstantinou had apologized to Matthew for the macabre double purpose of the fish plant. He said that he had personally fought to have a conventional morgue built as an annexe to the station. He said proudly that finally Athens had agreed and he was awaiting the paperwork. He said it as if his sharp cynicism was switched off when it came to analysing the changes coming out of his beloved Athens, his cherished modernity.

The *Guardian* carried the article on the third page, and the presence of Matthew's name in the text had impressed Konstantinou more than he cared to show. The description of him as 'a reclusive Hampstead millionaire' had also subtly changed Konstantinou's attitude.

The air inside the police station was hot and dry, and Matthew guessed that Konstantinou must have been shedding gallons of sweat beneath his neatly pressed suit, blazing white shirt and vest, even though he looked as dry as an island lizard. A black armoured insect the size of a small bird clung to the wall but only Matthew seemed to notice it. Between Matthew and Konstantinou there was a phone and a fax, and when Konstantinou wasn't studying the desk sergeant with disdain, he was looking anxiously at the fax machine.

'We've only had direct lines to Europe for two years,' Konstantinou said, to kill a little time. Outside, the hot cobbles rang with the sound of iron-shod donkey hooves, and the polite slap of tourists' sandals. Matthew was already beginning to find the silent curiosity of the endless procession of visitors unnerving. 'I had the fax installed a month ago,' Konstantinou said, trying not to sound too proud, 'I told them that it would be needed and now you see it is needed. I was right.'

Konstantinou shrugged, as if it was only natural that he had been proven right. After reading the article in the *Guardian* which had corroborated Matthew's bizarre story, Konstantinou had put in a call to Joyce in London. According to the Flying Dolphin timetables, Callow had been shot between 5.00 a.m. and 7.00 a.m. Greek time, eleven days earlier. Matthew had explained that it would have been impossible for him to have fired the shot because by 2.00 p.m. English time the same day, he was being interrogated in his own home in London by Joyce. Konstantinou had put the call through to Joyce to verify the story and to prove to Matthew that he could do it. A desk sergeant in London had taken Konstantinou's number and promised that Joyce would call back. Until he called, Konstantinou explained, Matthew was in custody and was the number one suspect for the murder of the guy who had come to the island in pieces.

'Hey, how come,' the desk sergeant said suddenly, pointing with his nose to the paper.

'How come what?' Konstantinou said, without taking his eyes off the fax machine.

'I'm talking to him,' the desk sergeant said, turning to Matthew. 'How come Manchester United are not in the First Division.'

Konstantinou sighed. The desk sergeant showed Matthew the sports page of the newspaper which carried the English football league tables. He pointed with a nicotine-yellow finger at the table marked First Division.

'How come Manchester United are not there any more?'

Matthew explained that the English football league had changed, that there was a new league called the Premier and that Manchester United were in that. Matthew pointed out the premier league table to the desk sergeant, who went back to scraping the gaps between his teeth with his paper-clip, neither satisfied nor dissatisfied with the explanation. Konstantinou murmured something to him in Greek which Matthew took to be a mild rebuke. The phone rang.

Matthew leant back in the badly sprung, revolving typing chair and lit one of Konstantinou's Greek cigarettes, as Konstantinou listened to Matthew's alibi being confirmed. When Joyce asked why Konstantinou needed to know, Konstantinou said that it was official Skiathos police business, and that if the

British police needed to be informed, his 'bureau' would be in touch. By fax.

3

Konstantinou had Matthew sign three separate forms, all in Greek, and he very deliberately tore up a fourth form which Matthew and the desk sergeant had signed earlier. The procedure was necessary, Konstantinou explained, to release Matthew from custody and to restore his freedom. The desk sergeant watched the short ceremony of tearing and signing forms with fascination and puzzlement.

'I'd like to buy you a drink,' Matthew said.

'I don't drink in the day.'

'Coffee.'

'I arrest this guy and accuse him of a murder he didn't commit and now he wants to buy me coffee,' Konstantinou said to the desk sergeant in English. The desk sergeant shrugged.

'I think we can help each other,' Matthew said.

Konstantinou was still swallowing Matthew's story and it wasn't yet properly digested. He ran through all the details as they walked through the narrow sloping alleys towards the harbour, stinking of donkeys and rotten fish and broken sewers, freshened by wild sea breezes. The theory Matthew had worked on through what was left of the night before, was that his half-brother had somehow learnt about his mother's £25 million legacy and had begun to do some digging of his own, and had maybe even stumbled across the truth of where the money had come from. So the same people who shot Tanya had shot Callow.

Konstantinou stopped walking and nodded at his shoes.

'Wait a minute. How long since your daughter was shot?'

Matthew's momentum was stopped short, like stepping off a cliff. For two hours, maybe even longer, this thing had been a puzzle in which the solution was the only priority. For two hours he hadn't even thought about Tanya and now he cursed himself for forgetting her. In order to function he had to freeze all images of her, store her away like the body of Callow in the fish plant.

'Eleven days,' Matthew said.

'So your daughter and Peter Callow were shot the same day.'

'That's right.'

'So it can't be the same person.'

'People,' Matthew said. 'Plural. There's more than one person involved.'

'How do you know?'

'I don't. I'm guessing. But I'm right. If Callow was my half-brother he was on the same trail as me. So they shot him.'

Matthew began to walk quickly down the cobbled alley. Konstantinou followed with his hands in his pockets, still asking questions. Matthew pointed out that it made sense that if Callow was coming to Skiathos to retire, whoever was protecting the secret of the inheritance would want to kill him before he arrived in case he discovered something.

'But your mother died ten years ago,' Konstantinou said, as if he'd caught Matthew out in a lie. 'If he inherited the villa ten years ago, why wait until now to visit it?'

'I don't know. That's why I need your help.'

'It doesn't make sense.'

'Forget sense. None of it will make sense until we have the whole picture.'

'We?'

'I'm hiring you,' Matthew said. 'I like you. You wear a suit in a hundred degrees.'

Konstantinou didn't like to appear wrong-footed, but Matthew could tell that he was already intrigued. He'd guessed that Konstantinou was the kind of man who didn't like things that didn't make sense. For something to say, Konstantinou said, 'It isn't a hundred degrees today, it's ninety-five.'

'There, you see,' Matthew said. 'You know things like that. That's good.'

As they strolled past black doorways, proprietors called out greetings, which Konstantinou acknowledged by jutting his chin upwards.

'So you got a cassette and it was posted here in Skiathos,' Konstantinou said, as they waited for a tiny moped to bump up a set of limestone steps that led down to the harbour.

'It was a death threat. The British police didn't take it seriously.'

Konstantinou shook his head with exaggerated disbelief.

'I take everything seriously,' he said and Matthew said, 'I noticed,' and laughed out loud. For the first time in many years, Matthew felt open-hearted like, a sea shell opening up in warm sunshine.

They sat beneath a huge sunshade canopy and stared out into Skiathos harbour. There were yachts moored in the harbour, and copper-skinned tourists lay full stretch on the wooden slat decks, as if too rich and tired and bored to haul themselves ashore. The waiter who brought coffee to their table bowed when he saw Konstantinou and waved his hand when Konstantinou offered to pay. Konstantinou laid some coins on the table anyway.

'In the barber's shop,' Konstantinou said suddenly, 'I knew your story was true. I didn't need to read the paper to know. I knew it was true all along. Only a madman would make up a story like that. And I don't think you are a madman.'

German and Dutch and English tourists drifted by their table, clutching their leather bags and purses, peering into each of the cafés on the harbour front as they walked by. There were a dozen cafés, all almost identical, with identical menus of fresh local fish and salads and with squid the size of a man's chest draped inelegantly to dry over wooden frames. It was mid afternoon, and the whole island was being grilled by the sun and the freshly killed squid were beginning to cook in their own ink. There were no islanders on the harbour front except for Konstantinou who seemed to keep European office hours as an act of defiance.

'If Peter Callow was your half-brother,' Konstantinou said, 'there would be a genetic match. I can check that. I can get some blood and tissue sent to Athens. I'd need some of your blood too. I could send the samples and check that you were related. Did you know a test like that existed?'

'I've heard about it,' Matthew said.

'There's a laboratory in Athens attached to the office where I used to work. I can send the samples there and they will have an answer in two days. I'll fax them and tell them to expect something . . .'

Konstantinou broke off in mid-sentence and shook his head in disbelief over Matthew's shoulder. A few moments later, a girl of eight or nine appeared at Matthew's shoulder with her hand outstretched. She was dressed in brightly coloured calico with a mass of uncombed black hair. Her face was the colour of red gold and her bottom lip protruded as if she were about to burst into tears. Konstantinou clicked his fingers and hissed through his teeth. The waiter who had been reading a paper in the cool of the café suddenly got to his feet and began to yell. The little girl stood her ground, looking only at Matthew. Konstantinou seemed to be embarrassed by the girl's presence.

'Put your hand on your wallet, Mr King,' Konstantinou said, swatting his hand at the child as if she were a mosquito, 'she's an island Gypsy. Don't give her any money.'

The waiter was scurrying between tables, yelling. Matthew noticed an exotically dressed young woman with a gold front tooth standing just beyond the awning with a basket hooked over her arm. She looked like an Indian or a Tibetan, a splash of green and gold set against the electric blue of the ocean. Konstantinou yelled something to her in Greek and she bared her teeth at him like a cat and sucked hard. Matthew reached into his pocket and put three crimson notes into the Gypsy girl's hand. She ran to her mother and showed her the notes with a grin as they set off down the harbour road.

'You just gave her a month's wages,' Konstantinou said with flat astonishment.

'Really?'

'You just gave her more than I get every month.'

Konstantinou didn't sound angry, but the sight of the money being handed over had taken his breath. His mouth fell open and he pushed his sunglasses up on to his brow. Then a sudden realization seemed to strike him and he softened.

'I'm sorry,' he said, suddenly deflated. 'I understand.'

'Understand what?'

'Nothing. It doesn't matter.'

'What do you understand?'

'I suppose your little girl . . . your daughter . . . I suppose she was around the same age.'

Konstantinou wasn't good at sympathy. His efforts made Matthew smile.

'I'd say that girl was a little older,' Matthew said. 'But pretty, just like Tanya. And persistent when it came to treats . . .'

Matthew chuckled and peered into the distance. Konstantinou nodded and looked away dreading what might come next.

'But that wasn't why I gave her the money.'

Konstantinou glanced in Matthew's direction and Matthew narrowed his eyes.

'In eleven days I've learnt something, Inspector,' Matthew said. 'When they take your baby away, when they take her away for good, it's the same as if she was never there in the first place. As far as the whole world is concerned, it's the same as if she'd never even existed. So it's you against the whole world. Just you against the new reality. You want to go back to that world where she did exist. This new world is hell but you have to live in it. It's like the whole world is digging the grave and you are trying to fill it in. That's how it feels. But that isn't why I gave that little girl the money.'

There were only two responses to what Matthew had to say next. Either Konstantinou would be filled with awe and begin fawning or he would be consumed with jealous hatred. He decided to put Konstantinou to the test.

'I gave her the money because it really makes no difference to me,' Matthew said. 'I have so much money that it means nothing at all to give it away. That wasn't generosity. I just couldn't be bothered to sort through the notes.'

Konstantinou was peering at the Gypsy girl as she skipped

over mooring ropes, waving her money in the air and shrieking. Matthew needed to get Konstantinou's attention.

'Once, two years ago, I actually burnt some money,' Matthew said and he stared at Konstantinou to check his reaction. 'I took £200 in twenties and I burnt it in an ashtray. I was drunk but it made me feel good to do it. It was like pissing on fresh snow, or taking a carving knife to a Picasso. You know those people who do that kind of thing? I can understand why they do it.'

Matthew raised his eyebrows at Konstantinou to show him that it was true. The waiter saw that his quarry had gone and turned on his heels and slouched back towards the shade of the café.

'You burn your money if you want to,' Konstantinou said, 'that's your business. But you should never give money to Gypsies. That girl's father will get drunk tonight. He might drive his truck over a cliff.'

'That isn't my problem. Money is a chemical. What people do with it is their problem.'

'Maybe you are a madman after all.'

'Maybe I am. I just thought you ought to know what kind of man you're dealing with. I used to spend £500 a week on cocaine.'

Matthew leant back into the sun. He felt the orange glow on his eyelids.

'You spend £500 on the stuff then you roll up a fifty and you suck it up your nose. For me that was the finest way of spending money. Direct payment for happiness. Cut out the middleman, the car dealer, the travel agent, the guy selling you the suit. Cocaine and heroin are the only things in this world that are worth what you pay for them. Everything else is a rip off.'

When Matthew leant forward again, he expected to see a look of puzzlement on Konstantinou's face, or a look of contempt. Instead, Konstantinou was peering down at his coffee, stirring the froth, as if he hadn't even been listening.

'You won't find cocaine or heroin on my island, Mr King,' he said softly.

'Really?'

'And if you've brought any to the island I swear I'll arrest you.'

'Relax. I gave up. Eleven days ago.'

The oblique reminder of Matthew's loss made Konstantinou back off. He sighed and stirred his coffee.

'If you hate your money so much, why don't you give it away?'

'I intend to. All of it. That's why I'm here. And inspector I intend to give some of it to you.'

Konstantinou puffed out his cheeks as if he'd expected this too, but he hadn't. He stared out at the yachts shining like cut glass and diamonds in the sea glare.

'I intend to spend all of my money on finding out who it was who killed my daughter,' Matthew said.

'That will be my monument to her. I'll fill the hole with the bodies of the people who shot her. And the first thing I need to find out is where my mother got her money. I'll need access to bank statements, records of money transactions, whatever you can get . . .'

The Gypsy woman and her daughter were approaching another table of tourists in the next café. The tourists waved them away, the café owner leapt to his feet, the little girl sobbed, an exact re-enactment of what had happened at Matthew's table. Matthew and Konstantinou were both watching the re-enactment, but Matthew knew for sure that he had all of Konstantinou's attention.

'And if you find out where she got her money,' Matthew said, 'I'll give you a million pounds. Cash or cheque.'

Konstantinou choked on his thick syrupy coffee and some of the black juice dribbled down his chin. He began to dab his chin with a napkin and Matthew felt the throb of the engine inside which had the power to crush the rock of Konstantinou's authority, the power to put virtue to flight.

'You really are insane,' Konstantinou said.

'No I'm not. If you want I can have a money order drawn up now, before noon. I can have the money transferred direct to your account from London or Zürich.'

Konstantinou flicked his sunglasses back over his eyes.

'Fuck you,' he said.

'That's more like it.'

'Mr King, I don't work for you. I work for the State Department of Athens.'

'You want that yacht there in the harbour. The big blue one. It's yours. And the woman lying on the deck too if you want her. People are like anything else, some are cheap some are expensive. I'd say that she would be expensive because someone has bought her already. That fat old guy in the hat. He probably doesn't want to sell, but if you want her I'll buy her for you.'

Konstantinou stood up quickly. He hitched his trousers up over his skinny hips.

'As I said, Mr King, I'll need some of your blood.'

'You can have my blood and my money.'

'Call in tomorrow morning. I'll have a nurse there. She's my sister. She'll take some of your blood and we'll send the sample to Athens.'

Suddenly, Konstantinou seemed to be in a hurry. It had taken a while, but Matthew had got to him in the end. Matthew could see that if there was one thing Konstantinou hated more than anything else in the world it was confusion in his own mind. Through sheer force of habit, Matthew wanted to nail him.

'For one million pounds I want you to give priority to finding out about my mother. You can tell Athens that it is your own line of inquiry. In my opinion Callow was killed by the same people who killed my daughter. If you want to find the people who killed her, you have to start with my mother's accounts. It wouldn't even be a detour.'

Konstantinou mumbled something in Greek and then turned on his heels and walked quickly towards the shaded alley that led up the mountain from the harbour. Matthew rubbed his hand through his short-cropped hair, felt the smoothness of his newly shaven chin, and felt at last that he was dealing now with certainties, simple statements of fact which he was neither responsible for nor was guilty of having created.

The Gypsy girl had broken free of her mother's hand and was grinning at Matthew with her hand shading her eyes. Matthew waved at her and smiled from behind his sunglasses. From this distance, with her mop of dark hair and her shadowy smile, she really did look like Tanya, and Matthew felt his heart swell with recognition. Maybe he could pay the girl's mother to let him hold her for a while, just to feel that weight in his empty arms. He dismissed the thought quickly. That girl wasn't really his daughter, but maybe she was what her spirit had become, here on the spirit island of Skiathos.

4

Matthew went back to his hotel room and sat in the shade of his patio, staring out at the ocean. He checked that the cash was still inside the safe, and stuffed a few bills into his pocket. He still had no idea how much most of the notes were worth, but he was now aware that the crimson ones were big currency.

Twice he picked up the receiver to call Sarah, but both times he put the phone down again. If his enterprise was going to work, he decided, he couldn't speak to Sarah until he had everything in place, until he had some kind of trophy to present to her. If he had to travel the whole world, he would do it, and he wouldn't stop until he had dived all the way to the bottom of the ocean and hauled it up to the surface.

Matthew called room service and ordered fish and champagne. He gave the waitress two large crimson notes and urged her to take them. He knew that already he would be getting a reputation around the hotel and that his reputation would work for him. Word would spread around the island and soon he would be able to get anything he wanted with just the nod of his head. Cars, boats, co-operation, information. And it wouldn't be long before he wouldn't even have to pay. That was the final absurdity of wealth. After a while, the reputation was enough, the actual bank notes became irrelevant.

When the sun began to set he ordered a taxi and drove down to the harbour to eat. He found a taverna and saw a public phone box across the cobbles. His resolve failed him.

'Hello Sarah, it's me . . .'

Matthew had his finger in his ear. The customers in the taverna opposite the public phone box were filling the small white-washed square with a constant babble of sound, voices speaking in a dozen languages all at once. Matthew had had to make the call through the international operator, and the line was bad. Sarah had agreed to give Matthew the number of the apartment where she was staying in Gibraltar on the condition that Matthew would only call in case of emergency.

'What is it, what's wrong?' Sarah said.

'Nothing. Nothing's wrong. Is Tanya OK?'

Matthew had asked through sheer force of habit. It felt like biting on a rotten tooth. The line crackled.

'I'm sorry . . .'

The tourists all laughed uproariously at the same time. The evening was warm and perfumed with the smell of goat and lamb roasting on open charcoal. In the flickering electric lights of the tavernas, the tourist's sunburnt skin shone dark orange, making the whites of their eyes and their teeth flash.

'Where are you?' Sarah said, when the laughter died down.

'I'm in a public phone.'

'Are you still in Skiathos?'

'Yes. A lot has happened. I can't tell you it all now. I'll write to you. Give me the address.'

There was a long pause.

'Just tell me what's happened.'

'I can't tell you over the phone. Give me the address.'

More silence.

'I've found out some things about the money. Sarah, I have a brother. A half-brother. Or I did have a half-brother, but he's dead. He's been murdered. It's the same people. It has to be.'

Matthew thought he heard Sarah sigh.

'Matthew . . . are you OK?'

'Yes, give me the address. I'll write to you.'

Matthew knew that Sarah didn't want to give him her address in case he appeared on her doorstep. He was about to give her some reassurance when the international operator came on the line and demanded more money. Matthew fumbled in his pocket and began to pump drachmae into the phone.

'Hello? Sarah?'

The coins fell from the phone in a shower. The line went dead. When Matthew called back the phone went unanswered. He went and sat at an empty table outside one of the tavernas and ordered beer and some grilled sardines, most of which he fed to the stray cats who purred and pleaded around his feet. He tried not to think about the way he'd asked after Tanya, but he knew it would bother him all night.

After he had drunk a few beers, he felt his anxiety dissipating. It felt good to have urgent business which put Tanya's death to the back of his mind. He paid for his meal leaving a handsome tip, then took a taxi across the island to settle his more urgent business.

CHAPTER TEN

I

Konstantinou's sister squeezed Matthew's finger until the tip of it turned scarlet. Two tiny drops of blood fell into a small glass dish. She spoke to Konstantinou in Greek.

'Rina says you don't bleed very well,' Konstantinou said. 'She says you've got bad blood pressure.'

Rina squeezed hard and a fat droplet of blood formed on his finger. She shook his hand to make the droplet fall into the dish. Then she dabbed the pin prick with a cotton wool swab dipped in surgical spirit. The smell of the antiseptic filled the station office. Konstantinou took the blood sample, screwed on the glass lid, and put it into a padded envelope. He then nodded at the desk sergeant who was unusually sombre.

'We have a severed hand in the fridge,' Konstantinou said, wiping his mouth. The desk sergeant walked across to the fridge with great solemnity. When he opened the fridge door, Matthew saw a package sealed in a plastic sheet. There were two cartons of milk beside it. The desk sergeant took the package and held it like high explosive. Konstantinou helped him stuff the package into the padded envelope. The desk sergeant then put on his police crash helmet and snapped the visor shut with determination. He put the padded envelope under his arm and walked quickly to the door. He had obviously been told that there was no time to lose. They heard his moped fire and then there was a squeal of tyres.

'He'll put it on the next hydrofoil to Athens,' Konstantinou explained. 'We should have an answer by tomorrow afternoon.'

Rina kissed Konstantinou on both cheeks. She had the same neat, sharp features as Konstantinou. Her uniform was brilliant white, with a blue cross woven on to the front. She also put her helmet on and strapped it tight beneath her chin, her big, bulbous helmet making her uniform look ludicrous. She nodded curtly at Matthew and then left.

'She goes all over the island,' Konstantinou explained with pride he could hardly disguise. 'She gives innoculations. The people in the mountains think she is a witch. She goes to the Gypsies too. She tries to patch up the livers of the men. They drink too much. Too much easy money from the tourists.'

Konstantinou sat down and began to make an entry in his log. Matthew found himself smiling at Konstantinou's brusque efficiency, the way he couldn't let any matter drop, not even something as trivial as giving money to a gypsy.

'So what have you found out about my mother?' Matthew said, and Konstantinou reached for a cigarette. His hands shook a little.

'If we establish that Peter Callow was your half-brother, I will begin the investigation,' he said and busied himself with his log.

'But do we have a deal?'

'What deal?' he said casually, flicking through the pages of his log.

'You know what deal.'

Konstantinou pecked the page with his pen to make a full stop and closed his log.

'I have faxed an initial report to Athens,' he said. 'I have mentioned your story and told them that I think it is worth investigating. They offered to send me backup but I told them to go to hell.'

'Good.'

'If they agree that your story is worth investigating I might decide that I need to find out more about your mother. If they don't, I won't.'

Konstantinou stood up and put his file away. The large black insect was still clinging to the wall in the same place above the filing cabinet. Konstantinou began to hum to himself. Matthew knew that he wasn't really looking at the files at all. He decided that Konstantinou hadn't slept too well that night.

'I assume then that we have a deal,' Matthew said. 'One million if you find out where she got her money. Half a million if you try and fail.'

Konstantinou said nothing. When the phone rang, he seemed to be relieved at the interruption. Matthew watched him with amused curiosity as he spoke quickly in Greek. When he put the phone down, he rubbed his tired eyes and then straightened his tie.

'Mr Rook is dead,' he said flatly. He swallowed hard and took a deep breath, resting his hand on his desk for support. Matthew's look of amusement didn't fade.

'What the hell is happening here, Mr King?' Konstantinou said.

2

When Konstantinou leapt into his tiny black Fiat, he seemed to assume that Matthew would come with him. They took the same mountain road Lot had taken on his motorbike, and the Fiat choked and coughed its way up the mountainside until there was a vast panorama either side of the road, the shimmering green of the island, the lighter green of the shallow waters around the coastline, the dark blue of the deeper ocean. Matthew and Konstantinou drove in a silence which was filled with uneasy voices. Konstantinou's face in the rear view mirror was a murderous conversation.

Once they had reached the small fishing harbour at the other side of the island, Konstantinou left the road and took a dirt track through spiteful, chirruping scrub land towards a whitewashed villa. The iron gates of the villa were already open, and Konstantinou parked beside a defunct well. The place looked neglected, half consumed by the heat and insects.

In the shadows inside the villa there was a housekeeper with swollen legs, patting her chest and fighting to get her breath. She pointed into the shadows towards a shuttered bedroom. There on the bed lay Rook, naked, striped by sunlight from the shutter, his face placid, his chest split by a fresh scar, a broken knife hanging by a twist of metal from the tip of its blade which was buried in his heart. The housekeeper began to wail as Konstantinou wiped his face and stared down at the bloody, twisted sheets.

'Do you mind if I take a look around,' Matthew said calmly. Konstantinou tightened his tie again, even though it didn't need to be tightened. The heat in the shuttered room had already begun to ferment the blood and oil inside the body and the air was sickly with the smell of it. Konstantinou flicked his hand to clear the flies from the wound. He mumbled to himself in Greek.

'Inspector, I'd like to take a look around,' Matthew said again, with a hint of impatience. 'There may be letters or files. He was a close friend of my mother's.'

Konstantinou turned to Matthew in the darkness with a look of incomprehension which quickly turned to anger.

'Wait for me in the car,' he said softly.

'Inspector, I'd appreciate it if you'd just give me five minutes looking through his things.'

Konstantinou strode towards the bedroom door and held it open. The housekeeper was now shrieking in the sitting-room.

'Wait for me in the car,' Konstantinou said again and Matthew could see that it was still too early to exercise his power. He went outside and stood in the burning sun. When he closed his eyes, he saw Rook's lifeless features burnt on to his eyelids, a sight he'd seen many times in his dreams of revenge. It was a shame that he hadn't been fat as he had been ten years before and it was a pity that Sarah wasn't here to see the pain and incomprehension on his face.

3

The conversation beside the well was conducted in whispers, even though there was no one for miles around apart from a few green-eyed lizards and the housekeeper, and she was wailing and praying so loud that she wouldn't have heard Matthew and Konstantinou talking anyway.

Konstantinou was bathed in sweat and when he emerged from the villa he had his handkerchief to his mouth.

'From the smell I'd say he was killed at around eight or nine last night,' he said, relieved to get back to his textbook learning. He looked up at Matthew who was peering into the overgrown garden, almost identical to the garden at his mother's villa.

'Where were you last night between eight and nine, Mr King?' Konstantinou said quietly.

'I was in my hotel,' Matthew said. 'Ask anyone at the Skiathos Palace. They all know me well.'

'OK, so what do you know about what happened?'

Matthew took a packet of cigarettes from his shirt pocket and lit one. He offered one to Konstantinou, but he simply glared at the packet.

'As I understand it,' Matthew said, 'he was very unpopular with the local fishermen. That was a fish-gutting knife in his chest, wasn't it?'

'I have been chief inspector here on this island for three years. Not a single murder. Not even a serious assault. So why do the fishermen suddenly start putting knives into people's chests?'

'I have no idea.'

'You're a liar. Who did you pay to kill him? The housekeeper said she saw a Gypsy hanging around here last night.'

'Then go and speak to some Gypsies.'

Matthew dragged on his cigarette and blew smoke into the air.

'Can your sister issue death certificates?' he asked. Konstantinou didn't answer.

'If she can, I suggest you call her and get her to certify the death. Mr Rook was a very sick man. He was dying anyway. She could say that he died of a heart problem, which I suppose in a way would be the truth.'

Konstantinou slapped the cigarette out of Matthew's hand and grabbed him by the shirt collar, pushing him over the cool, dark abyss of the well. Now was the time, Matthew thought, when he would see if Konstantinou could resist the power of the engine. He shoved Konstantinou off and retrieved his cigarette from the ground, blowing off the dust.

'OK, Inspector, look at it this way,' he said. 'Let's say you call Athens and tell them there has been a second murder. Two murders in a week. How will that look?'

Konstantinou seemed to be one step ahead of Matthew already. He knew how it would look.

'They'll assume that you can't cope,' Matthew said. 'Fax or no fax. This place will be crawling with detectives from the mainland. And both the victims were British citizens. Maybe they'll even call in Scotland Yard.'

The housekeeper had stopped praying and the air came alive with the sound of insects. Konstantinou took one of his own cigarettes and lit it. His hands were shaking more than ever.

'If Athens come snooping around, they'll find out that Rook was the biggest dealer in heroin in the whole of the Sporades islands. You didn't know about that, did you, Inspector.'

Konstantinou froze, his face filled with horror.

'You've been here how many years? And you didn't even know. Take a look around his villa. See what you find. My guess is you'll find enough raw opium to keep this island happy for ten years. The guys from Athens come and they find that out. They find out that with your fax and your phone links you had no idea. Maybe they'll guess that you knew and you were taking a rake off. Do you think you'll get your morgue then?'

Konstantinou's whole world was beginning to sink into the sea. Now all Matthew had to do was save a little outcrop of rock for him to perch on.

'Rook was evil,' Matthew said softly to the mountain top. 'He admitted as much himself. And he would have been dead within a month anyway.'

Skiathos mountain shone emerald and grey above their heads, and Matthew could almost believe that the spirit of the mountain was giving him momentum, finding the words for him to use.

'There's £250,000 for your sister if she comes up with a death certificate,' Matthew said and Konstantinou began to shake his head in silent despair at the enormity of what was happening to him.

'If she doesn't want the money for herself, then I can make a donation to her medical unit. She can get herself a jeep instead of a moped. She can buy needles, vaccines, maybe even employ someone to help her. Think of the good that will come of it. Think of the gypsies who will be saved. It will be the only good that ever came out of Mr Rook's life. It will be a redemption to make up for all the wicked things he did when he was alive. They might even take it into account when he gets to the gates of heaven.'

The insects kept on chirruping as Matthew waited for Konstantinou to reply. Matthew hid his anxiety with a look of sober concern, directed at the mountain top.

'Let's say that it was fate that killed him. It got to him before his heart gave out by itself.'

The housekeeper began to wail again. Somewhere away on the mountain road, a motorbike was beginning its fast descent. Matthew knew that Konstantinou, whose face was hidden by his hand, needed one more shove.

'If you check your account at the National Bank of Greece you'll find I've deposited £500,000 already. I did it this morning because you didn't say no. When I asked you if we had a deal you didn't say no.'

Konstantinou was stuck like an insect on a pin. If Konstantinou faltered he'd make the offer two million. He was sure that a million was enough but he was still getting used to the currency of corruption. He still wasn't sure of the exchange rate when it came to the men's souls.

'What about the housekeeper?' Konstantinou said at last and Matthew felt his relief like a landfall down the side of the mountain. He put his hand on Konstantinou's shoulder.

'Perhaps you could take care of her,' Matthew said. 'After all, you are a very rich man now, Inspector.'

CHAPTER ELEVEN

I

No one touched their food that evening. Not Rina, not Konstantinou, not Matthew. They sat in a little circle of lamp light on the patio of a restaurant in Skiathos village which seemed to be out of bounds to tourists. Even the insects seemed in sombre mood and left them alone. The only other diners were two middle-aged Greek men with steel-coloured hair, distended bellies and relentless appetites for fish. Konstantinou explained in passing that they were oil men, fabulously wealthy, taking a break from the chaos of Athens. Matthew recognized their looks of lonely resignation.

Rina and Konstantinou spoke to each other calmly in Greek, occasionally glancing at Matthew, who in spite of the fact that he couldn't understand what they were saying, presided over their conversation. Rina had acquiesced to falsifying the death certificate without a word, simply because her brother had asked her to. She seemed to assume that if Konstantinou asked her to do something, then it must be right. Now she needed an explanation, and Konstantinou was labouring to give it to her. Finally, when something seemed to be resolved, they began to speak in English.

'I have explained to her,' Konstantinou said, lighting his tenth cigarette of the hour, 'that the larger investigation into the murder of Peter Callow would be jeopardized if Rook's suicide were to become public.'

'Suicide?' Matthew said involuntarily.

Konstantinou put his hand on Matthew's hand.

'I have explained to her about the suicide note that the housekeeper found. About how Rook put the knife into his own chest because of the pain he was living with after his operation. She says that patients living with chronic pain often take their own lives . . .'

Konstantinou implored Matthew with his eyes to go along with the deceit. Matthew nodded and smiled at Rina, who had huge dark eyes the colour of varnished oak.

'You knew Mr Rook?' she said with great concern. Matthew nodded.

'He was a friend of my mother's.'

'You must be upset.'

Matthew took a deep breath.

'Yes. Yes I am. As I understand it he was a great patriot in his time. A hero.'

Konstantinou glared at Matthew for his elaboration, and Matthew met his gaze. He guessed that Konstantinou had already checked his bank account and that the half-million was now hanging around his neck like a lump of granite. His head was bowed. Matthew had noticed that Konstantinou wasn't terribly good at deception, but decided that he would be a quick learner.

'But perhaps,' Matthew said, 'you should tell her about the donation.'

Konstantinou shook his head at Matthew.

'There is no need for any donation,' he said quickly.

'I would like to reward her for her co-operation.'

'She doesn't need any reward.'

'I would like her to have it. It would be for a good cause.'

Rina asked a question in Greek and Konstantinou dismissed it. It was obvious that Konstantinou had decided to shield his sister from Matthew's offer of payment, and he had invented the lie about suicide so that she could sign the death certificate and keep her integrity intact. If Matthew had told Konstantinou two days earlier that a quarter of a million pounds could be a burden from which loved ones must be protected, he would have laughed.

'I still want her to have it,' Matthew said. 'Tell her that I am eccentric.'

'Leave it,' Konstantinou declared and Matthew hissed in his ear.

'When I said I wanted the money to go to a good cause I meant it. I'm not just doing this to see you people squirm.'

Matthew had spoken too quickly for Rina to understand and she asked Konstantinou for a translation. He struggled to conjure up another lie.

The two oil men stood up at their table and bowed humbly at the waitress who had served them. They trooped towards the gate of the patio and disappeared into the night without a word. The cats who had been begging at their table scampered over to where Matthew was sitting. He tossed them a pinch of fish flesh.

'OK,' Matthew said with a smile, 'perhaps you would prefer it if I had a home built for stray cats.'

'Don't joke because this isn't funny,' Konstantinou said and he banged the table. Rina recoiled in shock.

'I think it is,' Matthew said, 'I'm feeling very light hearted.'

'Well, I'm not,' Konstantinou yelled. Matthew stopped smiling and apologized, saying he knew exactly how Konstantinou must be feeling.

2

Next morning, Matthew was swimming in the cool, clear water of the bay below the Skiathos Palace Hotel. It was still early and the water fizzed with cold. Matthew dived under the calm surface into the brilliant, sunlit underworld that hummed in his ears. He remembered the blue and crimson fish that swam above the green lawn of seaweed from the times he had been here with Sarah. She had lost a silver ring swimming here and he thought that it would be a good omen if he were to see it glinting in the cleft of a rock somewhere.

All night the spirit of the mountain had troubled his dreams, but in the restful moments between nightmares, he had been submerged in this sparkling slow-motion world and in his dreams Sarah had been swimming with him. There had been no need to come up for air. They had been locked in an embrace beneath the water, the warmth of their bodies against the colours of the whole ocean.

When he surfaced, his ears unplugged to a rushing noise like the sound of a train, which was soon transformed into the gentle ruffle of a breeze around his ears. He wiped the sea water from his eyes and saw Konstantinou standing on the beach beside his pile of clothes. He was wearing his suit and leather shoes, and he looked unshaven. It was just after dawn.

'We will have to go to Athens,' Konstantinou said, handing Matthew his hotel towel. Matthew dried himself, still tingling from the cold of the water.

'Why do we have to go to Athens?'

'I've been working through the night. I traced your mother's accounts through statements in the file I took from Rook's villa. Did you know that he was her executor?'

Matthew dried the salt water from his ears and smoothed his short-cropped hair to his head.

'No, I didn't know that.'

'Right up until a week before she died he was down as the executor of her estate. Then she changed it. She wrote out a new will. The villa went to Peter Callow, the rest went to you.'

'You found all this out from Rook's files?'

'No. I accessed the State Department computer in Athens. All transactions over $50,000 are recorded . . . for the past ten years . . . are you listening to me, Mr King?'

Matthew had pushed out his chest to breathe deeply: a great chestful of sea air. The first of the tourists were tiptoeing along the rugged path that led down to the beach from the road. Matthew sat down on the sand and began to strap his sandals. The sand was already too hot to stand on in bare feet.

'Yes, I'm listening.'

'You don't seem too concerned for a man who is paying a million pounds for information.'

Matthew looked up at Konstantinou's haggard features, his

coarse growth of beard, the dark rings around his eyes. Konstantinou reached into his pocket and handed Matthew a cardboard ticket.

'We're on the midday hydrofoil,' Konstantinou said.

Matthew took the ticket, peered at it and then got to his feet. Konstantinou was still struggling to justify himself.

'I need to go to Athens on official business anyway. I need to go and get the results of the genetic tests from the lab.'

'I thought they could fax you.'

'There's a problem. I need to go there in person . . .'

'And looking up my mother's accounts will be like a little freelance work on the side,' Matthew said, smiling at Konstantinou's self-deception. 'You should remember, Inspector, in the whole world you can be honest with me.'

Konstantinou's face suddenly ignited and he punched Matthew hard across the chin, sending him spinning into the hot sand. Konstantinou was breathing fast, fighting the urge to follow up with a kick. Matthew sat in the sand and checked the joint of his jaw with his hand.

'What was that for?'

'That was for you talking to me like you own me. I'm taking your fucking money for my son, not for me. If it was just me I'd have told you to fuck yourself. But it's not for me it's for him. So don't talk to me in that way again.'

The tourists creeping down the beach trail had taken fright and stood in a line, shading their eyes to see what was happening. Matthew stood up a second time and dusted the sand from his arms and hair.

'So what am I paying for, an education?'

'An operation.'

'I'm sorry . . .'

'Just get dressed.'

Matthew began to take off his swimming trunks and Konstantinou turned his back while Matthew pulled his trousers on. The tourists set off for the shaded part of the beach, giving Matthew and Konstantinou a wide berth. There was something creepy about a man in a suit on a beach.

'So what else did you find out?' Matthew said, watching them pass and nodding to them, simply to scare them.

'I found out that the money was paid into your mother's account in Athens every month. It was £200,000 a shot. Every fucking month.'

'From where? You can turn around now.'

Konstantinou turned to see Matthew zipping up his trousers.

'From where, I don't know yet. That's why we need to go to Athens. There are some people I can talk to. But I have to go to the lab first.'

'On official business,' Matthew said with a smile. Konstantinou was about to ignite again, but Matthew grabbed his arm.

'Listen to me, Inspector. I've been at this for a lot longer than you. There's one thing I've learnt. Money is only good for buying things that aren't for sale.'

Konstantinou looked at Matthew for a long time, blinking hard.

'What the fuck's that supposed to mean?'

Matthew grinned.

'I've got no idea. It just sounded good.'

He threw his wet swimming trunks over his shoulder and set off towards the path. Konstantinou shook his head and mumbled, 'The guy's a lunatic.' Then he hesitated, looking down into the sand.

'Hey, you dropped your hydrofoil ticket.'

'I didn't drop it, I threw it away,' Matthew said, carrying on ahead without turning round. 'Hydrofoils are bad for my health. It runs in the family. Besides, I'm in a hurry. We'll hire a jet.'

3

When Matthew ordered a taxi from the hotel lobby, three cars arrived within seconds. His reputation as a big tipper had spread quickly. When they arrived at Skiathos Airport, the Leah jet which Matthew had chartered was shimmering on the tarmac.

There was a regular business flight to Athens once a day, but Matthew made some calls and brought the flight forward a few hours, paying five times the fare for the privilege. He and Konstantinou were to be the only passengers, and as they walked across the airport apron in the impossible morning heat, Konstantinou was still shaking his head.

'You're insane, you know that don't you?' he said.

'Yes.'

'And ever since I've met you, I've been insane too. I haven't slept for two days.'

'It's something you get used to.'

Konstantinou was labouring in his suit and tie. Matthew was wearing a T-shirt, Chinos and sandals. When they climbed the steps into the jet, the smiling hostess assumed that Konstantinou was paying the bill, and gave him her warmest smile. He glowered at her. The grey leather interior was cool from discreet air-conditioning.

'So are we going to talk to each other or are you just going to grunt and tell me I'm insane?' Matthew said as Konstantinou fiddled with his seat-belt clasp.

'I can't get this thing buckled.'

'The hostess will help.'

'We should have taken the hydrofoil.'

The hostess helped Konstantinou extend his belt and fasten it. He wiped his face and looked out at the watery haze of the tarmac.

'Look, Mr King,' he wiped his face, ' I don't have a son who needs an operation. I just said that because I didn't want you to think . . . I didn't want you to think that I was just taking your money for no reason. I was angry, OK? It was a wicked thing to say.'

'You don't have to justify anything to me.'

'Fuck you.'

The hostess looked up sharply from her perch in front of the cockpit and smiled as if she hadn't heard a thing.

The jet was cleared for take-off and soon they were climbing over the electric blue sea, the engine cutting to a murmur at the top of its ascent. The hostess brought them gin and tonics and a plate of tiny sandwiches glazed in aspic. The plane was built for maximum physical comfort and maximum mental discomfort. The hostess smiled constantly, the pilot occasionally turned from his dazzling console to smile the same smile. The slightest raising of an eyebrow brought the hostess to her feet. Konstantinou sat uneasily in his grey leather seat, still strapped in, while Matthew took a swig of gin and looked down at the nameless green islands below.

'That must be Skopelos,' Matthew said.

'Yes, it must be,' Konstantinou said without looking down.

'You were born on Skiathos?'

'Yes.'

'And trained in Athens.'

'Yes,' Konstantinou grunted, chewing a finger nail. Matthew nudged him.

'This is the only way to travel, isn't it, Inspector?'

'As a matter of fact, I hate flying.'

Konstantinou looked queasy. He unstrapped himself and hurried to the cramped executive toilet at the back of the jet where he was sick. Half an hour later, they were circling around Mount Olympus, like Zeus and a still disbelieving Hermes.

4

Whatever had gone wrong at the forensic laboratory wasn't being explained to the satisfaction of an overheated Konstantinou, who was punctuating his exclamations of disbelief with slaps on the desk. A female laboratory technician with large owlish glasses had consulted her clipboard and said that as far as she was aware, the severed hand had never arrived.

Konstantinou showed her the dispatch receipt from the hydrofoil which proved that the package was put on board, and another faxed confirmation from the dispatch company in Piraeus that the package had been collected from the hydrofoil. He had even called the lab himself to confirm that the package had arrived and he had been assured that the hand was in cold storage. Now it seemed the hand had simply vanished into thin air. Konstantinou translated all of this for Matthew's benefit with disbelief.

'These fucking people!' Konstantinou declared, waving his hand at the window of the third-floor office, signifying the whole of the City of Athens. 'They call us fish-guts because we come from the islands. But these people!'

The owl-eyed technician studied her clip board. She had already explained that all the people Konstantinou had mentioned as being friends of his who worked at the forensic laboratory had left to work elsewhere. The senior forensic doctor was away on holiday in Italy. The boy who logged packages was at home because his girlfriend had left him. Konstantinou looked heavenward. He occasionally glanced at Matthew as if to convey to the technician that this man was an external witness to a whole nation's incompetence. Finally, speechless, Konstantinou swept out of the office and out of the forensic building, with Matthew in pursuit.

Furious anger seemed to be the only appropriate emotion for a hot day in Athens. The entire population of the city was blinded by anger, hooting their horns, throttling their engines, sucking their teeth and yelling at each other. Matthew and Konstantinou found a newly built roadside café near to the forensic laboratory and they sat at the table on the pavement, letting the roar of traffic wash over them like the breaking of mighty waves. Every radio was turned up full, every dog had visible ribs and a frantic erection. It could have been a thousand miles away from the stunned tranquillity of the beach at Skiathos where Matthew had bathed only a few hours before. But Matthew had grown accustomed to the way that wealth speeds up transitions, makes the world a small place.

'I'm not hungry,' Konstantinou said almost as soon as they had sat down. 'Come on, let's go.'

'Go where?'

'Find out about your mother. Let's get it over with.'

He set off at a fast walk and then hailed a smog-stained taxi. The cab pulled away even before Matthew had time to close the door.

After the glaring heat of the Athenian traffic, there was a kind of tranquillity inside the offices of the Department of Finance, a huge brown monolith near the National Archaeological Museum. The snarling of the city outside could still be felt as a kind of tremor in the cool, ancient air. A sleepy-eyed soldier had waved Konstantinou through the marble entrance hall after Konstantinou had flashed his ID. The walls of the records office were stained yellow, and the plaster pillars were as grey as pencil lead. The central library consisted of a large hexagon of corridors leading away from a central atrium, in which, it seemed, a hundred yellow-skinned clerks had long ago died and begun to gather dust. Konstantinou hurried into this tomb with his eyes blazing.

'There are certain advantages,' he said loudly, not caring how much his voice echoed, 'to living in a country that used to be governed by a military junta. They leave a legacy of suspicion, especially of foreigners. Until five years ago all financial transactions involving foreign nationals resident in Greece were monitored. And there were currency restrictions too, and certain tax laws. I would say . . .' He held open a large coffee-coloured door for Matthew to walk through, '. . . that the answer to your question will be in here somewhere.'

Matthew and Konstantinou brushed by another desk manned by an armed soldier who was smoking a cigarette and reading a paperback. The further they went into the tomb, the cooler the air became, and Matthew doubted that any sunlight had ever penetrated this far.

The thickness of the walls refrigerated the corridors and sealed in the echo of every voice and footstep. Matthew imagined that any word anyone had ever said inside this building was still reverberating somewhere in the vast chamber of the records office, and every footstep could be counted and logged. Konstantinou said vaguely that real oppression took place in buildings like this one. Matthew had gleaned that he was a socialist, maybe even a communist.

'Now we are in the foreign nationals section,' Konstantinou said, quickening his pace. Before them there was another set of double doors, which Konstantinou held open with his foot. He seemed to be in a tearing hurry to get this business over with.

'Can I help you?' said a voice in English. A face had loomed up at them out of the shadows on the other side of the door, a pair of gold spectacles and a bald head like a shiny brown moon. Konstantinou answered in Greek and showed his identity. The moon nodded quickly and pointed to a collection of desks further along the corridor.

'There is something else about oppressive regimes,' Konstantinou said, hurrying on. 'They leave a legacy of respect for badges. They make everyone scared of anyone whose authority might be higher than their own. With this badge I could get almost anywhere in Athens. If they knew that I was from the islands, that I was . . .' Konstantinou broke off and became thoughtful. 'Of course, that is something I have always fought against.'

'Until now,' Matthew said.

'Now is different,' Konstantinou said firmly, as if at last he had resolved something in his own mind. 'Now I am making an exception and for a good reason. When this is finished, I will explain why I have agreed to do this. Why I have agreed to take your money. I worked it all out in my head last night. I made up the story about my son because I don't think you deserve to know the truth. Here. These are the files.'

Konstantinou began to scan a set of black, iron filing cabinets, which looked to have lain undisturbed for centuries. They were all marked with yellow labels, typed in Greek script.

'What was her name?' Konstantinou asked.

'Mathilda Margaret King.'

Konstantinou prowled the length of the filing cabinets, half-humming to himself.

'And I suppose we can pick any year between . . . when . . .?'

'She died in '85,' Matthew said. 'So try '82 or '83.'

Konstantinou lighted on a draw and tugged it. It didn't move. He tugged again.

'Locked,' he said. 'So why didn't the guy tell me?'

Konstantinou hurried away to get the key. Matthew was left alone, facing the regiment of black, iron filing cabinets. It seemed ludicrous that it had only taken a few hours to get this close to the truth, that there was a single key, held by a frail old man, which would unlock it. When Konstantinou returned, the man with the moon head was with him, tiptoeing and holding the key to the cabinet in front of him. Konstantinou put his hands on his hips and sighed as the old man unlocked the cabinet.

'OK, OK, OK,' Konstantinou mumbled as he began to rifle through the files. He was moving as feverishly as a bank robber and he was sweating even in the cool air of the tomb. He pulled a file, impossible for Matthew to decipher. He stopped on a page and ran his finger down it. The file referred to another, which Konstantinou pulled and riffled. He was now mumbling to himself in Greek. Finally he flicked the file.

'Here! Mathilda Margaret King. Guest resident on the island of Skiathos . . .'

As he read, Matthew looked at the file over his shoulder, even though the words on the page meant nothing to him.

'You see there, two hundred grand . . . December, January, February, the fifth of every month. Direct transfer.'

'Where from . . .'

Konstantinou frowned at the page and then called out to the old moon-headed man who was shuffling back down the corridor. The old man turned and came back to study the file over Konstantinou's shoulder. They spoke quickly in Greek.

'What does it say?' Matthew asked.

'Beside the entry for "source" it says *Embisteftigos*".'

'What does that mean?'

'It's something like "confidential", except it's worse than that. It means it's restricted information. My friend here says that it probably means the money came from the military or from the government. Did your mother have any links with the military?'

'What military? The Greek military?'

'I don't know. Or the government . . .'

Konstantinou spoke sharply to the old man who answered him with an apology in his voice.

'He says that he has no authority for this. He says I should take it up with the ministry. He says it must be classified information. Shit! Shit! Shit!'

Konstantinou kicked one of the filing cabinets and the sound reverberated through the whole building. The old man looked up at Matthew with grave misgivings in his eyes.

'I was sure it would be here,' Konstantinou said to the ceiling.

'Hey, relax,' Matthew said.

Konstantinou took a deep breath and the old man took the file out of his hands. He placed it carefully back in the filing cabinet. Konstantinou had already set off down the corridor. He seemed to be filled with shame for reasons Matthew couldn't begin to fathom. Matthew thought that it was possible that he was angry that he hadn't been able to earn his money in one shot, but he knew deep down that Konstantinou was more honourable than that. Even doing this discreditable work, Konstantinou was a perfectionist and he had wanted to do as good a job as he could. Matthew thanked the old man in English and set off in pursuit of Konstantinou, following a trail of swinging double doors that he had shoved open on his flight out of the building.

CHAPTER TWELVE

I

Konstantinou made some calls from a public pay phone to some people he knew who might have access to the ministry. Matthew waited outside, listening to the smooth hum of traffic. They were standing on the edge of a park, Matthew taking cover from the sun beneath a lime-tree.

'We'll have to stay in Athens tonight,' Konstantinou said when he had finished his calls, still furious, still embarrassed. 'There's a guy in the Ministry of Culture who knows someone in Fisheries, who knows someone else in the Naval Institute. I'll have answers for you tomorrow. I know a cheap hotel. I'll stay there, you stay wherever you want.'

Konstantinou was about to walk away to join the rest of the furious, feverish Athenians who all had their own unfinished business, but Matthew grabbed his arm.

'Wait a minute, where shall we meet?'

Konstantinou glared at Matthew's hand on his arm, and then calmed himself.

'Name a place.'

'Why don't we go for a beer somewhere,' Matthew asked. 'You can show me round Athens.'

Konstantinou laughed. At last the sun was beginning to lose some of its heat and the lime-trees above their heads sighed softly in the breeze, as if they too were relieved that evening was drawing on.

'I just wanted to get this thing done and over with,' Konstantinou said.

'I can see that.'

'I don't feel good about any of this.'

'Neither do I,' Matthew said. 'So what? Show me a place where they sell cold beer. And fuck the cheap hotel, I'm staying in the most expensive hotel in Athens. Which hotel is that?'

Konstantinou shook his head.

'What's wrong?'

'I want you to know that no matter what happens, I only want the money you've given me already. I don't want the other half. Even if I succeed. Half a million is enough. It's too much. I can give you half of that back . . .'

'Whatever you say.'

'It's fate. You came along and offered me money just when I needed it. Any other time I wouldn't have taken it.'

Matthew nodded and laughed.

'And this is going to stay a secret.'

'What?'

'The reason you need the money.'

'You wouldn't understand.'

'You don't want to tell me, but you want me to know that you're not just some shyster island official who can be bought and sold.'

Konstantinou hitched up his trousers and pushed his sunglasses up the bridge of his nose.

'Something like that, yeah.'

'Well I know that already.'

'Then that's good.'

'If I'd thought your integrity was already for sale I would only have offered you five grand. A million pounds you should be flattered. Let's go and have a beer.'

Konstantinou hesitated and then they both set off towards the nearest bar, their shadows crossing the width of the road which was empty of traffic. A hundred yards behind them there was another shadow and the shadow hurried to keep up as they headed towards the expensive part of town.

The bar that Konstantinou chose was the venue for a wedding, and they sat at the only table that wasn't reserved for guests. When they arrived, just as the sun was setting, the bar was filled with the sound of traditional Greek music, played on a tape deck, but now there were three teenage boys in their wedding suits tuning up electric guitars on a small stage.

The bride was spinning round and round to take kisses from old uncles with big bellies and lascivious smiles. Two waiters laboured hard in the dark heat to keep everyone's glass filled and they left a cloud of stale sweat odour every time they hurried by. The boys on the stage had put their ties round their heads and their guitars growled and buzzed. There were three old ladies with blue-grey hair dressed in black sitting near the stage, and they chewed constantly even though they had nothing in their mouths.

'We can go somewhere quieter,' Konstantinou said.

'This is fine.'

'Whatever you say, Mr King.'

'My name is Matthew. This beer is awful.'

'So let's have wine.'

Konstantinou clicked his finger at a waiter and was ignored.

'I'm nobody in this town,' he said, then he smiled. 'I like it like that.'

When the wine arrived, they began to drink it in big tumblers, and Matthew could feel his insides turning black from the cheapness of it. The band started playing, the music was badly played pop, sung in English with thick Greek accents. The bride was dancing so hard that her hair was wet with sweat.

'I thought they pinned money to brides here,' Matthew said.

'That comes later.'

'Have some more wine. I don't even know your first name.'

'In London they called me Tony. Jesus, this music's bad.'

The whole bar was now vibrating with the bass notes. The boys on the stage were shrieking into buzzing microphones. A short, fat, middle-aged man came and sat at a table near the door to the kitchen, half-hidden in shadows. He was wearing a suit and tie and Matthew and Konstantinou hardly noticed him. He looked like any other wedding guest.

'So how long were you in London?'

'Ten years,' Konstantinou said, the music almost too loud for him to be heard. Matthew had to shout to ask him what he had thought of London, but Konstantinou cupped his ear and shook his head. Then the music stopped with a collapsing of guitar chords. Someone's voice boomed into the microphone.

'Thank fuck for that, they're taking a break,' Konstantinou said. Greek bouzouki music took the place of the guitars and it was just as loud. The older wedding guests all shrieked and began to drag each other on to the dance floor. The old men in their dark suits and the golden-skinned ladies looked like leaves and debris blown across a clearing by the sound of the music. The middle-aged man in the shadows took a fat Greek cigarette.

'You know about our mythology,' Konstantinou said, lighting a cigarette.

'What mythology?'

'What mythology? Greek mythology. I was thinking about the fates. Do you know the story of Atreus.'

Matthew shook his head. The fat man in the shadows had stood up and was approaching with his unlit cigarette in his mouth.

'I studied the myths at school,' Konstantinou said. 'The story of Atreus reminds me of you . . .'

The fat man had reached their table and he leant over their bottle of wine, asking for a light with his eyes. His fat belly stretched against his shirt. When Konstantinou offered him his lighter, the fat man took a light and glanced down at Matthew's face.

'When I was a kid and I was studying the stories, I used to think they were all bullshit. But now I know that the old gods existed once. They had blood in their veins. Skiathos had a god living on the mountain.'

The dancing on the dance floor had turned into a whirl of

shrieks and dresses. The fat man had stepped back a little way from the table and had his eyes fixed on the side of Matthew's face. He reached into the inside pocket of his jacket.

'Atreus,' Konstantinou said, blowing out smoke.

'I know the story,' Matthew said.

'Are you sure you don't want to go somewhere quieter?'

'Yeah, why not.'

Konstantinou's face suddenly froze, and when he leapt to his feet, Matthew thought that he was getting up to leave. Instead, he grabbed the table and threw it forwards, knocking Matthew to the floor. Between the legs of the table and an overturned chair, Matthew saw some faces turning, saw the bride twirl around in her silvery white dress. Then he saw Konstantinou pushing forward with his head down like a bull. The fat man fell back and then fell sideways on to a table full of bottles and glasses. The glass smashed like the crashing of a cymbal and as Matthew got to his feet, the fat man stumbled into the crowd of wedding guests. Konstantinou was about to follow, but Matthew grabbed his arm. Konstantinou looked at Matthew with horror. The dance floor had been punctured by the flight of the fat man.

'He had a fucking gun,' Konstantinou said. 'The guy had a gun pointing right at your head.'

They both pushed their way through the throng of drunks and bridesmaids, but by the time they reached the street door, the fat man had disappeared into the dark confusion of Athens, where there were a thousand fat men and many thousands of loaded guns.

3

'So you didn't believe somebody wanted to kill me before,' Matthew said.

'I didn't think about it either way before. I've been thinking about the money.'

They'd checked into a cheap hotel near to Piraeus harbour.

Konstantinou pointed out that if the fat man wanted to track down Matthew King, he'd go to the most expensive hotels first, so they should use a cheap one. They'd found a coffee-coloured *pension* which at least had mosquito grilles that weren't punched full of holes and air-conditioning of a noisy, 1930s variety. The port of Piraeus was greasy with the heat, and Matthew's hotel room overlooked the slick, oily water of the harbour.

Matthew was staring out at the ships docked along the harbour wall. Konstantinou was pacing up and down the tiny room, pushing his hands through his hair. His room was down the corridor, but they'd been talking in Matthew's room for four hours. It was nearly 1 a.m. but the City of Athens wasn't sleeping.

'How come he knew where to find you?'

Matthew shrugged. There were seven ships docked, all of them with mighty, rusted hulls. They had come from Sierra Leone, Barcelona, London . . . For some reason the sight of big ships, their vast ugly majesty, their huge anchor chains disappearing into the blackness of the sea, always made him shudder.

'He must have followed you from London.'

'If that were so, why didn't he try to shoot me on Skiathos. Like he did with Callow.'

'Maybe he never got the chance.'

'Or maybe he didn't know where to find me until I got here.'

'How? Who else knows you're here?'

'No one.'

Konstantinou sat down on the bed. The warm air left sea salt all over the furniture and the bedclothes. The naked bulb was driving the flying ants and mosquitoes beyond the mosquito grille wild. Matthew realized that Konstantinou had been right to insist on rooms that had protection against insects. The air was so full of cigarette smoke that lighting another seemed pointless, but Konstantinou lit one and Matthew lit one too.

'I've been thinking about the lab,' Konstantinou said. 'They never lost things when I was there.'

'Maybe their standards have slipped since . . .'

'I mean it. How come they lose a hand? You saw her face.

That technician was telling the truth. She said the hand had never been registered. Somebody lost the stuff on purpose.'

Matthew sat down on the coffee-table, the only place to sit other than the bed. He flicked ash on the carpet because it was that kind of room, and because the ashtrays had all been stolen.

'Somebody at the lab tipped him off,' Konstantinou said with certainty. Then he looked at Matthew with great seriousness. 'Do you think I'm being paranoid?'

'No.'

'You're pretty calm. It was your head he was aiming at.'

'I know. I'm not calm. But I knew all along that someone wanted to kill me. Before, you didn't believe it. Now, you're just shocked.'

Konstantinou took his turn looking out of the window. There was something about the dinosaur cargo ships rotting in the harbour that was compulsive on a hot night.

'And now that you know it's real,' Matthew said, 'now that you believe me, you should get out. You should leave me to it. This is going to be dangerous work.'

Konstantinou turned around with a look of genuine puzzlement, the yellow lights of the harbour lighting up his face.

'Get out? Are you serious? Don't you understand, I'm glad that this happened.'

'And you say I'm insane.'

'At least now I get a chance to earn the money you're giving me. I saved your life. That's got to be worth something.'

'Yeah. Let's call it a reward. It's a reward now, not a bribe.'

Konstantinou's face brightened, even though Matthew had been joking.

'Let's do that,' he said. 'Let's call it a reward.'

'OK, it's a reward. Jesus Christ . . .'

'It's important to me.'

'Then fine.'

'How can you laugh when there's someone out there . . .'

Konstantinou jerked his head at the mosquito grille on the window. The fine mesh was alive with insects trying to find a way through to the light. Matthew washed his cigarette end into the sink.

'You were telling me about Atreus,' he said. Konstantinou left his lookout post by the window.

'Some other time,' he said. 'I need to get some sleep.'

'So you'll sleep tonight?'

'Yeah, I think I will.'

'The dignity of honest labour.'

'Something like that. You'd better lock your door when I leave.'

CHAPTER THIRTEEN

I

The Ministry of Culture was a modern, smoked-glass building which was still being completed. The top two floors were still girders and hard hats, open to the blazing sun. Konstantinou's friend worked on the third floor, which already had air-conditioning. It was the air-conditioning, Konstantinou's friend said, which was making him sneeze. Matthew and Konstantinou stood behind him, one at each shoulder, staring at his computer screen. The characters on the screen were all in English.

'He wants to know if we're sure about '82.'

'She lived on Skiathos in '82,' Matthew said.

'I've already told him that we saw the records in the old files yesterday. He says that maybe they got thrown out when the files were put on to disc.'

Matthew had been puzzled that their first stop that morning was the Ministry of Culture, but Konstantinou had said that any government clerk could access almost all government records through the new computer link system. He said that the whole thing was like a spider's web, but he had predicted even before they entered the half-tiled entrance hall that the system wouldn't work properly. They left without even thanking the clerk who had spent an hour punching in the same information and shrugging his shoulders.

Next they took a cab to Fisheries Ministry to find that the system hadn't reached Fisheries yet. Then Konstantinou said that if they couldn't go through the back door they would have to go in through the front. They would have to go to the Ministry of the Interior, but for that he'd need a higher clearance from the police department of Athens. He said he had friends who could fix it for him.

'You want what?'

'I want clearance to enter the foreign nationals surveillance records for '79 to '82. It has direct bearing on a murder investigation.'

They'd caught up with a friend of a friend in a sandwich bar near some other government building that was hidden behind a parade of advertising hoardings. This friend of a friend spoke half English and half Greek, winking at Matthew every time he broke into English. He was the same age as Konstantinou, heavier and more weary. Matthew imagined that this was how Konstantinou would have looked if he'd stayed in Athens. Konstantinou had explained the night before that he left his position in Athens and returned to Skiathos because he thought he could do some good for his native island. The friend of a friend had a mouthful of sandwich.

'So why are you telling me?'

'You work in the Ministry of the Interior, don't you?'

'Yeah. So what?' He spoke quickly in Greek and tore another piece of crust off his long French roll.

'He says a lot of the old stuff has been dumped. He says it was sensitive.'

'Yeah, that's the word,' the friend said, 'sensitive.' He asked a question in Greek.

'My wife's fine,' Konstantinou said. 'Can you help me or not?'

The friend shrugged then shook his head. Someone he knew came into the sandwich bar and he yelled and introduced Konstantinou. Konstantinou sighed and went through the ritual of remaking an old acquaintance before leading Matthew back out into the street, which was blinding white with sunlight.

'Everyone will be at lunch for the next two hours,' he said, looking at his watch. 'Maybe we should try and dig up that law firm you told me about.'

'Xianthos and Luggi.'

'Yeah.'

'I've told you, they went out of business.'

'Let's check.'

'It's so fucking hot here.'

'You're the one who said you're in a hurry.'

Konstantinou stretched out his arm and another grey-stained taxi swerved across the carriageway to a torrent of insults and hooting horns.

Matthew kept the address of the law firm which had dealt with his mother's will in his wallet. It was a hairdressing salon now, and it was closed. Above the shop front there was a large window with Greek lettering.

'You're sure this was the place?'

'See for yourself.'

Matthew showed Konstantinou the scrap of paper with the address. He was sweating so much that the backs of his knees and his armpits were becoming sore. The air was too hot to breathe, and Matthew stood in the shade of the hairdressing salon's awning, wafting air into his sodden shirt.

'I've got another idea,' Konstantinou said suddenly and he set off quickly in search of a taxi.

The taxi took them back to the laboratory they had visited the day before. This time Konstantinou took them through a back entrance which was patrolled by a single guard, who looked no more than twelve years old. Konstantinou showed his ID and the child soldier spent five minutes poring over it. When he finally let them through, Konstantinou said that he had high hopes for the next generation of his country-men.

They entered a cool labyrinth of corridors painted battleship grey. Konstantinou led Matthew down some iron stairs into a basement where the air trembled with the hum of machinery. Konstantinou obviously knew the building well, holding open the innumerable sets of double doors which all had hospital style porthole windows.

'What is this place?' Matthew asked.

'It's the morgue. There's an old guy here. I used to give him cigarettes.'

Konstantinou turned his back on another set of double doors and bumped them open with his back. There was a blast of hot air and a sweet, sickly smell, the same smell Matthew had smelt in Rook's villa. Inside, the room looked like some kind of un-hygienic canteen.

Konstantinou whistled loudly, but the place seemed to be deserted. Then a door opened and there was a loud rumble of machinery. A pale orange light glowed beyond the door, and the sweet, sickly smell grew stronger. The furnace roared loudly until the door swung shut. An old guy, in his sixties, with silver-blue hair and a grey overall which matched the walls shuffled in. He took one look at Konstantinou, mouthed something to himself under his breath and then hugged him like a son. He held Konstantinou by the shoulders and spent a few moments staring into his eyes. Konstantinou nodded in silence.

They spoke for no more than two minutes in Greek. Matthew saw Konstantinou clutching his hands at his wrists. The old guy showed him some paperwork that was pinned to a cork noticeboard.

When they left the morgue, Konstantinou slapped his palm with the back of his hand and gave a little yell of triumph.

'Two days ago he got a hand,' Konstantinou said. 'They sent a hand for him to burn. That's got to be our hand. And guess who signed the paperwork. Kossandrou. The guy in charge. The guy who went to Italy the next day.'

Suddenly they were back out in the heat of the afternoon. A fat woman wrapped in a black *chuddar* with her face hidden brushed past the door of the morgue, a walking shadow in the blinding heat. The air outside smelt of meat and decay. Matthew had decided that Athens wasn't a city at all, it was a suburb of hell.

'So that makes it my business,' Konstantinou said. His eyes were ablaze. 'I send forensic samples to the lab and they burn them. It's a cover-up. Me and you are after the same people.'

Matthew was leaning against the wall of the morgue and cold, rank air from inside blew around his ears.

'So now I got to find the right person to report to,'

Konstantinou said. 'I've got to make sure I go high enough. Maybe I'll go straight to the Ministry.'

'Maybe it was the Ministry that wants this thing covered up,' Matthew said.

'I thought about that.'

'And . . .'

'And I was hoping it was just me being paranoid. But you think so too.'

Matthew nodded his head. The heat of the city was making him dizzy. He suddenly felt a long way from home.

'We should think about this,' Matthew said.

'You're right.'

The woman in the yashmak stopped walking, turned around and doubled back, her sandals slapping the hot tarmac. On the shaded side of the street a truck was reversing at an impossible angle into a tiny gateway. The street was filled with noise, heat, possibilities. The ventilation duct from the morgue stopped blowing.

'We don't have any idea how big this thing is, do we, Mr King?' Konstantinou said, eyeing the black-robed woman. 'We don't know what we've got ourselves into.'

'We don't. Or who we're up against.'

'We should get out of here.'

'Yeah.'

The woman in the robe passed by and Matthew and Konstantinou were both on tiptoe waiting for her to pull a gun, a knife, even explode in front of their eyes. The truck driver seemed to be acting strangely too. And now a taxi had pulled up at the end of the street, blocking their exit.

'We're just scaring ourselves,' Konstantinou said, not taking his eye off the Muslim shadow.

'Yeah. Let's get out of here.'

'Out of this street or out of Athens?'

'Out of Athens.'

They both walked quickly in the direction of Piraeus harbour, not trusting any taxis that cruised by, but waiting to find a taxi rank. This feeling of panic, this sudden realization that maybe they were taking on a whole city, had hit them both at the same time, but it was a feeling they would have to get used to. They didn't speak all the way to the hydrofoil, but their eyes were wide open.

2

There could have been no finer antidote to their sudden attack of panic than the hydrofoil journey back to Skiathos. They had booked their tickets in false names, not even conferring with each other before they did it. There was a scrum to get aboard, but most of the tourists got off at Aegina and after that the boat was almost empty. The cabin crew in their starched white uniforms sat near the front smoking cigarettes. Matthew and Konstantinou took seats on the viewing deck at the back as the sun began to set over the endless sea.

The air was silent except for the throbbing of the engine and the tumult of white water in the boat's wake. They headed west past a hundred nameless islands, the evening air as soft as a child's breath. Matthew threw a cigarette into the wake.

'Did you pick up all of him?'

'Who?'

'Callow.'

'We got the right side of the upper torso, the lower left leg, the hand, the heart. Some pieces must still be out there.'

They both stared at the smooth surface of the ocean.

'His sister is flying in tomorrow morning to identify the remains. I'll have to move him out of the fish-packing plant and get her to him before he thaws.'

Konstantinou scratched his head with disgust and then laughed at his predicament.

'Can I speak to her?'

Konstantinou thought about this for a few moments, still clinging to the last shreds of procedure.

'We'll both speak to her,' he said at last.

Darkness came quickly, and soon, Konstantinou was just a pale outline set against the crimson sky. Matthew had begun to wonder what his half-brother had looked like, what kind of man he was, how much he knew. He had always somehow known that there was somebody his mother loved more than him. And when he was a boy he had often tortured himself with the idea that the reason his mother had left was because she hated him. Now he knew that his absurd childhood fantasy was the truth.

Matthew had felt her hatred when he had visited her in Skiathos. She had been fighting hard to control it, but he could feel it in the air around her. He had mistaken it for evil intent.

But none of these thoughts affected the throb of his own engine, the one that was powering his quest through these islands. It hummed like the propellers of the hydrofoil, chewing up each new fact as if they were sticks of driftwood. It was still Tanya that mattered. Tanya and Sarah.

'So what do you suggest we do now?' Matthew asked. A slow-moving ferry was cruising by, an island of lights and strangers heading in the opposite direction. A little girl waved from the upper deck.

'I will make some calls when I get back to my office,' Konstantinou said. 'We'll be safer on the island. It's my territory.'

'I meant it when I said you should get out of this. You've earned your money.'

'And I meant it when I said that this was my case too now. I've got friends who went to college with me. Some of them are in the administration. They were communists like me. They might have changed, but then again they might not. Something like this might appeal to them.'

The ferry and the little waving girl had already left in the hydrofoil's wake. She had run to the back of the deck to wave the hydrofoil goodbye. In the last blush of sunset, the little girl was suddenly transformed. She stood up on tiptoe and as she did, Matthew saw that it was Tanya waving at him through the half-light. The thud of the hydrofoil engine subsided and he heard her voice calling to him as clearly as if she were calling his name from the shadows at the bottom of their beautiful garden at home in London. Matthew had to grip the rail to stop himself getting to his feet and yelling back, or leaping into the foam to swim to her. For a few seconds he felt the agonizing need of an abandoned child, seeing her father again for the first time and yelling for him to rescue her. For those few seconds the islands dissolved into the sea and into the crimson light and he felt that Tanya was only inches from his grasp, ready to be pulled back from the underworld. Then the distance between the hydrofoil and the ferry became too great and the image of the little girl was swallowed by green darkness. The lights of the ferry winked in the sunset.

'. . . If Kossandrou really is part of a cover up . . . who knows? We could be digging up something big.'

Matthew leant over the back of the boat and stared into the tumult of white water. Salt air fizzed around the propellers and made his eyes sting. He hoped that he could pretend to Konstantinou that it was the salt air that was bringing the tears to his eyes.

'Are you OK, Mr King?'

'Yeah, I'm fine.'

'What's wrong? Do you get seasick?'

'Yeah. Seasick.'

Matthew sat down heavily on the slatted bench. He turned to Konstantinou and smiled.

'You have to be very hard to even carry on, don't you?' Matthew said.

'What do you mean?'

'It doesn't matter.'

Konstantinou looked hurt.

'You mean me? You mean I'm hard for taking your money?'

Matthew shook his head.

'That's not what I meant at all.'

'Well I have my reasons. OK?'

Konstantinou was squaring up for an argument. He wanted so badly to tell Matthew his reasons for accepting his bribe, but something was stopping, and the constipation was unbearable.

Matthew straightened up and sighed.

'I really wasn't referring to you at all. I was talking about myself. I was talking about how hard I have had to become to carry on with this.'

Konstantinou wasn't convinced.

'Yeah, sure.'

'OK, if it bothers you so much, tell me your reasons.'

Konstantinou thought for a long time, as the hydrofoil banked north towards the distant lights of Skopelos, and beyond them, the high mountain of Skiathos.

'Not yet,' Konstantinou said.

'But it is for a child?'

'It's for a child who hasn't been born yet.'

CHAPTER FOURTEEN

I

The engine of the hydrofoil was cut and the huge, steel mosquito hull sank slowly into the water of Skiathos harbour. With the motor idling, the hydrofoil was just another boat, its gleaming metal skis hidden beneath the waves.

When they reached the harbour wall a crewman jumped on to the key, fastened a mooring rope and began to wind the boat into dock. It was almost midnight and there was a cool breeze blowing but Matthew wasn't sleepy. Konstantinou waited for him to step ashore.

'I'd like to take a look around Rook's villa,' Matthew said.

'Now?'

'Now. I won't sleep anyway.'

'Do you want me to come?'

'No. This is personal.'

As Matthew and Konstantinou walked up the quay towards the harbour front, they could see a dozen sea-front cafés, all crowded with tourists beneath long strings of night lights. The tourists in the cafés were shrieking and laughing, and a small family of Gypsies was working its way through their tables. Matthew and Konstantinou walked through the crowds of tourists, and this time the café owners were all too busy hauling trays of food to pay homage to their police chief.

When they got back to the police station, Konstantinou switched on the lights and locked the door behind him. There was a full ashtray and the smell of fresh smoke, but the desk sergeant had gone home. The fax light was winking, but no one had called. Konstantinou sat at his desk and massaged his neck. Then he unlocked a drawer and handed Matthew a set of keys.

'The big key is for the gate, the other for the front door. The little keys, I don't know. I think they are for his bureau and his drawers. What is it you're looking for?'

'I don't know yet. I think Rook knew more than he told me.'

'Is that why you had him killed?'

Matthew waited a long time before he answered.

'I've told you already. It was fate that killed him.'

'That isn't an answer.'

Matthew headed for the door and Konstantinou stood up quickly.

'I need to know the truth, Matthew.'

Matthew waited with his back turned, his hand on the door handle.

'Rook raped my wife. He ruined my mother's life, and my father's too. That little Gypsy girl I gave the money to in the café, she introduced me to her father. I gave him a handful of notes and he did the killing for me.'

Matthew turned to see how Konstantinou would react. Konstantinou had his head bowed.

'So you didn't have the courage to do it yourself?' Konstantinou said.

'I wouldn't have made a very good job of it. The Gypsy knew his craft. I told him that the killing was an act of vengeance and so he said he would make sure that Rook's spirit wouldn't come after me. There is a ritual that they carry out to banish evil spirits. I think he is the first man I have spoken to who really understood what this whole thing was about.'

'And you believe in evil spirits?'

'Yes I'm afraid I do. Inspector, why don't you go home?'

Konstantinou stood up and loaded some paper into his fax machine. Matthew thought that maybe the fax machine was the only solid thing left in Konstantinou's world.

'I'm going to make some calls,' he said. 'Some of my friends will be drunk at this time of night. There's no communist like a drunk communist.'

Konstantinou smiled and Matthew knew that he was forgiven, even though in Matthew's mind, there was nothing to forgive. Killing Rook was simply another step on the path into the impenetrable darkness, a routine command spewed out by the engine of his grief. There would be more deaths along the way, and Matthew hoped that he would meet other people as sober and honourable as the Gypsy to help him carry out his work. When he stepped outside, the small whitewashed alley was still warm from the day's heat and Matthew walked down to the harbour in search of a taxi.

The taxi took the new coast road around the mountain. Matthew got out at the end of the shale path that led to the villa and gave the driver triple the fare.

'I'd like you to wait here for me,' Matthew said as the driver counted the money. He didn't seem sure.

'How long will you be?'

Matthew gave him another handful of notes.

'That long,' he said and the driver switched off his engine.

It was difficult to stick to the path in the darkness, and the cicadas all stopped chirruping as Matthew passed by. The mountain above his head seemed to give off its own grey light and the bottle-green sage scrub almost glowed in reflection. Matthew unlocked Rook's rusted gates and they creaked as he stepped into the garden.

In the darkness this was a different place altogether. The weeds in the defunct well sprouted into the shape of an old woman with a black shawl over her head. A wrecked moped that was lying near to the door had grass growing between the spokes of its wheels, but Matthew imagined that it had been moved since the last time he saw it. When the wind blew, it blew a fine grey dust into Matthew's eyes and made him realize how tired he was. He should have gone back to his hotel first and got some sleep, but he was sure that Rook still had secrets that he hadn't divulged. The night air was filled with the staccato clicking and whistling of fruit-bats.

Matthew turned the lock on the front door. For some reason he tried to do it without making a sound, as if there were something inside the villa that shouldn't be disturbed. He felt the rough plastered wall for a light switch and then the living-room emerged in a sickly, yellow light.

The door to the bedroom where Rook's body had lain was still ajar, opening on to darkness striped with the grey light from outside. Matthew forced himself to go into the bedroom first, because he knew that if he waited, his imagination would create an inhabitant for the darkness in the room. He went into the bedroom and found that the bloody sheets had been removed. He guessed that Konstantinou had burnt them.

The kitchen was just a grease-caked stove and a sink with water dripping on to a cracked ceramic bowl. When Matthew switched on the kitchen light, cockroaches ran for cover. Matthew went back into the living-room and saw a water-colour on the wall of a bowl of fruit, badly painted, almost identical to the painting his mother had sent him when he was a young man. Matthew thought that maybe Rook had loved his mother after all, to give pride of place to such a monstrosity.

Matthew looked around for the bureau and saw an ancient-looking mahogany box half-hidden beneath a lace shawl and discarded clothes. There was something frozen about the whole house, as if the house itself had died when Rook had died, and all the things he'd casually tossed on to shelves and cupboards were now sentenced to stay where they had fallen for ever, a single moment of a man's existence turned into an ugly still life. The heavy mahogany chest looked out of place among the flimsy whicker and whitewashed plaster of the villa. It was an import from home, a little piece of England, locked and forbidding.

The second key that Matthew tried fitted the chest. When he pulled open the roller he found a pipe, a glass jar, an envelope full of white powder, lots of dead matches and a silver cigarette lighter. This was where Rook sat to smoke and to dream. To escape from all the wicked things he had done.

The third key fitted a trunk in the bedroom which seemed to be of the same vintage as the mahogany chest. Matthew got down on his knees and opened the trunk to find two neat piles of papers. The air from inside the trunk smelt like a desert tomb which hadn't been opened for centuries.

There were two piles of paperwork and receipts concerning the Costa Rica bar and another bar on Skopelos called the Blue Bird. It seemed odd that Rook should keep straightforward accounts, when everything else he did was so crooked. There were also dispatch receipts from the hydrofoil, packages sent to Athens, packages received from Hydra and Aegina.

Matthew scanned all the paperwork and then dug deeper. At the bottom of the trunk there was a pink folder bound by an elastic band. Matthew took the elastic band off and began to open out the sheaves of paper.

There were a dozen A3 size sheets, and Matthew instantly recognized the diagrams on them. They were the sailing boats and thin dark tubes he had seen in his father's desk when he was a child, burnt into his memory by the blow across the head that his father had given him. They weren't the exact same diagrams, but they were laid out in the same way, with the same annotations. Matthew now recognized the thin dark tubes as the hulls of submarines, some side on, some in profile, some opened out to offer a precise diagram of the complex interiors.

The paper was yellow with age, but the design work was still clear. Matthew felt a lock turning in his head. A vivid childhood memory becoming real before his eyes. Matthew had very little knowledge of ship design, but he guessed that they were Polaris, or maybe prototypes of the next generation after Polaris.

Along with the blueprints there was an envelope full of photographs. The photos were all black and white and fading. From the clothes he guessed they were taken in the late 1940s and early 1950s. There were some of Rook in military uniform, but mostly they were of Rook with Matthew's mother and father. In one of the shots, Matthew's mother was sitting on his father's shoulders, captured in mid-scream, horseplay on a chilly-looking English beach. Beside them stood a young Mr Rook, not smiling at all, perhaps already guilty of betrayal, his trousers rolled up to his knees. Rook looked tanned and fit in the photographs – time had been cruel to all three of them. Matthew studied the photograph for a long time, a simple holiday snap that told a long and bitter story if you looked closely enough at the eyes. Matthew's mother, shrieking and scared, Matthew's father struggling under her weight, and beside them Mr Rook, knowing more than either of them.

As well as the photos of Matthew's mother and father there was a single, over-exposed photograph of a new-born baby. Matthew put the photo into his pocket.

In the sleeve of the envelope there were three sheets of negatives. Matthew held them up to the light bulb, but they were so old and faded that he couldn't make out any picture. He put the negatives into his pocket, along with the photo of Peter Callow, who'd just arrived on earth and was innocent of the horrors his new life would cause.

Matthew stood up and his head buzzed. It had been a long time since he had slept properly. He turned towards the bedroom door and heard footsteps on the shale path. Then he heard the front door open and saw a shadow fall across the living-room floor. His heart pumped fast, but the engine inside the mountain made him stay cool. He reached out and grabbed an ugly, blue marbled vase that Rook had kept by the bedside.

He stepped out into the living-room and heard a scream. Matthew yelled too. When the first few seconds of terror had passed, Matthew saw the cowering figure of Rook's housekeeper. Her eyes were enormous as she stared at Matthew, seeing perhaps in her terror the ghost of Mr Rook. She had her hands to her mouth and then she crossed herself. Matthew put the vase down and the housekeeper began to weep. She sat down on the floor and fought for breath as Matthew whispered to her in English that everything was OK and that she was going to be fine.

'I saw lights . . .' she said in English.

'I was a friend of his,' Matthew said. 'I was just sorting out his things.'

She seemed suddenly to remember something and leapt to her feet.

'It was he kill himself,' she said firmly. 'He put the knife into himself.'

With that she turned and fled into the night. Matthew had

wondered how much money Konstantinou had given her to make her stick to her story with such alacrity. And he wondered how long the ghost of Rook would haunt her for telling one simple lie.

2

That night, Matthew slept without dreams. As the sun rose, his phone rang and he woke up to see the grey light of dawn pressed against his shutter blinds.

'Hello?'

'We have a call for you, Mr King. Detective Inspector Joyce from London, England.'

Matthew sat bolt upright in bed. His skin was dry and hot. Athens had burnt him more than he had realized and the skin on his back chaffed against the pillow.

'Put him through.'

When Joyce came on the line, he sounded contrite and almost humble. He explained that Ali Farhouk, the Jordanian student who had been charged with Tanya's murder, had been released. A witness had unexpectedly come forward and confirmed Farhouk's alibi. Joyce said that for want of other lines of inquiry, his superiors had agreed to follow up Matthew's story.

'You should understand, Mr King, that the last time we spoke I had been given an absolute cast-iron assurance that the evidence against Farhouk was overwhelming . . .'

Matthew rubbed his eyes. The sleeve of negatives was beside the bed on the bedside table and he held them up to the light of dawn.

'So you don't think I'm insane any more, Mr Joyce,' Matthew said.

'I never did. It was just that your story was so . . .'

'Bizarre?'

'Exactly.'

'You know, there are policemen in this world who hear a

143

bizarre story and realize that it's true simply because it is so bizarre.'

Joyce mumbled something. Matthew could see white lines cutting vertically and laterally across a black square. He stood up with the phone hooked between his chin and shoulder, and pushed open the shutter blinds. In the first sunlight of morning, the image on the negative came into sharper focus, but still made no sense. He scanned the four frames, all of them lines and rectangles of darkness. No faces, no human form.

'I suppose I should apologize to you, Mr King.'

'There's no need.'

'Well, I'm sorry anyway.'

Matthew sat down on the bed, flicked on the bedside lamp and studied the negatives through the electric light. Joyce explained that if Matthew was agreeable, he would send two of his people out to Skiathos to interview Matthew about the cassette. Matthew saw what looked like the outline of a ship.

'Would that be OK, Mr King?'

'Send who you like. But I have to tell you, Mr Joyce, I have been doing pretty well without you. The police here are extra-ordinarily helpful.'

The shape on the second negative now looked like a sub-marine, a long, dark cigar, rounded at both ends. It was a photograph of the same A3 diagram he'd seen in Rook's villa. Joyce said that two detectives would be arriving on the island on the first flight the next morning. They would visit Matthew in his hotel room.

'Around midday, Mr King. Will you be there?'

'I have no idea.'

'I need to know for certain.'

'If I'm not in the hotel, I'll be around. It's a small island.'

Matthew thought he detected a sudden note of panic in Joyce's voice, which he tried hard to disguise.

'Then it's agreed. Midday at your hotel.'

'Midday at the hotel.'

Joyce rang off quickly. Matthew wanted to enjoy this small triumph, but the eagerness in Joyce's voice had already begun to unnerve him. He slipped the negatives into his wallet and dressed for the murderous heat that would surely follow the cool of the dawn.

Matthew visited three wide-fronted general stores on the harbour quay, where they sold beach-balls, mosquito sprays, sandals, bread, vicious-looking sea knives, fake pearls, soap and coffee. Everything the tourists needed for their temporary lives. They also developed film.

All three of the store owners peered at Matthew's strip of negatives and said that the film type and grade were too old for the equipment they had. Then he discovered that they all sent their film away to the same developer anyway. He hiked up through the sweltering limestone alleys towards the dog-leg of unmarked shops that the islanders used. He found an apothecary which hadn't invested in anything at all since the end of the Second World War, not even new stock, and the old guy who ran the place said that he would have the film ready by that afternoon.

Back on the beach, Matthew stripped down to his swimming trunks and splashed into the water. There was an old German couple swimming slowly and elegantly with short, deliberate strokes, parallel with the shore, occasionally calling out to each other in rasping German. There were English and French families, some Italians panting and gleaming on the rocks, copper-skinned Athenians smoking and flicking their cigarette ends into the hot sand. The whole of Europe was here on this beach, not even glancing at each other, all separated into their own little islands of towels and iceboxes.

Beneath the water, Matthew was freed from the heat and voices, and he explored the green and crimson world, searching vaguely for the silver ring that Sarah had lost. Something told him that it would be gleaming up at him in the cleft of a rock, or in the soggy embrace of an anemone. He didn't know why, but he felt that if he could find the ring, then something would be resolved, and as he searched he imagined that the Gypsy whom he had paid to take care of Rook would have understood. The Gypsy had said that he would use the money to pay for his daughter's wedding, and Matthew thought that that was a fine way to spend it. There was something joyous about this world beneath sound and air, and his chest ached before he reluctantly found the sand beneath him with his feet and looked around the beach.

The mountain shimmered above his head, its shadow moving slowly around the island. As Matthew stared up at the mountain, a seagull shrieked, and a sudden realization struck him.

'The money was a secret because she dealt in secrets,' he said softly, as if the words themselves would have the power to make the mountain tremble.

'S'beautiful, isn't it,' said the German swimmer, who had stood up to empty water from his swimming goggles.

Matthew splashed the water, transfixed by the mountain, and superimposed on to that, the outline of the diagrams he'd seen in Rook's villa and in his father's bureau.

'Yes, it is beautiful,' Matthew said, filled with awe. 'It's fucking perfect. She photographed the contents of his desk. She photographed the diagrams and then sold them. Only a government would pay that kind of money . . .'

The German swimmer looked puzzled. He peered up at the mountain as if there would be some explanation there.

'Are you English?' he said at last.

'Yes.'

'My wife and I had bets . . .'

'Jesus Christ, that's it! And Rook too. She brought him the photographs and he made copies of the designs and brokered the deal. That's how she took her revenge on my father.'

Matthew suddenly turned to the German with a look of open-mouthed joy and horror. The German swimmer mumbled something and launched himself into a hasty crawl towards the shore.

Matthew dived down beneath the waves. A shoal of brilliantly pink fish scattered in front of his face and many disparate possibilities began to take shape.

Matthew came up for air again. Konstantinou was standing on the brow of a small dune in his suit and dark glasses, waving

and shading his eyes. Matthew dressed quickly, while Konstantinou told him that Peter Callow's sister was on the island, and
that she had something for Matthew to see.

Konstantinou led him to a small chapel, sunk into a thick
limestone wall a few metres up from the harbour. Konstantinou
said that Maria Callow had already had to endure the ordeal of
seeing the chopped up pieces of her brother's body, and that as
an exercise in identification, it had been a waste of time. There
were hardly enough pieces to make a quarter of a man, no head
or teeth, nor even any rings on any fingers. However, she had
been able to confirm that her brother had written to her a month
before saying that he was quitting his job and going to live in
Skiathos. She said that she had been shocked at his decision, and
also hurt that he had specifically told her not to come and visit
him. The letter had said that Peter Callow had decided to erase
his past entirely and begin his life again as a painter. But she said
that her brother had always been a very precise and determined
man.

'Have you told her who I am?' Matthew said.

'Some. I told her that Peter Callow was your half-brother. She
said she would like to meet you.'

Inside the church the darkness was cool and scented with lavender and the smell of extinguished candles. At the altar, a
dozen candles still burnt, and the ancient stone effigies of Christ
and the Madonna smiled and wept in the shifting light. Maria
Callow was kneeling near to the altar, her head resting on the
black wooden bench in front of her.

'Maria?'

She turned. The candles made the tears shine on her cheek
and there was a look of despair on her face, which she tried to
turn into a smile. Matthew liked her immediately and he sat
down beside her.

'The inspector said it would be OK to talk.'

She sniffed hard and eased herself up on to the pew.

'I don't know why I'm here really. I'm not a believer or
anything.'

'At least it's cool in here,' Matthew said and he couldn't

believe that he had already drifted on to the topic of the weather, as two English people meeting in a hot place must always do.

'It was just the way he looked,' Maria said, tidying up her tears with a handkerchief. 'It made me think that Peter couldn't possibly belong to those fragments. They were so torn. I thought he must be somewhere else.'

Matthew nodded and looked down at his feet.

'You don't believe either, do you?' she said.

'No, I don't.'

'Shall we talk somewhere else?'

'If that's what you want.'

'I thought I wanted this . . . but what I really need is a bloody strong gin.'

Matthew grinned and led her out of the darkness into the blinding white light of the day.

They sat in the harbour café and Maria sipped her long, iced gin and tonic with great purpose. Matthew drank beer and the café owner, who had seen Matthew in the company of Konstantinou, gave them the best seats in the place, looking out on to the harbour. The wealthy tourists were still sunning themselves on their decks, the islanders were hopping down into their rigs and hauling up boxes of fish.

'We knew he had a half-brother,' Maria said, after she had drunk half her gin. 'Peter's real mother wrote him a letter. She left it with a solicitor, with strict instructions that he shouldn't read it or even know about it until he was twenty-one.'

She had already explained that she and Peter were both adopted. She had been left at a railway station when she was a few months old. Peter had come along a few years later, offered to her father and mother by a friend of a friend in the diplomatic service. They had both been raised in Nigeria and then Kenya, where her father had been the British High Commissioner. Maria had the ramrod straightness of a tough colonial woman: her hair was silver blue, her face lined by years of foreign sun. Her accent was almost aristocratic, and Matthew wondered how she would have looked, what she would have become, if she hadn't been left at the railway station, at the mercy of the whole world.

She said that Peter had graduated from Cambridge and taken a job in Glasgow working for Brown's, the shipbuilders, as a designer. Then he moved to Canada and finally to the United States, where he worked as a naval architect.

'I'd rather lost contact with him lately. He was always very ambitious and I am quite the opposite. No reason why we should be similar, I suppose. Then he wrote me this odd letter saying that he was giving it all up and coming here. I suppose he had worn himself out. I didn't realize until I heard he was dead that I still think of him as a little boy.'

A cloud passed over Maria's face, and Matthew could see that she was afraid that he would think her silly. Matthew smiled.

'Would you like another gin?'

She shook her head.

'What was she like, your mother . . . Peter's mother?'

'She was a fine woman. She liked to paint. I understand Peter liked to paint too.'

Maria sipped her gin as if the subject were something that shouldn't be dwelt on.

'I imagine that the urge to paint was genetic. He certainly had the urge. Unfortunately, his genes hadn't given him any talent.'

'His mother was pretty awful too.'

They both giggled, sharing an illicit joke at the expense of the sacred dead.

'The Inspector said you would want to see the letter,' Maria said.

'If you don't mind.'

'I brought it with me to bury with him. He said he wanted to be buried here, so I'm making the arrangements. He said he wanted to be buried beside his real mother. She's buried up on the mountain, isn't she?'

'Yes, I believe she is.'

'Have you not visited her grave?'

Matthew shook his head and looked out across the harbour where fish boxes were being sprinkled with ice and loaded aboard trucks and on to the backs of fly-ravaged donkeys. Destined for the same freezer that had housed Peter's remains.

Maria fussed in her handbag and then handed Matthew a torn envelope. The envelope was addressed to Peter Callow, c/o the British Africa Mission, Lagos, Nigeria. The ink on the envelope had turned turquoise with age. Inside, the handwritten letter was still clear, the ink as deep blue as the day it had been written. Beneath Matthew's home address, there was a date: 16 February 1965.

CHAPTER FIFTEEN

I

Dear Peter,

I can hardly begin to express the pain that I feel.

You were born at six o'clock in the morning and I held you in my arms for a whole day. When it went dark outside they took you away from me. It has been dark ever since.

There is no excusing what I did, but I must tell you that I was left with no choice. Your father isn't my husband. That sounds so simple, doesn't it, but in those few words is a terrible tangle of feelings and pain.

Your Father is called Thomas Rook, he is a captain with the Royal Marines and he is a fine man. I met him after I had already married and I had no way of controlling my feelings for him. Our affair wasn't dirty or sordid, as you might think. It was a fine, happy thing. You have his eyes, I know that for sure. And the same wrinkle to your nose.

My husband works for the military too, except he is an intelligence officer. It was he who forced me to give you up, and he threatened all sorts of damnation if I didn't. I didn't love him before and now it takes an enormous amount of prayer and fortitude to stop me from hating him.

A year after you were born I had another baby. He is crying now in his room and I know that I should go to him, but I fear myself. I know that soon I shall hurt him if I don't escape. My priest has told me that it is unnatural for a mother to feel like this about her own child, so then I must assume that I am unnatural. Either that or all my love was used up on you, on that one day, when you and I were together.

I am writing this letter to you now because I have made my decision to rejoin your father. I will try if I can to persuade him to get you back. How I would love for us to live together, the three of us. He lives on a little Greek island and I know that you would love it there. I fear, however, that your father has too much loyalty to my husband to allow this to happen. If there is a miracle and he agrees to my plan, then we will be together soon. If he does not, you will already be a young man by the time you read these words.

I am writing to you from my bedroom in England. My husband is downstairs working, as always, and my poor son is still crying. I have a packed suitcase and an airline ticket. I must leave them both because now I have betrayed my husband in two ways. If I stay, very bad things will happen.

I don't believe that a single minute of any day goes by when I don't think about you, Peter. I hope they kept your name. You were such a sweet little thing and I gave you a whole lifetime's worth of kisses in just a few hours. It may be that you can never find it in your heart to forgive me, and for that I wouldn't blame you. But I can only tell you that I was given no option, and when you were lifted out of my arms, my heart was broken for ever.

I love you Peter. You were never a mistake.

All my love, your loving Mother

Matthew wiped his eyes with his sleeve. He imagined that he could remember the very evening that she wrote the letter. He recalled a night spent crying in his room, and the next day, his mother had gone. That was when his father had said that she was 'being rather silly'. Matthew handed the letter back to Maria.

'I'm so sorry,' she said softly.

'I knew already,' Matthew said.

'I'm sure she didn't mean those things.'

Matthew turned in his chair and called for the bill. His composure had cracked only briefly, but now the engine inside was working hard to plug the holes and shore up the damage. The only line that he should dwell on was the line which said that she had betrayed her husband in two ways. The first betrayal was sleeping with Rook. The second was espionage. Matthew laid two crimson notes on the table and the waiter thanked him profusely.

'So will you take on the villa, now that Peter is dead?' Matthew asked.

'I haven't even seen it. Is it pretty?'

Matthew shook his head and laughed.

'I don't think so. But then I'm prejudiced.'

Maria closed her bag firmly, as if the letter might give off a poisonous gas if it weren't sealed in.

'Mr King, do you have any idea who shot my brother?'

'Not yet. But I'm working on it.'

'The Inspector said that there was nothing he could tell me.'

'That is the truth. If we find out anything, I'll write to you.'

'But he never made an enemy in his life.'

'I don't think it was personal. That sounds crass, doesn't it. Murder is always personal, I suppose.'

'Yes, I suppose it is. But it's all so *unlike* him.'

Maria laughed at herself and Matthew laughed too. He had already decided that Maria was a woman who deserved to be shielded from the truth, and that she deserved some kind of reward, if only for her brother's sake.

'Do you know what my mother left me in her will?' Matthew asked.

Maria seemed to prepare herself for the worst. Perhaps she expected Matthew to say that she had left him nothing.

'She left me £25 million,' he said flatly. 'And now I know for sure that she did it to curse me. She knew what would happen. To the son she loved she left a crumbling little villa. To me she left more money than I can ever spend.'

Matthew stood up and Maria stared at him with bewilderment. Matthew could see that she didn't believe what he had said. He reached into his back pocket and produced his cheque book and a pen. Then he leant forward on the table and wrote the cheque and handed it to Maria.

'This is some of what I owe your brother,' he said. 'I suppose you should have it now he's gone. I would have made it more, but I know that any more than that figure is dangerous. It would only cause you harm. I am very familiar with the currency of these things now. There's enough there to make your life better, but not affect your sanity.'

Maria was staring at the cheque with her mouth wide open. The cheque was made out for a quarter of a million pounds.

'Mr King, is this some sort of joke?' she said.

'Take it to the bank and see if they laugh,' Matthew said, and he headed off quickly towards his hotel.

When the bellboy delivered the photographs to his room, Matthew was certain that his theory was correct.

The photos were the same as the blueprints that Rook had copied, except in the photographs, there was a signature scrawled at the bottom of each sheet. It was impossible to make it out, but Matthew was sure that it was his father's signature.

Matthew locked the photographs in the safe along with his English and Greek cash. Then he began to pace the room, as the sun set over the Aegean, turning the sea and sky the colour of cherries. There were two questions still to be answered. Why did she do it, and who bought the diagrams.

The first wasn't too hard to answer. It had been his father who had forced his mother to give up her child, and the pain of the separation had driven her to seek an easy vengeance. It would have been the easiest thing in the world to break into his bureau. And after the photographs had been taken, she fled to Rook, who would have had the contacts to shift that kind of merchandise.

The second question was more difficult and more urgent. Selling military secrets was something Matthew had only ever read about in books, but it would explain the huge sums of money involved. The only nagging doubt was, why would any government be prepared to kill innocent people simply to protect a secret that was at least thirty years old?

Matthew knew that he had strayed into deadly territory. He felt like a man who has climbed too high up a mountain and then realizes that there is no way down. There was a knock at the door and Matthew froze.

'Who is it?'

'It's me, Tony.'

Matthew let Konstantinou in and he immediately looked at Matthew's face and asked what the hell was the matter. Matthew said that there was nothing wrong, then he said that the letter had upset him a little.

'What is it?' Konstantinou asked. 'What is it you're not telling me?'

'There's nothing I'm not telling you,' Matthew said and he laughed. 'Why don't you go home?'

Konstantinou looked astonished.

'Home? What's wrong with you?'

Matthew ran his hands through his hair and turned his back on Konstantinou.

'Your part in all this is over,' Matthew said. 'You've done what I paid you to do and now I can take it from here on my own.'

'What the fuck is this?'

'You don't need to know. It's better for you if you know nothing.'

Konstantinou stood up and grabbed Matthew's shoulder, turning him around.

'How many times do I have to tell you that this is my investigation. The whole fucking world doesn't revolve around your cheque-book.'

'Yes it does.'

'You're such a fucking arrogant bastard.'

'So go home.'

'I want to know what this is all about. I want to know why the lab deliberately lost my forensic evidence. I want to know why someone tried to kill you.'

'You're the detective, find out for yourself. Except you won't survive to find out the truth. They'll kill you too. You have a wife, don't you?'

Konstantinou didn't answer. He still looked furious.

'If you have a wife and kids, then for their sake, leave this to me. I'm up against governments. Maybe the whole fucking world . . .'

Matthew pointed out to sea, where the sunset was reaching the peak of its glory. Konstantinou waited a few moments and then turned angrily towards the door.

'If that's how you want it . . .' he said. 'You don't need me, I don't need you. You've got a head start, but I'll find out before you do. I've got the contacts. I've got the fax machine . . .'

'Your precious fucking fax machine . . .'

Matthew wanted Konstantinou to get angry, so angry that he would decide to drop the whole thing.

'Why don't you just go back to handing out maps for the tourists.'

'Fuck you.'

'Yeah, fuck me.'

'And for your information, shit-head, I gave your money away. I gave it to a charity in Athens. I didn't like what I was becoming, so I sent them a cheque. I'm clean.'

Matthew looked up at Konstantinou's contorted face and smiled. It was true, he really did look clean.

'What do you want me to do, give you a medal?'

'Yeah.'

'You never even told me what it was you wanted the money for in the first place.'

Konstantinou was half-way out the door. A wave of hot air flooded the air-conditioned room.

'Or don't I deserve to know?'

'You don't deserve to know, but I'll tell you anyway, because I wouldn't want you thinking I took it for myself. My wife can't have kids. There's a place in Italy where she can get the operation, but it costs. I was going to give her the money to have the operation. But then I thought about the kid who would be born. What kind of kid would that be?'

Matthew turned his back and let the crimson light of the sunset bathe his face.

'You're an honourable man, Inspector. Any child of yours would have been OK.'

Matthew waited with his back turned, feeling the warm air from outside blowing into the room. After a few moments of silence, he heard the door slam.

2

After the sun had set, Matthew sat in his room in darkness, looking up at the stars which fill the Greek sky like a million pinprick holes into a better, brighter world. It was almost ten before he picked up the phone and called Sarah. He got a male voice on the answering machine, an American. Matthew could hardly remember what Saul had looked like, but he had a hazy image of a tall guy with spectacles, good looking, clean shaven, late forties, with a strong handshake and a blunt, humourless manner.

'This is a message for Sarah. It's me. Listen, I've found out some things. I can't tell you over the phone. I'll be coming to see you soon, when I've put together the whole picture. Rook is dead and I think I understand now why my mother was the way she was. When I come to see you, I hope Saul will give us some time alone. The other thing I've found out is that I really do still love you, Sarah.'

CHAPTER SIXTEEN

Matthew was woken by the sound of footsteps, heavy boots on the gravel path outside his hotel suite, not the kind of footwear you heard in this tourist resort. He immediately felt a deep panic and he leapt from the bed. There were more footsteps, and orders being barked in Greek. He put a towel around his waist and peered out of the door.

There were two Greek military policemen, one each side of his door, with machine guns slanted skyward in their arms. Across the small, dry garden of the hotel, he could see another military policeman taking up position on the roof of the other hotel rooms. A fourth policeman was jogging across the dusty rose bed near the pool. Other guests were peering out of their windows, or looking down from their balconies to see what was happening. Other uniforms appeared on the roof, a detachment of six men walking briskly past the pool.

'What the fuck's this?' Matthew breathed to one of the guards standing beside his door. The guard turned to him and shrugged his shoulders. A few seconds later, the hotel manager arrived, escorted by another policeman who had a folder under his arm.

'Mr King,' the hotel manager said. 'May I come in?'

The hotel manager was short and round and his face was shiny with sweat. He wiped his mouth and glanced at the policeman at his shoulder before he spoke.

'This is totally unsatisfactory,' the manager said. The policeman at his side glanced into the bathroom and then leant against Matthew's desk.

'I had no idea that you were involved in any kind of trouble. If I had known, I would have asked you to leave the hotel immediately.'

'What trouble? Who are all these fucking policemen?'

The policeman leaning against the desk didn't seem to understand English, but the manager apologized to him anyway.

'An order has been received from London that you are to be given 24-hour armed protection,' the manager said. 'I don't know why and I certainly don't *want* to know why. I have been assured that there are some people arriving from England today to take you home. Until then, I have been advised to tell you that you must stay in your room.'

The manager spoke sharply to the policeman and the policeman shrugged. Matthew sat down on the bed and lit a cigarette. Even through this, his coolness didn't desert him. The cigarette tasted like burning leather so early in the morning.

'I think someone has made some mistake,' Matthew said.

'Yes, me,' the manager barked. 'How does it look to my other guests?'

'So, I'm under arrest?'

The manager shook his head.

'I have no idea.'

'So, ask the flunkey.'

Matthew jutted his chin at the policeman. The manager winced.

'He is not a flunkey, he is a police captain.'

'So ask the police captain.'

The manager spoke to the policeman.

'He says you are not under arrest. You are in the protective custody of the Greek Government until the people arrive from London.'

'Where is Inspector Konstantinou?'

'I don't know.'

'Ask him.'

The manager had pulled open the door, desperate to escape. He asked the policeman the question from the doorway.

'He says that the local inspector has been temporarily relieved of his duties.'

Matthew stood up quickly. The police captain fiddled with the button on his holster.

'Why? Ask him why?'

'I have no idea,' the police captain suddenly said in clear English. 'We were only told that he is being questioned and that command of the island has been given to us. Just until you've gone.'

The police captain smiled and Matthew tore off his towel. He was naked beneath it. The police captain's smile disappeared.

'Do you want to stay here and watch me shower or do you want to wait outside?'

The police captain straightened his cap and looked politely at the ceiling.

'There are people out front too,' he said, turning towards the door. 'Please don't try to jump.'

'I have no intention of jumping. And I'd like some breakfast.' Matthew turned to the hotel manager. 'Send someone with a full English breakfast.'

The manager cursed under his breath and then nodded his head.

'Toast or rolls?'

'Toast.'

After the manager and the police captain had gone, Matthew picked up his phone but the line was dead. He switched on the shower and sat on the edge of the bath, thinking this thing through. He had no idea who had given the order to have him guarded or why, but he knew for a fact that he couldn't stick around and wait for the two guys from England. He should have realized that Joyce knew more than he was saying. The breakfast was his only way out and the idea had come to him from nowhere, in a flash of lightning. Matthew thanked the engine of his grief for giving him inspiration.

He peeked out of the window to see the guards standing on the lawn below his window. Outside the door he could hear the two guards talking and see their cigarette smoke blowing past the window. Matthew got down on his knees and began to unscrew the bath panel with his thumbnail. When the panel was half-free, he went to the safe and took out £10,000 in twenties, and a handful of Greek drachmae. He then pushed the panel back into position.

There was a knock at the door and Matthew prayed that it would be the bellboy he'd dealt with earlier. He put a towel around his waist and went to the door. One of the guards was lifting the silver lid on the breakfast tray and sniffing. Matthew knew that fate was still on his side when he saw the familiar face of the bellboy who'd put him in touch with Lot. Matthew quickly ushered him into the darkness of the room.

The bellboy looked sick and nervous. He tried to leave the breakfast tray and head for the door, but Matthew grabbed him.

'You want to earn some more money?' Matthew hissed.

The bellboy glanced at the door and shook his head.

'I got to go, Mr King . . .'

'Ten thousand pounds sterling for your uniform.'

The bellboy's eyes widened and he struggled to shake himself free from Matthew's grip.

'You give me your uniform, I tie you up in the bathroom with the belt from the dressing gown. You say I overpowered you. Come, look . . .'

Matthew pushed the bellboy into the bathroom and pulled the bath panel away from the bath.

'You see that? That's £10,000. Maybe another £1,500 in drachmae. You give me your uniform, I tie you up. Tomorrow you come back here and collect the money.'

The bellboy was breathing hard, staring at the cash pushed against the waste pipe of the bath.

'Do you want to count it?'

'Mr King, I've got to go.'

'Eleven and a half thousand. How much do you earn a week?'

The bellboy was hypnotized by the sight of the money, like a rabbit in torchlight. Matthew hissed in his ear.

'There'll be no come back. We'll make it look real.'

The bellboy wiped his mouth with his sleeve.

'What kind of trouble are you in?'

'I'm not in trouble. Those guys are just there to protect me. But I don't want protection. Take off your trousers.'

The bellboy whimpered and stared into Matthew's eyes. Matthew nodded.

'It's got to be now. Ten more seconds and the guards will get suspicious.'

'I've got a girl in California . . .'

'So, go and visit her.'

'She hangs around with some guy who owns a jeep . . .'

'So buy a jeep of your own.'

The bellboy thought for a few more moments. Matthew heard one of the guards asking the other a question. The bellboy began to unbutton his tunic and Matthew helped pull it off.

When he was undressed, Matthew tied his hands behind his back and pulled the belt of the dressing gown tight. The bellboy winced.

'Sorry. It's got to look real.'

'Sure. You want to hit my face or something?'

Matthew smiled.

'No. Say I threatened you with a knife.'

'A knife, got it.'

Matthew pushed the bath panel back into position with his foot and the bellboy sat down on the lavatory. Matthew pulled on his trousers and buttoned his tunic, then pulled the crimson hat down hard over his face and tied the red sash around his waist.

'How do I look?'

'It's a pretty good fit.'

'Thanks. Hey, are you going to tip me or not?'

The bellboy laughed and Matthew checked his face in the mirror. If he tucked his face down into his collar, he'd look OK.

'Give my regards to your girl in California.'

'I will. Is it OK to tell her?'

'You tell her. And remember this. Tell them I told you to say that Konstantinou knows nothing about anything. Do you understand? Tell them Konstantinou knows nothing and they should set him free.'

The bellboy shrugged and nodded. Matthew took the remaining money and the photographs from the safe and then headed for the door. He took a deep breath before opening it. The two guards had their eyes fixed on a woman in a flimsy bikini on a balcony across the garden. Matthew tucked his head into his collar and set off at pace towards the pool. A few yards down the petal-strewn path, one of the guards called out to Matthew in Greek. Matthew kept on walking and raised his hand and mumbled, '*Yassou.*'

Down on the beach, Matthew took off his uniform and hid it beneath a sage bush. He was wearing his swimming trunks and looked like any other sunbather. He walked quickly across the hot sand to Lot's beach bar, where Lot's wife was struggling to feed breakfast to a café full of hungry tourists. He caught up with her as she trotted back to the bar to fetch another tray of rolls and coffee.

'I need to see Lot.'

Lot's wife was startled by the urgency in Matthew's voice.

'Lot is sleeping.'

'So wake him up.'

'He has only just this minute gone to bed.'

Matthew had all his money folded in his wallet in the pocket of his trunks. He took out a handful of crimson notes and showed them to her.

'Tell him it's me and that it's urgent.'

Matthew heard Lot swearing in German as his wife tried to rouse him from his slumber. Finally Matthew was waved into a small dark hut which had been built on to the back of the bar as a kind of rush and driftwood annexe. The air inside the hut smelt of bamboo and rotten fish. Lot was lying on a couch, in his vest and underpants. He stared up at Matthew blearily.

'You're a pretty dangerous guy,' he said with a chuckle, scratching his tangle of long hair. 'I introduce you to Rook and next day he's dead.'

Matthew took his wallet out of the pocket of his trunks and counted out some sterling.

'Five thousand pounds. I need a boat out of here.'

Lot swung his legs off the couch and gave Matthew an admiring smile.

'You're in a hurry?'

'You could say that.'

'Where do you want to go?'

'Gibraltar.'

Lot laughed.

'You're a pretty funny guy too.'

'I'm serious.'

Lot stood up and sipped from a can of beer beside his bed. He belched loudly.

'My boat doesn't have that kind of capacity.'

'Six thousand pounds. And I'll buy the fuel.'

'Where would we harbour?'

'You drop me off wherever you can. I'll swim if I have to. Seven. Seven thousand is my limit.'

Lot's wife put her head around the door of the hut and asked a question in German. Lot yelled at her and threw a sandal in her direction. She hurried away.

'You really want to go to Gibraltar.'

'I really do.'

'When?'

'Right now.'

Lot scratched his chin and thought for a few moments. Matthew knew that he didn't need to offer any more money, because it wasn't the money that appealed to Lot. He had guessed that Lot was the kind of guy who liked a challenge, just so long as it was something illegal.

CHAPTER SEVENTEEN

I

'This journey has a fine classical precedent,' Lot said, grinning and sweating under the weight of a gasoline barrel. They'd made a fast dash across the channel to Skopelos, where there was a hardware store which Lot often frequented. There was a bar, a section for fishing tackle and nets, a gasoline dump and a shop that sold provisions. Lot eased his barrel on to the deck of his boat which was called *Europe*. Matthew laid his own barrel beside it. His hands were greasy with spilt oil and the reflected glare from the quayside was making him squint. He didn't have a watch, but he guessed it was around half an hour since he'd left his hotel room.

They'd know by now that he'd gone, but Lot didn't seem to have any sense of urgency.

'It's the journey of Hercules,' Lot said, taking up position straddling the blue body of the outboard motor. 'From the centre of civilization to the end of the known world. The journey to the Pillars of Hercules.'

Matthew set off down the gangplank to fetch the last barrel of gasoline. Each barrel was as heavy as a man, but Matthew had enough strength in his arms to carry two at a time if he had needed to. By hauling the heavy weights with such vigour, he hoped he could impress on Lot that he was in a hurry. Lot had produced a spanner from the back pocket of his shorts.

'OK, let's get out of here,' Matthew said. Lot grinned and removed the shiny outer casing of the outboard.

'Oh yeah? And what do we eat for the next three days before we make the next port?'

Matthew didn't even wait to argue. He set off back down the

gangplank and walked into the shade of the general store. There was an old guy who had greeted Lot earlier with a shifty smile. Lot had handed him a roll of notes and a sealed package. Lot had already explained that this was where he got his provisions and his fuel for his fast dashes to Turkish waters, where he often used to pick up his packages for Rook. Lot had assured Matthew that the guy who ran the general store was safe.

'I need food and water,' Matthew said when he reached the counter. The phone rang and the old guy answered it. As he did, he waved Matthew towards a yellowing chest freezer. Above it there were stacks of canned fish. Matthew took a large box and began to throw anything to hand into the box. Sardines, pilchards, cheese from the fridge, two bunches of green bananas, more tins of fruit and vegetables. He hauled the box to the counter and waited. The old guy looked puzzled. He grunted down the phone and then eyed Matthew from head to foot. Matthew quickly laid some bills on the counter and carried his box of food to the boat. Along the way he picked up two flagons of water.

Back on the boat, Lot had the outboard in pieces, and was wiping the guts of the thing with a cloth. He glanced up at Matthew as he laid the provisions on the deck.

'We'll need more water,' he said and then turned back to his engine.

'Fuck the water,' Matthew said, 'the old guy is on the phone. I think he knows who I am.'

Lot seemed unconcerned. He wiped his oily hands on his vest.

'I've told you, the old guy is fine.'

'You don't seem to understand, I've got to get away from these islands now.'

'Sure, we go now. The harbour patrol see my boat and they think, what's *Europe* heading out to sea for when it isn't even midday? I wait an hour and a half and I can tell them I'm going after Ionian tuna. They feed around two. They'll believe me if it's after midday. If we set off now they'll check the boat.'

Matthew wanted to push Lot into the slick, treacly water beneath the jetty. Instead he fumbled for a cigarette in the voluminous pockets of the big-waisted khaki trousers Lot had lent him. He lit his cigarette and Lot tapped the engine with his spanner.

'We'll need a couple of cartons of cigarettes too. And more fish. So that's water, fish, cigarettes. What are you waiting for?'

The heat on the deck was unbearable. The *Europe* was a two-berth fishing skip with a seven by seven cabin and twin outboard motors. The back of the boat was a tangle of nets and lines, the front of the boat dipped under the weight of the gasoline and the provisions. This twenty-foot piece of driftwood didn't look strong enough to reach the mainland, let alone Gibraltar, but Lot had assured Matthew that his ship had a good heart and a fine spirit, which was better than glue and resin. Since Matthew had no choice, he had to believe him.

He went back to the store and shopped at a more leisurely pace, glancing occasionally at the old store owner, who was busy with his accounts. One suspicious glance, one move towards the phone, and Matthew would have fled.

A little after 1 p.m. Matthew and Lot were sipping coffee that Matthew had brewed on the ancient Calor stove in the cabin. The cabin itself smelt of damp wood and fish guts, and everything aboard had a thick film of grease that left black smudges on his hands and bare feet. They sat beside the shell of the outboard as Lot told Matthew the story of the Pillars of Hercules, which he said was what they used to call Gibraltar.

'We got fifteen hundred miles ahead of us,' Lot said with relish. 'We'll take in Carthage, Syracuse, the Atlas Mountains that hold up the sky. It's like taking a truck on to a very old road. The spice route, the slave route, the route the Gods took. And beyond the Pillars of Hercules, Atlantis. Do you believe in Atlantis?'

Matthew shook his head and blew on his coffee, hardly hearing what Lot was saying. Lot had guessed that the journey to Gibraltar along the length of the Mediterranean would take eleven days minimum. If there had been any other way out, Matthew would have taken it. He didn't think he could stand eleven days of Lot's classical philosophy.

'You'll understand when we get out there,' Lot said, gazing out towards the ocean. 'Even you, with your head full of shit. You'll feel it. Hey, maybe we'll even catch sight of Athena or Cadmus. You know Cadmus? He built the temple to Poseidon on Rhodes . . .'

Matthew threw the dregs of his coffee into the water.

'No, I'm afraid I don't know Cadmus. How soon before you get your engine fixed?'

'This stuff bores you, doesn't it?' Lot said with a huge grin.

'I'm sure it's fascinating, but I've got a lot on my mind.'

Lot shrugged and drank the last bitter dregs of his coffee down. He gasped and slapped his chest hard.

'You think I'm crazy, but when I've been out at sea I've seen Poseidon with my own eyes.'

'Great. That fills me with enormous confidence.'

Lot chuckled and slapped Matthew on the shoulder as hard as he'd slapped himself.

'We're going to have a ball. Pass me that piece of fuse wire, I've got to lash up the motor.'

It was almost two before Lot took up his stance over the outboard motor and tugged hard on the starter cord. The engine spluttered into life and then choked on its own fuel. He pulled the cord again and this time the engine fired and began to hum smoothly. Lot appeared to be proud of his handywork.

'I had to change the flow of the fuel,' he said loudly above the thud of the engine. 'For fast journeys, when you might have to make a run for it, you can have the fuel pumping quickly. For a long journey like this one you have to calm the whole thing down a little. It's like a marathon instead of a sprint. The fuel is like a runner taking breath.'

Matthew took his seat on the slatted bench that ran all the way to the cabin. He'd borrowed a frayed straw hat which Lot kept inside the hold and he pulled it down over his eyes. Lot suddenly whooped loudly at the sky, making Matthew start. He yelled something in German and then turned to Matthew.

'I just asked Poseidon to be kind to us,' he said. 'I told the old bastard that we are two desperate adventurers who are putting our lives in the hands of the fates . . . you know anything about the fates?'

'Please Lot, let's get a move on.'

'Yes sir! Let's move!'

Lot deftly unhooked the mooring rope from the boat and then danced across the debris on the deck towards the cabin. Inside, his face lost all its wildness and he took the wheel with calm assurance. He backed the boat away from the jetty, shifted a gear lever, and the *Europe* began to turn through one hundred and eighty degrees until it was pointing out at the gleaming, molten expanse of the sea. Stretching ahead there was just blue and green and light, nailed down to earth by the sharp escarpments of tiny islands. Beyond the islands, the curve of the earth, an empty horizon. Lot had said this would be a journey to the end of the known world, and already, Matthew had some idea what he meant.

2

They saw only one harbour patrol boat, a few miles off the coast of Skiros island. Its immaculate blue and white livery and its erect machine-guns cut a neat silhouette against the glare of the afternoon sun. Lot's expression never changed as long as he was at the wheel, and he maintained his course towards the patrol boat, and even waved, as the *Europe* bobbed fussily in its wake. Soon there were no boats to be seen at all, just occasionally a swarm of windsurfers sticking close to the coastline of the small islands, like spindly sea insects. The *Europe* made good time and Matthew felt a surge of well being. He laid his head down on the wooden bench and looked up at the sky through a mesh of eyelashes.

Above, there were seagulls wheeling. Beneath his outstretched body, the calm throb of the engine, gulping fuel. Lot might have been crazy, but he seemed to know the sea. It was as if the ocean welcomed the boat to itself, and filled the deck with a sunny feeling of contentment.

Suddenly, Matthew's face was in shadow. Lot was standing over him grinning.

'I've lashed up the wheel to head west. I'm going to do a little fishing. You want to try?'

Matthew and Lot went to the stern and Lot began to untangle two thick lengths of fishing line. He hummed some tune to himself as he quickly knotted two hooks the size of curtain rings to the ends. Then he fetched a bucket filled with sand eels and flies feeding on their rotting bodies. He dipped his hand in.

'What do you want to eat tonight, mullet or yellowfish?'

Matthew smiled.

'You decide.'

'OK, mullet.'

Lot hooked a sand eel through the eye and then trailed his bait into the water. He nodded at Matthew to go ahead and Matthew stuck his hand into the moist guts of the bucket. He hooked up an eel and dropped it on to the sparkling ocean. They both sat back against the sides of the deck, and Matthew held his line gently between thumb and forefinger, the way Lot showed him. Within a few minutes they both had diamond-bright mullet dangling on hooks over the deck, their silver bodies like pieces of water and sun mixed for just half a second. Lot dispatched them to eternity and the miracle of their vigour and unearthly brightness quickly faded into ordinary flesh.

Lot left his post at the back of the boat for long enough to light the stove in the cabin, and he fried five mullet in their own fresh juices, before making up a pot of coffee and breaking open the cigarettes. After they had eaten, he peered at Matthew, as if checking on how the experience had affected him.

'Pretty good life, huh?'

'Yeah, it's pretty good.'

'I hate the land. On land everything is so slow.'

Matthew tossed his cigarette into the water, which was darkening behind them in the twilight. Ahead, the western ocean was the colour of the mullet's scales.

'So how come you haven't asked my why I'm in such a hurry?' Matthew said.

Lot shrugged.

'You don't ask, you don't know. That's OK with me.'

'What will your wife say when she knows you've gone?'

Lot laughed and whooped.

'She knows me. I take off all the time, Sometimes I chase a single fish all the way to Turkey. She says, "How do you know it's the same fish?" and I say that I just know. And sometimes the son of a bitch gets away and I'm drunk for a whole week.'

Lot felt between his feet in the recess under the bench and produced a styrofoam icebox. He pulled out two beers and handed one to Matthew.

'Yes sir, this is a fine life. If I had my way, I would spend my whole life on the run. There is no feeling in the world like it.'

Matthew said he was new to it, but being on the run did have certain dubious advantages. This made Lot shriek out like a hungry gull.

3

After dark, the feeling of well-being vanished. The hum of the engine was the only constant, and Matthew listened to every variation in its pitch, as if at any minute the outboard might splutter and die. He soon became expert in the engine's voice, the way it seemed to panic in the face of a head-on wave, the way it purred contentedly when the wave had passed. Lot had lit a hurricane lamp in the cabin and he was checking his sea charts. Matthew felt the first chill of night and went into the cabin to join him.

'I guess eleven days was about accurate,' Lot said, smoothing the sea chart on the tiny oak desk beside the wheel. 'We'll make first port in two days, then stop off somewhere here, in Sicily, for water and food . . .'

Matthew peered over Lot's shoulder at the chart and felt a sudden panic.

'What the fuck is this?'

Lot stroked his unshaven chin in consideration.

'It's our route to the Pillars of Hercules.'

Matthew had only glanced at the chart, but he had already seen a city marked 'Carthage'. Where Sicily should have been the map said 'Syracuse'. Where Morocco should have been the map said 'Numidia'. Even Sparta and Babylon were marked in handwritten italics.

'Wait a minute,' Matthew said with alarm. 'This isn't the map you're using to navigate, is it?'

Lot seemed unconcerned.

'Sure, why not?'

'Carthage?'

Lot craned his neck to look up at the night sky.

'Lot? Fucking Carthage? Babylon?'

Lot nodded and smiled.

'I made this map myself.'

Matthew leant back against the salty glass partition that separated the cabin from the deck. Suddenly the ocean was enormous, the sky was the face of eternity.

'But you do have a proper navigational map, don't you?' he said with horror.

'This is a navigational map. It was good enough for Hercules . . .'

'Oh Jesus fucking Christ.'

Lot stepped out of the cabin on to the deck and stared up at the night sky. Matthew joined him. The sight of the billion points of white light above their heads stilled his panic for a moment, and the majesty of the sight made him whisper, even though he was becoming frantic.

'Lot, your fucking map has mermaids marked on it.'

'Sure. Maybe we'll see one.'

Matthew instinctively turned to look all around. All he could see was darkness, all he could hear was the hum of the engine. He realized quickly that at least for tonight, he had no choice. He had to have faith.

'You see that star?' Lot asked. 'That's not a star, that's Jupiter. We head for Jupiter.'

Matthew sat down heavily on the greasy bench. The mullet was suddenly in turmoil in his belly.

'So you navigate by the stars.'

'Sure I do. You've got to understand my friend that everything on this earth changes, but the stars never change. They stay the same. When you're out in the ocean, the only thing you can trust is the stars . . .' he turned to Matthew with a grin that flashed in the lamp light, '. . . and the skill of your captain.'

Lot went back inside the cabin to consult his chart. Matthew watched him as he began to make careful notes in a ledger beside the wheel, a straggly haired seafarer, picked out from the black expanse of nothingness by a single flame.

This whole thing had been a bad idea. Maybe we should have waited for the guys from London. Maybe everything that had happened in the past couple of weeks had been some kind of dream. Matthew heard the voice of his old self telling him that he should order Lot to take him to the nearest port so that he could simply hop on a jet and fly home to London. But Matthew also knew that his old self was wrong. The man he had once been had no place interfering out here, and he knew that he had no choice but to carry on.

CHAPTER EIGHTEEN

I

Daylight brought no lifting of Matthew's spirits. He'd spent an uncomfortable night lying on a small couch tucked into the back of the cabin, beneath one of Lot's overcoats that smelt of dirty hair and fish. The boat had hit some kind of squall at around 3 a.m. and Matthew had been tossed effortlessly from his couch on to the hardwood floor.

Shortly before dawn, the sky had begun to growl and Matthew opened his eyes to see a thread of lightning fizzing between sky and sea. A wave of electrically charged air hit the boat and Matthew's skin tingled.

'That's Zeus,' Lot had whispered, still steadfast at the wheel. 'But Zeus has no business with us. There are more wicked men on the sea tonight than us.'

When Matthew had slept his dreams had all been of Tanya and of Sarah. He was already beginning to believe that the closer he got to Sarah, the more his resolve to take her back would grow.

He'd also tried to work out a plan of action of what he would do when he got to Gibraltar. There was no way of knowing if the British police were involved in the conspiracy, but even though Gibraltar was a dependency, Matthew hoped that the lines of authority would be blurred.

He'd decided that his only protection now would be publicity. If he could go public with what he knew, then the hands of whoever was trying to kill him would be tied. He remembered the flashing lights of cameras outside his home in London, the intense power that those guys generated when the chase was on. He had told them once that the murder was nothing to do with

Farhouk. Maybe next time they would believe him and he would be able to keep the lights flashing.

Sometime, a few years before, Sarah had introduced Matthew to the mother of a schoolfriend of Tanya's who worked as a journalist for the *Sunday Times*. If Sarah still had her number, Matthew would call her and fly her out to Gibraltar, all expenses paid. If that didn't work, he'd dangle his story in the water like a sand eel and see who bit.

Lot came into the cabin with a large, grey fish, still struggling for life. He saw Lot casually whack it against the wheel and then proceed to filch its guts with a knife he pulled from the back pocket of his shorts. Within seconds the fish was in the pan. Somehow, the smell of frying flesh didn't have the same appeal that it had had the day before.

'I'll just have coffee,' Matthew said, getting to his feet.

'Then you're crazy. This is a snapper. The sweetest fish in the Aegean.'

Matthew went out on deck and breathed in the sunlight. To the south the horizon rippled with mountains, which Matthew took to be Africa. To the north, there was just the ocean.

'Where are we?' Matthew called out.

'We're on a boat in the sea,' Lot answered, above the spitting of the frying-pan. A few minutes later he joined Matthew on deck and began to devour his fish holding it in his bare hands.

'That must be Africa,' Matthew said, pointing vaguely to the south.

'Yeah, it must be,' Lot said casually. Matthew lit a cigarette.

'You're getting nervous,' Lot said, his mouth full of hot fish.

'You noticed.'

'Don't be. What you see to the south isn't Africa, it's Crete. We're just now slipping between Crete and the mainland which is . . .' he raised his head and made a fast calculation, 'seventy-seven miles to the north. In around an hour I'll turn *Europe* due west north-west, towards Sicily. Tomorrow night we'll dock at Palermo and pick up more gasoline. Then we'll pick up the African coast at Cape Bon and follow it all the way to the Rock of Gibraltar. I won't use the old names because you might jump overboard. And you should be glad that I'm not some straight naval school captain, because if I was I wouldn't let you smoke on deck. Not with all this gasoline around . . .'

Matthew quickly threw his cigarette into the water and Lot wiped the fish oil from his hands on his bare legs.

'I use the oil to stop my skin from burning. You're pretty dark, but you need something on your neck and face. I've got some sunblock in the cabin. And you should wear your hat. I don't need you hallucinating on me. If something happens to me, you'll have to drive this thing. Which reminds me . . .'

Lot suddenly got to his feet and leapt into the ocean. Matthew's mouth fell open. He jumped to his feet and looked over the side, but Lot was nowhere to be seen, there was just a trail of bubbles where he had disappeared. The engine panicked against a wave and then began to hum. The trail of bubbles began to recede into the distance.

For a few agonizing seconds, Matthew was alone with the ocean, the boat, the throb of the mindless engine. Finally Lot's swirl of blond hair surfaced and he shook his head like a dog.

'Turn her around!' Lot yelled, splashing the water around him.

'Lot, you fucking lunatic!'

'Turn her around!'

'I don't know how to!'

'So learn. Go to the wheel and turn her around.'

Lot's head was receding at an alarming rate, as if the engine had decided to pick up speed just at that moment. Within seconds Matthew had leapt into the cabin, cut through the lashing that held the wheel steady with Lot's fish knife, and was man-handling the wheel through a severe rotation. The strength of the resistance took Matthew by surprise and he had to heave the wheel through ninety degrees with all his strength. He felt the boat sway and he fell to the floor, the wheel spinning back wildly as if it had a direction of its own. Matthew got back to his feet and grabbed the wheel. This time he turned it more gently, feeling the slap of the waves against the hull with some part of his body he couldn't quite recognize. He eased the boat around and then the engine began to rev frantically, before finally cutting out.

The silence was the silence of the grave. It was finally broken by the sound of Lot's voice somewhere far away yelling to him.

'Start her up and turn her around!'

Matthew ran to the stern and grabbed the starting cord, which was still wrapped around the hub of the engine. He tugged it hard and the engine sneered. He tugged again and water spluttered from the exhaust funnel. He could hear Lot's voice ebbing away and he yanked the cord with all his might. At last, the engine fired.

He ran back to the cabin and took the wheel. He suddenly felt in total control of the boat, and took up a wide-legged stance to maintain his balance. The nose of the boat began to turn and Matthew made a wide arc towards the south.

When he was sure he had turned her through one hundred and eighty degrees, he searched for the throttle. The boat seemed to be moving at half-speed and he urged it on with his knees and elbows, all the time scanning the waves for a sight of Lot's long blond hair. The ocean seemed to be empty and Matthew cursed Lot's insanity.

After a minute, Matthew was sure that he'd gone too far, or maybe even sailed over Lot's head and cut him to pieces. He looked behind him to see if the water was stained with blood, but there was only blue and emptiness. Now he wanted to slow the boat down and he found a gauge which he turned. The boat revved wildly and Matthew turned the gauge the other way. The engine began to beat out a slower rhythm and began to idle.

Matthew ran out on to the deck and scanned the waves again. Finally he saw a hand waving just a few yards from the stern. Lot looked up at Matthew and grinned before diving down beneath the waves. He didn't resurface and Matthew felt like leaping into the water after him to drown him. Then a hand slapped against the deck rail and Lot heaved himself up out of the water and flopped down on to the deck in a pool of his own water, whooping with delight.

Matthew had him around the neck, prone on the hot wood of the deck.

'Don't you ever fucking do anything like that again, not ever!'

Lot grinned.

'So now you know what to do if something happens to me,' he said.

When Matthew had calmed down, Lot showed him the rudiments of boat craft, how to refill the fuel tank while the engine was still running, something the textbooks said you should never even contemplate, but Lot said, what the hell.

All that day they took turns steering the boat, with Lot's casual instruction ringing in Matthew's ears.

'Head away from the sun before midday. Head towards the sun after midday.'

'What do you do *at* midday?'

'You have lunch.'

At sunset, Lot took over and guided the boat by the motion of the stars. Matthew had begun to ease into the situation, and even though he knew that Lot was insane, he trusted him with the ocean. After all, it was Lot's life on the line too.

Just after midnight, Lot joined Matthew on the deck, where Matthew was studying the crescent moon, which had never looked so close before, and never so vividly silver.

'Now we've got Africa to the south,' Lot said. 'Kind of.'

'That's good.'

'Sure it's good. We're making better time than I thought. We should make Sicily tomorrow night. Do you have a passport?'

The question hit Matthew like a girder. Lot grinned.

'That's O K. I know some people in a little fishing port. They'll get us fuel and provisions and they won't ask too many questions.'

Matthew had left his passport behind in the hotel room. When he had made his dash for freedom, the idea of something as mundane as a passport hadn't even occurred to him.

'But when we get to your destination,' Lot said, 'you're on your own.'

Matthew nodded at the moon.

After a few minutes of listening to the beat of the engine Lot said, 'So what's in Gibraltar that's making you go through all this?'

'I thought you didn't want to know.'

'This is a long journey, we've got to talk about something. You don't want to hear about Athena and Cadmus.'

For the first time since they had left Skiathos, Matthew felt that Lot deserved some kind of explanation.

'My wife is in Gibraltar,' he said.

'So why not just send her flowers. Or take a plane.'

'It's a long story.'

'We've got all the time in the world.'

Matthew reviewed all that had happened in his own mind and decided that it might help him to think things through if he told Lot everything. Now that Skiathos was a long way behind them, his unaccustomed steadiness and caution had begun to desert him.

'Two weeks ago, someone murdered my daughter . . .' Matthew said, and the story of what had happened since curled up into the night along with their white cigarette smoke.

2

It was forty-eight hours before the dark folds of Sicily appeared on the horizon. The night before, Matthew's sleep had been disturbed by the sound of Lot speaking in Italian on the ship-to-shore radio. He told Matthew that he was making arrangements for fresh fuel and supplies to be waiting for them when they arrived.

As *Europe* neared Palermo, the sea began to fill with small pleasure craft and rusting freighters which drifted on their moorings in the hot, early-evening wind. Lot had raised a Greek flag on the small mast of the boat and conversed fluently with the coast authorities.

'I told them I'm on holiday,' Lot said. 'I told them we're a pleasure craft.'

'That's true,' Matthew said, 'it's been a pleasure.'

Lot pursed his lips and said, 'So far.'

Lot steered the boat due west of Palermo and the coastline became craggy and barren. He stayed close to the shore until darkness fell and then headed for a small sprinkling of lights at the foot of a small, river valley. The harbour wall was laced with lights which shimmered in the slick, oily water of Italy. Somehow the night in Sicily seemed darker than it had in Greece.

'You know, it's weird,' Lot said, concentrating more than usual on his steering as he negotiated the harbour wall, 'your story about your wife. The rape. I called this boat *Europe*. Do you know why?'

'I have no idea. Because you're a good European?'

'It's not named after that Europe. That Europe is just bullshit.'

Lot broke off to wave in the direction of a small, brightly lit hut on the spur of the harbour wall. A uniformed coastguard waved back at him and tossed a cigarette into the water.

'I named it after the Goddess Europa. She was raped by Zeus one night. They call it the Evil Evening. But Europa had four sons and they went away to found the four great civilizations.'

Lot glanced at Matthew looking genuinely troubled. Matthew decided that this was just part of Lot's insanity and urged him to look where he was going. The cluster of small boats was nearing, *Europe* was idling.

'So what?' Matthew said.

Lot thought for a while then shrugged.

'I guess it's nothing.'

When Lot finally killed the engine, Matthew realized that its hum had been a constant for three whole days. When the engine was switched off, he felt an unreasonable jolt of panic. Then the silence became normal and was filled by the sound of gulls and the gentle lapping of waves. Lot turned the wheel sharply and the boat nosed its way into a tiny berth, no more than ten yards wide. All that ocean, that vastness, reduced now to a numbered length of concrete in some half-deserted Sicilian fishing village.

Lot stretched and yawned and then puffed out his cheeks.

'I think it's best if you stay aboard,' he said. 'I'll go ashore and pick up the supplies.'

'I'd like to step on dry land,' Matthew said, his body suddenly filled with strange aches and twinges now that the motion of the boat had stilled.

'If you step ashore someone will want to see your papers. Just keep your head down here.'

Lot looked nervous and scratched his chin.

'I'll be two hours, no more,' he said and went to step up off the deck on to the concrete steps that led to the harbour. Matthew stopped him.

'Won't you need money?'

'Yeah, I guess I'll need some money,' Lot said as if he'd been caught out in a lie. 'Give me maybe £200. I'll change it in a hotel.'

Matthew had hidden what was left of his cash in a knapsack underneath the couch where he slept. He counted out three hundred and handed it to Lot.

'Buy us some more beer,' Matthew said with a grin. 'And some wine. When we get to Gibraltar, we'll have a party.'

Lot took the money and stuffed it into the back pocket of his shorts. He glanced up quickly at Matthew before hurrying up the steps and disappearing beyond the harbour wall.

Matthew sat in the cabin, enjoying the smell of dust and pine sap which he hadn't smelt for three days. There were gulls roosting in a small hollow in the concrete of the harbour and Matthew said hello to them out loud, just to have someone else to speak to other than Lot. The gulls nestled into their feathers.

He'd been asleep for maybe half an hour when he heard footsteps on the deck. He sat up expecting to see Lot. Instead, he saw a starched white uniform, the gleam of a braided cap, the dark leather of a holster.

Matthew got to his feet quickly. The coastguard called out in Italian and Matthew twisted the wick of the hurricane lamp to extinguish it. The only light was the reflected orange light of the harbour.

'Hello,' the coastguard said.

Matthew realized that the coastguard had already seen him.

'Who is it?' Matthew said.

The coastguard was a young guy and he appeared to be alone. He ducked into the cabin and smiled. He extended a hand for Matthew to shake and Matthew shook it.

'English?' he asked.

'American,' Matthew said.

'I have a message for an Englishman called . . .' he took out a rolled up fax and read the name, '. . . Matthew King.'

Matthew hesitated. The coastguard looked a little puzzled at the silence.

'This is the *Europe* out of Skiathos?'

'Yes it is.'

'I have a fax from the inspector of police in Skiathos for Matthew King on board the *Europe*. It was sent to Palermo, but we heard the *Europe* was docking here so they sent it on to us. The inspector said it was very urgent that Matthew King sees it.'

Matthew peered into the coastguard's eyes and saw that he was genuine.

'I'll see that he gets it,' Matthew said.

'He's a friend of yours?'

'Yes he is.'

The coastguard suddenly seemed suspicious, but he handed the fax over anyway. As Matthew took it, he looked around the cabin.

'It's pretty cramped in here. Why don't you go ashore Mr . . .'

'I've got things to do,' Matthew said.

The coastguard raised his eyebrows. Any second he would ask to see Matthew's passport.

'Actually, I'm waiting for someone. A girl. Her father doesn't know . . .'

The lie came from nowhere and Matthew grinned to add sauce to deceit. The coastguard grinned too.

'I'd say this is pretty romantic, wouldn't you?' Matthew said.

The coastguard looked around at the greased woodwork of the cabin, the fish blood, the empty cups and beer cans. There were a few more seconds of suspicion before the coastguard shrugged his shoulders and smiled. Then he saluted and ducked out of the cabin. Matthew listened to his footsteps disappearing along the harbour before he sat down to read the fax.

As soon as he'd read it, he leapt to the back of the boat, fired the engine, and somehow found reverse. He steered the boat out of the harbour and back out to the open sea at speed.

CHAPTER NINETEEN

I

Matthew almost smiled at the thought of it. Konstantinou using his precious fax machine to save the day. He must have sent it more in hope than anticipation, but it had worked.

The fax said:

Matthew,
Lot is selling you to the highest bidder. He sent a message to me via Palermo to arrange the arrest. Get away quickly.
Regards,

Konstantinou

PS I have new information.

Matthew's knowledge of the sea was restricted to two days' worth of vague advice from Lot, and maybe a hundred kilometres' worth of steering. But the engine was running and the boat was making good speed. There was still half a barrel of gasoline aboard and the tank was almost full. He had no idea how far the fuel would get him, but he knew that he had no choice other than to leave the harbour and head towards Jupiter.

Jupiter shone out like a headlamp in the western sky. Lot had been right about one thing. Everything on earth changes, but the stars stay the same.

Matthew gripped the wheel as he pointed the boat into the darkness. His only hope was to keep the boat within sight of the shore so that when the fuel gauge hit empty he could head inland and maybe beach the craft. He had no idea if there were rocks or sand bars beneath his feet, but he couldn't risk straying too far out into the ocean. Out there was eternity, no landmarks, no direction, just floating at the mercy of God knows what rip tide or current.

'This is OK,' Matthew said aloud to himself. 'This is OK because the land is there and I can always turn towards the lights. The sea is OK and the boat is OK, so all I have to do is keep steering towards that fat little star up there and I'll be OK. And in the daytime, I'll head away from the sun in the morning and towards the sun in the afternoon.'

He was gripping the wheel so hard that his knuckles ached. He thought about Tanya and cursed the thought and banished it to hell.

But soon the lights of the Sicilian coastline dissolved and there was only darkness, apart from the light of the hurricane lamp in the gloom of the cabin which he had relit but which was already beginning to flicker. Matthew told himself that the darkness didn't matter, that the light would be restored soon enough.

2

At dawn, Matthew consulted Lot's ludicrous ancient chart. He realized that he would need to steer a little to the south of Jupiter, because then he could pick up the African coastline and follow it all the way to the Pillars of Hercules

Every so often, Matthew would laugh at his predicament, because he was having to reduce his navigation to 'left a bit' and 'right a bit' to try to make sense of the layout of the map.

He had worked out a rough scale (by using his thumb to measure the distance between Skiathos and 'Athene' on the map) and figured that he would have to travel around sixty miles before Cape Bon on the African coast came into view. And yet he knew that overnight he'd travelled at least fifty and still there was no sight of land. He laughed hysterically at the sight of

Carthage on the map, the ink sketches of mermaids. The dawn gave way to the full heat of morning and Matthew sought out the flagon of water. There was enough for two days, maybe more. Along the way he could drink the juice from the tins of fruit and even catch a few fish if he had time.

Once Africa was in sight he'd head inland and scour the coast for any sign of life. If he came across a tourist resort (in Morocco? Algeria?) he would buy fuel and press on. He couldn't risk travelling overland without a passport. The only real resource he had apart from water and tinned food was the £12,000 in his knapsack under the couch. Until he met another human being, it was just paper. But when he struck dry land, its magic potency would be rekindled.

Sometime around noon, Matthew searched through Lot's locker for cigarettes and found a revolver. There was also a box of twenty-five shells.

Matthew lashed the wheel into a westward setting and loaded the gun. He went out on deck and set about figuring out how the revolver worked. If he had to trust his luck on the African coast, there might be pirates, thieves, coastguards, even wild animals, and a revolver might prove to be useful. He knew nothing about firearms, but that was a tiny detail; he knew what guns did and he knew that in this new world in which he had found himself, where it was just fate and circumstances, the gun would even the odds. That's if there were any odds to even.

After Matthew had found and released the safety catch, he let off two rounds into the endless expanse of ocean. He tried again, this time aiming at a seagull which was bobbing around in the wake of the boat. Matthew took careful aim and to his horror and delight, the seagull exploded in a puff of feathers. The sight of the exploding seagull made him laugh until tears ran down his face. He was laughing too because he knew that if he lost his way and ran out of fuel and drifted for days and days, then at least he would have his own way of ending it all. The froth of feathers disappeared into the distance.

Matthew stowed the revolver and the remaining shells back in the locker and fed himself tinned tuna with his fingers as he steered towards what he hoped was Africa. He had money, food, water and a gun. And his wits. He knew now that his most precious possession in the face of this eternity of ocean was his own rational mind.

3

'You drink beer, you dry yourself out,' said an impish voice from the engine. 'The alcohol makes you drier than before you drank it. You shouldn't drink beer. It dries you out.'

Matthew had been at sea for two days and two nights and still there was no sight of land. The wheel was lashed to head west. The water flagon had just a few sips left in it. He had emptied the gasoline barrel sometime the night before. He had no idea when.

'I've got to drink something,' Matthew yelled, and the engine hummed its disapproval. It was late afternoon, the sky was mellowing into sunset and Matthew's lips were tight as violin strings. It hurt him to yell out but it was the only thing that stilled the voices. It was as if he had developed two ways of hearing things, with his head and with his ears. If he made a real noise himself then that superseded the noises in his head. He tapped the iron rail around the deck with his wedding ring to keep the voices quiet.

To the south there was only grey horizon. Soon the sun would set again and he would have to try and find Jupiter, his only friend. The night before he had heard Jupiter speaking softly to him from the sky and he had glugged down a whole day's ration of water. He had had sun stroke when he was a child and so he was prepared for the delirium it brought. He knew that shade and water were the only medicine but there was precious little of both. Even inside the cabin the reflections from the deck and the ocean burnt his skin. When his thirst forced him to open a can of beer, this new, impish voice of recrimination had started up, coming from somewhere inside the engine of the boat.

'Shut the fuck up,' Matthew growled and he swigged his beer. When the engine did as it was told and spluttered into silence, Matthew was sure that it was just another hallucination. The boat bobbed gently and Matthew could hear the waves slapping against the hull. Then there was the scream of a gull. This was no hallucination. The offended silence from the engine was real.

Matthew finished his beer, praying without words or expression that the engine would somehow start itself again. Then he tiptoed across the hot deck and examined the exhausted shell of the motor. The fuel cap was scalding hot so he wrapped his hand in his shirt-tail to unscrew it. The belly of the thing was empty and now the engine was as thirsty as Matthew himself. He double-checked all the gasoline barrels and discovered a cupful of the precious juice in one of them. He poured the dregs into the fuel tank but the engine just chuckled at him.

Now at last, Matthew was alone on earth. Alone except for Jupiter which he could no longer reach, and the revolver which he couldn't yet use. The night came on quickly.

4

In his thirsty fever, Matthew decided that time and silence were opposites. He lay on his back, soaking up the last warmth from the oily wood of the deck. The star-scattered sky absorbed all his attention, and the moon in its half-crescent seemed to bathe in the darkness. Matthew had decided that if he could only keep talking then he could keep time moving along. If he was silent then time itself would stop and he would sink unnoticed into eternity. As long as he could hear his own voice then he would maintain his connection with the world.

'Tanya, my baby, I want you to fetch me that lemonade from the fridge,' he said out loud to the night sky. 'Don't pour it into a glass because you might break it and hurt yourself. Just bring the bottle out into the garden and I will have some of it. You can have some too.'

Matthew saw Tanya struggling to lift a full bottle of lemonade to her lips. It was the bottle he'd gone to fetch the afternoon she was killed. The lemonade spilled and fizzed around her mouth and she shrieked. Matthew wiped his own dry lips.

'Your turn Daddy,' Tanya said, her voice as clear as the moan of the sea breeze. Matthew lifted himself up on to one elbow and saw the glint of Tanya's bare arms in the moonlight. He saw the flash of her big brown eyes and the sticky reflection of lemonade around her mouth. Matthew took the bottle from her and drank but the bottle was dry. Tanya seemed to be upset by Matthew's look of bitter disappointment.

'Hey, hey, hey, it doesn't matter,' Matthew said and he hooked his arms around her waist, which felt warm and frail. Then he had both his arms around her and she was crushed into his chest. Matthew wanted tears, but his eyes were dry. Tanya's face was wet with tears and Matthew kissed them.

'It's OK, baby, it's OK. Hey, where have you been? I've been worried about you.'

'I got lost.'

'Oh yeah, I forgot,' Matthew said and he stroked her hair.

'It's so dark, isn't it?' Tanya said, looking around at the emptiness of the ocean. 'Where is this place?'

'I don't know, baby. Somewhere. At least we're both somewhere in the world. And we're together again.'

He felt Tanya's tiny head nodding on his chest. Matthew breathed deeply and smelt the lavender shampoo that Sarah always used on Tanya's hair. Matthew would smell it most evenings when she came downstairs to kiss him goodnight after her bath and he had forgotten how powerfully that smell evoked her memory. Matthew kissed the top of her head.

'You were always mine, you know, baby.'

Tanya didn't raise her head.

'What do you mean, Daddy?'

'I mean you weren't Rook's. You were always mine. I know that for sure.'

Tanya mumbled, 'Who's Rook?' and Matthew shushed her.

'No one, baby. He's gone now. I should have trusted you all along, but sometimes I wasn't sure and I'm sorry. Do you understand? I'm so sorry that I wasted all that time not being sure.'

Tanya leant back and fiddled with the button on Matthew's ragged shirt, the way she always used to when she got bored of hugging.

'Where's Mummy?' she said.

'We're going to her. We're on our way to see her.'

Tanya noticed the anxiety in Matthew's voice. She suddenly looked all around the deck and the cabin.

'In this old thing?'

Tanya struggled out of Matthew's grasp. She looked horrified.

'I know it doesn't look much, darling, but this boat has got a good heart and a good spirit. It'll get us there.'

'But you don't have any fuel or water.'

Tanya looked down at her feet and began to rub her eyes. Matthew knew that Tanya was right. All was lost.

'We'll be fine, baby,' Matthew said out loud. 'I promise you. I'll make a promise to you right now, baby. We'll go and get mummy and we'll all go home again.'

Tanya carried on rubbing her eyes and shaking her head. Matthew thought that he had to dispel her doubts about the boat or she would disappear and leave him again. He wanted to lie to her about the boat and the fuel, but before he could speak, her white socks, then her legs and then her chest were consumed by shadows. Finally the black sheen of her newly washed hair melted into a refraction of moonlight coming from the calm water of the ocean. Matthew stared across the empty deck and called Tanya's name softly. Then he yelled her name and his voice echoed across the ocean. When there was no reply he decided that maybe the time had come to reach for the revolver. One shot and they would be together.

Just then the wind blew cold and Matthew noticed straight away that the wind carried with it the strong smell of oil and smoke. Then he heard a deep, baleful moan that stopped his heart. It took him a long time to summon the courage to turn his head and confront the monster which had made such a dreadful sound.

5

The sky directly above his head was filled with fire. Beneath the huge flame, the outline of an oil refinery loomed like the twisted carcass of some beached, iron-clad monster. In the moonlight beyond the flame, the intestines of the creature gleamed silver. Pipes, tubes of inhuman dimension, running in all directions to feed the bulbous black belly of the storage chamber. The whole thing was around half a mile across, with subsidiary flames burning exhaust gases high above the shoreline. The most terrifying thing about the beast was that it made no noise apart from the noise of the flame three hundred feet in the air, which flapped like a flag. Here and there blue lights burned, tracing the circular outline of the central tank and the straight lines of the supply pipes.

Matthew was on his feet, his hands clawed ready to fight or flee. How could he have drifted so close to this monstrosity and not felt its presence somehow? It took him a long time to put all the twisted pieces together and clear his head sufficiently to work out what it was. Over to the east there was a dock lit by searchlights. He could just make out the silhouette of a truck parked on the dock near the harbour, sucking gasoline from a hole in the concrete jetty. The hooter sounded again, louder this time and Matthew almost leapt overboard in terror. He realized that the sound was coming from a mile or so to the east and could just make out the outline of an enormous oil tanker, black and angular against the shimmering moonlight, hooting out a warning of its approach. If the tanker hadn't blown its horn, Matthew might have drifted past the refinery and never woken from his delirium.

A little to the west, there was a dark mass of land. Beyond the ugly silhouette of the oil refinery rose a range of mountains dark against the moonlight. Matthew had no idea how long he had been drifting in the shadow of this thing, or even if it was real. The deck was lit with flickering orange light from the flame in the sky and Matthew looked all around to see where Tanya had gone. Maybe she had hidden in fright.

'Tanya!' he yelled and the sound of his own voice restored his sobriety. He fell into the cabin and grabbed the revolver. He pushed it into the belt of his trousers and then hooked his knapsack full of cash over his shoulder. His bare feet stuck to the wooden floor of the deck. He saw an upturned fruit can, its juices glistening in the flame-light, and he realized it was the spilt syrup from the can which was sticking to his feet. Had he really been so delirious that he had wasted its precious juices?

Back on deck, he saw that the boat was drifting inexorably towards the patch of shoreline to the west of the refinery. He guessed that he was around a quarter of a mile from shore, and could make out the vast docking hooks in front of the storage chamber. He gazed at the refinery with awe, the moonlight and the exhaust flame turning it into a monstrous moorish temple with vast silver domes. *Europe* was at the mercy of an agonizingly slow current and the boat's painstaking progress made him want to yell out with frustration. There was another hoot from the tanker which made Matthew catch his breath. Each time the hooter sounded, he recovered a little more, as if the loudness of the sound was calling him back to consciousness.

He figured that this must be the coast of North Africa, somewhere west of Cape Bon. But how far west? Many years before, Matthew's advisers had invested some of his money in a refinery on the north coast of Algeria. Maybe this wilful current had brought him here to witness the ugliness of his investment. As the boat drifted past the hulk of the storage chamber, the patch of shoreline for which the boat was heading emerged as a stretch of grey sand. There didn't seem to be any rocks, just a shallow incline from ocean to land. Matthew raised his head to the sky, all the stars were erased by the light of the refinery flame, and he spoke out loud, thanking the gods for blowing him to safety.

It was almost an hour before the boat hit soft sand and

lurched to starboard. The landing was kind to *Europe* and the water was shallow enough for Matthew to wade ashore. The solidity of land made him feel sick and he had to sit in the froth of tiny waves that fizzed on the beach, holding his head between his knees and breathing deeply. A little way up the beach, there were two small fishing boats, resting at forty-five degree angles on the sand. The boats had masts and canvas sales. Matthew began to walk slowly towards the boats, cocking the trigger of his revolver.

Between moments of sobriety there were flashes of delusion. He thought about Lot's chart and fancied that he had washed up on the shores of Carthage. Maybe soon he would see a horseman in a scarlet turban, armed with a lance and cutlass, riding across the sand from the shadows of the oil refinery. The uncertain light from the flame in the sky filled the beach with images and possibilities.

Both boats were covered in thick sheets of grey tarpaulin. Matthew circled them and then approached from land-side. The smell of sand and oil was overpowering, his senses unaccustomed to any smell richer than salt and ocean. From the back he could see that both boats had outboard motors as well as sails and masts. The approaching tanker hooted again and Matthew began to think rationally about the danger of detection. He crouched down and began to creep towards the flickering orange hulls of the boats.

This could be Tunisia, Libya or Algeria. The smart thing to do would be to let off a few rounds from his revolver and draw the attention of someone in the refinery. Then he should turn himself over to the authorities. Even if this were Libya, they'd simply deport him back to England. His need for water was now critical and he knew that he was using up the last few drops of his energy. If he didn't find water soon he'd slip into permanent delirium and die within twenty-four hours. Even now, as he began carefully to untie the string holding the tarpaulin to the first boat, it kept crossing his mind that Tanya was still aboard *Europe*, or hiding somewhere in the shadows, and that if he did turn himself in, he'd have to find her and turn her in too.

'Tanya is dead, you fucking lunatic,' he hissed to himself, untying the last fastening. The sound of his own voice was still the only antidote to his delirium, but he had also noticed that the coolness of the air inland was sobering him up too. He pulled back the tarpaulin and peered into the shell of the boat. In the half-light from the refinery flame, he saw four blue plastic fuel containers. He shook them each in turn and found that two were empty, two were full. He unscrewed the lids and sniffed. The smell of gasoline almost made him pass out. Some insane voice in his head told him to drink it, but he resisted.

He hauled the two full containers on to the beach and then walked over to the other boat. He laid his revolver down on the sand to untie the fastenings with more ease. The tanker moaned out a warning. Matthew pulled back the tarpaulin and after a second of silence, the shadows inside the hull burst into life and a hand and then a face flashed in the flickering light.

'Jesus fucking Christ,' Matthew yelled and he fell instinctively on to his revolver. He spun around on the sand and pointed it up at the sky. Above him he could see a young boy, who looked no more than eight years old, scrambling out of the boat as if the devil himself were at his heels.

When the boy hit the sand, he set off to run towards the darkness inland. Matthew grabbed him by the shoulder and pulled him down on to the ground. The boy yelped with terror and Matthew pushed the nose of the revolver into his face. Without a second's pause the boy began to chant in some staccato language something that sounded like a prayer. Matthew held him down for a few moments and then let him go and got to his feet, still pointing the gun at the boy's face.

'Where am I?' Matthew croaked, his voice full of salt and sand. The boy shivered on the ground below him, his eyes enormous with terror. He wore white, baggy trousers and a Coca-Cola T-shirt. His hair was jet black and grew over his ears.

'Where?' Matthew said again. The boy seemed to have no comprehension of English. Matthew released the hammer on his revolver and pushed it back into his belt.

'I need water,' Matthew said, as softly as he could, then he pointed to his mouth. 'Agua . . . water . . . eau . . . glug, glug.'

The boy looked up at Matthew as if he were an apparition. Matthew guessed that his face would be blood red and disfigured with burns and sores. His hair was stiff with salt. His shirt and trousers were still damp with oil and gasoline. To reassure the boy, Matthew took out a handful of notes from his knapsack and then mimed lifting a bottle to his lips and drinking. The terror in the boy's eyes began to disappear by degrees.

'Water . . .' Matthew said again, 'thirsty . . . I have to drink. I want to buy water.'

The mighty flame above their heads flapped in the darkness.

'You want drink?' the oy said suddenly.

'Yes! I want drink! Water. You can take this money . . .'

The boy slowly got to his feet and dusted the sand off his trousers. Then he looked at Matthew and shook his head.

'No water,' he said solemnly.

'Shit.'

'Coca-Cola?'

'Yes! Coca-Cola!'

The boy hopped into the hull of the boat and produced a plastic bottle full of Coca-Cola. Matthew snatched it from him and twisted the top off. It was flat and warm, but Matthew drank the whole litre, stopping only twice to catch his breath and to curse the searing pain in his tongue and throat. Matthew realized that his tongue was enormous in his mouth and that his throat was swollen too. The pain of drinking didn't really hit him until he had drained the bottle, and then he held his jaws and grunted in agony. He felt as if his whole head were on fire. He was breathing hard.

'You don't like Coca-Cola?' the boy asked, a little puzzled. The pain in Matthew's mouth subsided and he smiled.

'I love Coca-Cola,' he said, breathing hard. Then he dropped the empty bottle on the ground and tried to push the money into the boy's hand.

'What else have you got in there?' Matthew said. 'I need food . . .'

Matthew shook the money as if he were offering straw to a donkey.

'This is a lot of money. A hundred pounds. I'll buy whatever you've got.'

The boy seemed suddenly uneasy.

'I don't sleep,' he said at last.

'Sleep?' Matthew said, not sure he had understood.

'I don't sleep,' the boy said again. He eased himself back against the boat and appeared to be planning a fast get away.

'Listen this is serious,' Matthew said, 'I need food and water.' The boy shrugged, now filled with anxiety at the sight of the money in Matthew's hand. There was an impasse and Matthew took a step towards the hull of the boat. In a flash, the boy had reached into the boat and produced a knife which he held up in front of him, his hand trembling. Matthew hesitated. The boy was a quarter Matthew's weight, his arms so thin that even if he'd tried to use the knife, it wouldn't have been more than a scratch.

'I don't sleep,' the boy growled.

'What do you mean, you don't sleep?' Matthew said. The boy glanced at the money in Matthew's hand.

'I mean, I don't sleep with you,' the boy said.

Finally, Matthew realized what it was the boy was trying to say. He ran his hand through his matted salty hair and then sat down on the sand and puffed out his cheeks.

'It's OK,' Matthew said wearily. 'I don't want to sleep. You can put the knife away.' The boy stood still as a statue, not dropping his guard. 'I said you can put the knife away, I don't want to sleep with you. Jesus . . .'

One realization led to another. Matthew had often heard how Northern Europeans used parts of North Africa as some kind of lawless brothel. There were plenty of children living in doorways and on beaches who needed their money badly enough. But as far as Matthew was aware, this kind of thing was most common in places where tourists were welcome. That ruled out Libya, and it pretty much ruled out Algeria. Matthew looked up at the boy sharply.

'Where am I? What country is this?'

The boy shrugged, still brandishing the knife.

'Listen to me, I came here on that boat . . .' Matthew pointed out to sea where *Europe* was bobbing gently in the shallow water. 'I got lost. I ran out of fuel. I've been drifting for three days. You understand? I need to know what country this is.'

The boy lowered the knife at last. Matthew pointed at the sand between his feet.

'Here . . . this place . . . is it Libya . . . Algeria . . .'

The boy thought for a moment and then said, 'Maroc.'

'Morocco?' Matthew yelled.

'Marocco,' the boy said.

Matthew leapt to his feet and the boy raised the knife again. Matthew snatched it out of his hand and tossed it back into the boat.

'Where in Morocco?' Matthew said holding the boy's twig of a wrist. 'Where . . . I mean what town is this?' Matthew pointed at the refinery. The boy shrugged. Matthew knew that it didn't really matter which town it was and that he wouldn't be able to find it on Lot's map anyway unless the refinery had been built by Alexander the Great. What mattered was that he was perhaps five hundred miles further west than he had thought he was. If this was the Moroccan coast then at most he was only two hundred miles from Gibraltar.

Suddenly the Coca-Cola and glory of the realization took effect. Matthew yelled at the top of his voice and raised his face towards the flickering flame above their heads. He wanted to dance around in the sand and let the coolness of the earth soak up his fever.

'I'm almost there,' Matthew hissed staring at the boy with insane intensity. The boy's look of fear had turned to one of wry amusement.

'You like Morocco?'

'I fucking love Morocco.'

Matthew ruffled the boy's black hair as familiarly as he dared.

'How far to Gibraltar?' Matthew said quickly. 'Do you know?

Of course you don't, but it doesn't matter. If I steer north-west I'll hit the Spanish coast and follow it west . . .'

Matthew fumbled in his pocket and took out the hundred pounds he'd offered earlier. He laid the notes down carefully on the sand.

'This is for you. OK? I'll buy whatever you've got. And it's for the gasoline too. I took two tanks from the other boat . . .'

The boy stared down at the money on the sand.

'You sure you don't want to sleep?' he said incredulously.

'No, for Christ's sake . . . I need gasoline, water, food. Are these your father's boats?'

'Father?'

'I'll give you money to give to your father for all his gasoline. And I'll buy the outboard motor too. You know English currency? Look, I've got enough here to buy the engine. If you want to go and fetch your father, I'll wait here. OK? Do you live near here?'

Matthew hadn't had a chance yet to speculate why a young boy should be sleeping inside the hull of a fishing boat all alone. He had guessed that the boy was acting as some kind of night watchman. But then the more obvious possibility occurred to him. Matthew suddenly felt a wave of compassion.

'Do you have a house near here?' Matthew said and the boy shook his head. 'So where do you live?'

The boy pointed over his shoulder with his thumb into the boat.

'In the day I work. At night I sleep here. I have to get out before light. Before the man comes.'

There was a long silence, broken only by another hoot from the oil tanker making its stately progress towards the refinery. The boy seemed to be offended by Matthew's sudden look of sympathy.

'The boat is OK,' the boy said with some pride. 'It's dry and I am left alone. I have my own business. I sell Coca-Cola. Look.'

The boy hooked his hands over the side of the boat and lifted himself to peer in. Matthew looked over his shoulder. He saw five bottles of Coca-Cola wrapped in a small towel.

'I sell it on the hotel beach,' he said. 'The police chase me away, but someday I'll get a licence. I speak good English, don't I?'

'Yes, you do.'

'It's good drink, Coca-Cola,' the boy said proudly, as if he had brewed it himself.

Matthew nodded in agreement. Alongside the bottles of Coca-Cola tucked into the hull of the boat there was a half-eaten banana, a toy truck with flaked orange paint and a pair of tiny straw sandals. All the boy's worldly possessions.

'I've even got the uniform,' he said and he tapped his Coca-Cola T-shirt with great pride. Matthew wiped his mouth. It was as useless to succumb to this feeling of compassion as it was to fire off bullets into the ocean. There was an infinity of sadness between Skiathos and Gibraltar, and more beyond. But Matthew couldn't help the choking feeling in his throat.

'How old are you?' Matthew said and the boy held up eight fingers.

'OK, Mr Businessman, I'll buy all your bottles,' Matthew said and he grabbed a handful of notes. He thought about handing the child the whole knapsack, but he figured that he would need his money when he reached Gibraltar. He handed the boy £200, despising himself for being in a position where being good to someone was so easy and meaningless. The boy took the money calmly and Matthew guessed that he had no idea how much he was being given. The boy pretended to count the money out, then he stuffed it into the pocket of his trousers.

'I think it is a fair price. We have a deal,' he said very solemnly and extended his hand to shake. They shook hands and the child smiled shyly. Matthew held on to his hand for longer than was comfortable. He felt once more the softness of small fingers, the warm, uncertain grip. The boy finally snatched his hand away. Then Matthew felt a familiar feeling of foreboding.

'Can you change English money here? Will you be able to change it at a hotel?'

The boy mumbled, 'Sure', as if he wasn't.

'You be careful how you change it,' Matthew said. 'I don't

want you getting into trouble. Change it a little at a time or they'll think you stole it. Do you understand? Change it just one note at a time. There's a lot of money there. They are big denomination bills . . .'

The boy suddenly gasped and leapt into the boat. From the darkness inland, Matthew saw the beam of a torch, bouncing in time with footsteps. Then he heard voices. He froze.

'Who is it?' Matthew hissed, ducking instinctively.

The boy's head popped up from inside the boat for a few moments.

'Police,' the boy said. 'Beach patrol.'

His head disappeared again. Matthew saw a silver epaulette glinting in the orange light of the refinery flame.

'If they see me, they take me away,' the boy said, clambering back out of the boat. Matthew's first instinct was to go to the police officers and explain. But he had no passport, no papers, just a revolver and a sack of money. The boy had already raced around the front of the boat, his sandals and his half-eaten banana in his hands.

The torches were now sweeping the beach and he could hear two voices. Matthew saw the shadow of the boy flicker through one of the beams of light, but the policemen didn't seem to see. They were heading straight for the boat. Matthew had no more than five seconds to make up his mind.

He leant into the boat and grabbed the boy's towel. He stuffed two of the Coca-Cola bottles into his shirt and then opened a third. He drank down as much as he could in two gulps and then made a break for the second boat to collect the gasoline he'd left on the sand.

As he ran between the boats, a beam of torchlight caught him and one of the policemen yelled. He could hear keys jangling now as they ran. The gasoline containers were heavy and he tried to sprint towards the ocean with one in each hand. He could hear the jangling keys gaining ground. *Europe* was still bobbing gently in the shallow, but it was now at right angles to the shoreline, twenty yards out to sea. Matthew realized that as soon as he hit the water and began to wade, the policemen would catch up with him. He stopped, dropped one of the containers and reached for his revolver. He pointed it at the sky and fired two rounds. The jangling keys fell silent and Matthew raced into the water.

He half-staggered and half-swam to the boat, dragging the gasoline containers with him. When he reached the side, he threw them aboard and then grabbed the iron railing. It took a supreme effort to haul his weight out of the water, but he finally managed to hook his elbows over the deck. As he did, he heard a dry click and a deep thud as a bullet smacked into the hull of *Europe*. The sound of the bullet filled his arms with furious strength and he managed to leap aboard.

He ran to the back of the boat, almost on all fours, and unscrewed the fuel cap on the engine. There was another click from the shore, but this time the bullet missed the boat completely. The fuel tank drank the gasoline as thirstily as Matthew had drunk the Coca-Cola. Once the first container was empty, Matthew grabbed the starter cord and yanked it. The engine spluttered and another bullet thudded against the hull of the boat. Matthew closed his eyes and gritted his teeth and prayed for the engine to start.

The oil tanker horn wailed and Matthew ducked down instinctively. The air fizzed above his head and he guessed that if he had ducked a second later he would have been dead. From a crouching position, Matthew yanked the cord once more and the engine spluttered into life. He ran into the cabin, shifted the gear stick out of dislocated neutral and then found reverse. He hit the throttle so hard that the boat almost reared on its stern like a horse. Matthew turned the boat through one hundred and eighty degrees and headed out into the endless darkness once more.

6

While leaping aboard the boat, Matthew had managed to lose one of the bottles of Coca-Cola, which left him with just one litre to last him the entire journey. When the sun rose the next morning, Matthew took a couple of sips and smoked a cigarette. He had lashed the steering wheel to head north-west, towards what he presumed was the Spanish coast. If his calculations were right, he'd be at sea for another three days. He had no idea how long the fuel he'd taken on board would last out, and in the night, he had noticed that the engine seemed to splutter every ten or fifteen minutes, as if the new fuel wasn't suited to the motor.

By noon, when the sun was at its hottest, the temptation to drink down the whole bottle of Coca-Cola was almost irresistible. Now that he was out of sight of land again, the optimism of the previous night had vanished. Just before sunset the engine coughed and died, and Matthew discovered that the fuel tank was already empty. He didn't care to make the calculation. If the first container had only lasted a day, then the second would only last a day and he would run out of fuel around eighty miles short of Gibraltar.

When night fell, Matthew looked up at the stars as if they were old enemies. He had escaped and now he was back in his cell of darkness and Jupiter and the rotten stench of *Europe*. Even in his despair, he thought a lot about the Coca-Cola boy. In trying to help him, he had probably landed him in a lot of trouble. What would a hotel clerk or bank teller say to an eight-year-old homeless child with £500 in his hand? He just hoped that the boy had listened when Matthew told him to exchange the money one note at a time. Matthew laughed out loud at the irony of the fact that the curse of his money was still functioning, even through all this.

The litre of Coca-Cola was gone by sunset. When Matthew's second phase of delirium began just before dawn, he wasn't even graced by a visit from Tanya. Instead, he sat on the flat board at the back of the boat near the engine, treating every second it continued to run as a gift from the Gods. The only voices he heard were those of Jupiter and Poseidon, discussing in a calm and reasoned way whether Matthew King deserved to live, or whether he should be allowed to die

CHAPTER TWENTY

I

In the southern Spanish port of La Linea, the teenage boys who haven't smashed their brains inside their skulls with heroin make a living out of running contraband cigarettes between the duty-free port of Gibraltar and the Spanish mainland.

La Linea is a wild Gypsy town, ravaged by powerful winds that blow directly off the Atlantic and drive everyone a little crazy. The boys who work the cigarette runs retire at twenty-one, because they can afford to. They can make £10,000 in just one night of smuggling. Some of them don't reach twenty-one because the port authorities have an unofficial policy of ramming their boats.

The smugglers learn their trade on dry land, racing across the border between Spanish and British territory on foot, with their cigarette cartons under their arms, they're sometimes no more than ten years old and no bigger than the mountain of contraband they are carrying.

When they get a little older and have saved up enough money, they invest in a special kind of boat that La Linea produces for the purpose; sleek, black, rubber speedboats with huge Suzuki engines. The boats are streamlined and almost elegant, and there isn't a coastguard launch around that can catch them. The high-speed chases in the shadow of the rock are something of a tourist attraction. The black boats are invisible at night, but sometimes a random sweep of the waters on the frontier using high voltage search lights picks up a fast-moving black shape, and then the chase is on. The big coastal launches summon help and they try to manoeuvre their boats to cut off the smugglers' line of entry into British waters.

More often than not, the black boats melt into the darkness, their engines cut, the smugglers hiding the whites of their faces under their £500 black leather jackets. Sometimes there is a hit, a rescue attempt, sometimes a young Spanish boy washes up on the shore, along with 5,000 sea-soaked cigarettes.

The smugglers hang around a café called The Dog, which looks out on to that part of the ocean where the invisible frontier has been drawn. The smugglers moor their black craft openly and defiantly, flashing their contraband cigarettes to wholesalers who take them north to Madrid and even Paris. The Spanish authorities turn a blind eye because Gibraltar shouldn't be there in the first place, and if the British authorities are made fools of by a few boys in speedboats, then that's the price the British pay for hanging on to the last bare rock of their empire with their finger nails.

The Dog is owned by a fat Spanish Gypsy called Emmanuel, who is a kind of godfather to the smugglers. He opens his café at around eleven, but there are rarely any customers until after two. Most of his clientele keep late hours, not beginning their dangerous work until the sun and the moon have set over the Rock. The café has a rough dirt patio, which slopes down towards the sea and then turns slowly into shale beach. The café beach is the perfect launching place for the black boats and, as chance would have it, the first calm-water inlet on the granite dog-leg between the wild Atlantic and the more tranquil Mediterranean.

Various currents conspire to bring the debris of both seas to this one-hundred-yard patch of sand and driftwood. Sometimes the smugglers themselves are brought back here in death, deposited gently among the flotsam and jetsam for burial at their place of departure. This is also the place where wrecks are brought, Poseidon's very own safe haven for those who have trusted themselves to his mercy.

Three days after Matthew's flight from Morocco, Emmanuel saw a two-berth fishing skip flying the Greek flag, bobbing aimlessly two hundred yards out to sea. Not a smuggler, not a coastguard, not even a pleasure craft. The boat still looked to be in sea-worthy shape, and Emmanuel's first thought was to call some of the boys to take a boat out to it and see what could be salvaged. But, before then, he had to deal with the body lying on the beach because he was a Christian man.

Emmanuel dragged Matthew up the beach and sat him down at one of the yellow Formica tables. Matthew was still unconscious, but Emmanuel could tell from the salt deposits around his mouth that he needed fresh water. He opened a bottle of mineral water and began to dab Matthew's lips with a damp cloth.

Matthew opened his eyes to see merciful darkness. After so many days in the murderous glare of sea light, he never thought that his eyes would function properly again. Emmanuel spoke to him softly in Spanish and Matthew answered in English.

'I call someone,' Emmanuel said and Matthew's head flopped on to the table. A few moments later, there were three of the boys in black leather jackets and shades, standing around him, trying to figure out which of them spoke the best English.

'Hey, hey, drink some of this . . .' the oldest of the boys said; he was no more than eighteen. They had begun to pour brandy into his mouth and when Matthew spluttered they all broke up laughing. Emmanuel intervened and tried Matthew again with the water. This time Matthew grabbed the glass and gulped it down. Emmanuel poured some more and Matthew drank it so quickly that he threw up. The smugglers all yelled their disgust and danced away from the splashing vomit in case any of it got on their shoes.

Emmanuel went to the kitchen to prepare some broth out of the chicken pieces he'd saved from the night before. The smugglers began to feed coins into the jukebox and they danced around Matthew's table as he tried hard to focus, and work out where the hell he'd come ashore. He tried to speak to the boys, but they laughed at the dryness of his voice.

'What's he saying?' one of them said in Spanish.

'He's saying he wants to speak to his daughter,' the oldest one said.

Somehow, in his delirium, Matthew managed to stop Emmanuel calling an ambulance or the police. When he had sipped some broth, he told the boys that he had no passport and that he didn't want to speak to any policemen. Their attitude changed like the flicking of a switch.

One of them set off on his motorbike to fetch some cold soup that his mother had made which would cure a dead man. The other two helped him hold his spoon and wiped the salt from his brow. When the cleaning lady arrived to clear up the mess from the night before, they barked at her that the café was closed until further notice. Emmanuel had strolled back down to the beach to pick up the knapsack he'd noticed floating in the shallows as he was picking up the body.

When the broth was finished, the boys helped Matthew to the lavatory which stank of sweat and humanity and Matthew was promptly sick again. They helped him back to a table and directed a fan at his head.

'Sun sickness,' the English-speaker said. 'You drink some more water.'

Matthew's stomach slowly got used to holding water and his vision returned to normal. The English-speaker's English was no more than rudimentary, and his questions were unintelligible. Finally, the boy who had set off to fetch soup came back with his younger sister, who spoke English better than any of them.

She was around twelve years old. She spoke to him gently, asking him where he had come from, but all he could do was stare at her and hold her hand. Finally, he realized that his hand on her hand was causing the boys to stiffen in their jackets.

'Greece,' he said at last. 'I've come from Greece.'

'Are you in some kind of trouble?'

'Yeah. Lots of trouble.'

'Police trouble?'

'Police trouble.'

'What are you smuggler? *Droga*?'

The twelve-year-old girl mimed sticking a needle into her arm. Matthew smiled and shook his head. Emmanuel returned with the soggy knapsack in his hand, his eyes blazing. When the boys asked him a question, he shook his head, took the knapsack into the kitchen, and stuffed it in a small recess under the stove.

3

The only reason that Matthew had survived the final leg of his journey from Morocco to La Linea was because he had unfinished business. Matthew now knew the sheer power of his intent. The sunlight and thirst had stripped his soul down to one tiny flickering light which could not be extinguished.

On the third night he had taken the loaded revolver and asked himself a question out loud about the pointlessness of carrying on. Some other voice in his head told him to put the revolver into the knapsack along with the money, and wrap them in a cellophane sheet.

It seemed like insanity to seek to protect the money when all he needed was water, but he obeyed the voice anyway and he had tied the knapsack around his waist. He had licked crystallized sugar from the oily floor of the deck where the tin of fruit had spilled. Just before dawn he had passed out and woken to find himself sucking at the open neck of one of the gasoline containers, trying to drink the last few drops. The bitter taste of gasoline fumes had knocked him out once more. The next thing he knew, he was being helped into a chair by Emmanuel.

There was another memory too. Matthew didn't know when it had happened but one night he had opened his eyes and seen the God Poseidon rise majestically from beneath the waves, silver backed like a fish, wise like the stars, as huge as a mountain range. Poseidon had brandished his trident and spoken soothing words to Matthew in a language he didn't understand, but which gave him new hope. His heart kept on beating. Lot had been right about Poseidon.

The café began to fill up with boys in their leather jackets and the girls who hung around them. The jukebox played reggae and loud Sevillana flamenco, echoing across the beach and across the ocean. Emmanuel took Matthew into the kitchen and kept him supplied with water. A waitress appeared at three and began to cook and serve food, the fishy smell of the cooking making Matthew feel queasy. Eventually Emmanuel told her to take a break in the café because he wanted to speak to the Englishman alone.

Emmanuel took the still sodden knapsack out of the recess beneath the stove. Matthew's eyes widened at the sight of it and he made a grab for it. He'd almost forgotten the precautions he'd taken to preserve the money, and he could hardly believe that it had survived his ordeal. Emmanuel snatched it away.

'Give it to me,' Matthew said and he tried to rise up from his seat. His head was still split down the middle by sunlight.

'If I tell the boys, they steal it,' Emmanuel said, his eyes glinting.

'So don't tell them.'

'I'm older. I don't know who you are. You might be a danger-ous man . . .'

'I am.'

'But if you want help then I can help and you can pay me.'

Emmanuel held up the knapsack. Matthew didn't have the strength for this but he knew that somewhere deep down he would find the strength. He had the power of a whole ocean cur-rent at his back, driving him westward.

'I need to get to Gibraltar,' Matthew said.

'Without a passport.'

'Yes.'

'Then you are a lucky man. You're in the right place.'

'How much?'

Emmanuel clutched the knapsack.

'Fifty–fifty.'

'Sixty–forty.'

Emmanuel thought for a while then smiled. His head shone in the porthole light from the café.

'Sixty–forty it is,' he said.

Emmanuel handed the knapsack over to Matthew and Matthew struggled to unfasten it. Finally he pulled the Cellophane wrapping out and unwrapped the gun. It felt dry. He had no idea why he had felt the urge to save the revolver, but he only knew that he needed to keep it with him. It was like an ache in his body. Matthew began to count out the bills and separated £6,000. He handed the bills to Emmanuel.

'I'm trusting you,' Matthew said. Emmanuel quickly counted the bills and then frowned.

'You've given me half,' he said.

'The rest is a tip. And payment for the food and water.'

'That was on the house.'

'You saved my life. That has to be worth something.'

Emmanuel quickly stuffed the roll of notes into his pocket, just as the waitress barged back into the kitchen with an empty plate, yelling an obscenity behind her to the whole café. Outside the kitchen, the party was getting wild and Matthew could see some of the leather-jacketed boys dancing around on the beach, smoking and swigging beer. He waited for the waitress to disappear.

'What time do I leave?' Matthew said.

'After three. I'll get Ramirez to take you. He's the best and he's got the fastest boat.'

'Ramirez will be one of those fucking children getting drunk out there, will he?'

Emmanuel suddenly looked mighty offended, then his face filled with pride.

'If you were my own son and you wanted to get into Gibraltar, I'd tell you to go with Ramirez.'

The current had delivered him just in time, and although he didn't know it yet, it had delivered him to the only people in the world who could possibly help him complete his task.

CHAPTER TWENTY-ONE

I

Emmanuel's confidence seemed to have been misplaced. When Matthew woke from a half-slumber, there was a gaunt, sickly-looking boy of nineteen or twenty whose breath smelt strongly of stale brandy. He had a cigarette dangling from his lips and he grabbed Matthew under the armpits.

'Are we going now?' Matthew asked, getting to his feet.

Ramirez shrugged and said, 'No English.' Matthew looked around in the darkness for the knapsack and saw it lying on top of the stove. He quickly riffled it to check that the money was still there, and half pulled the revolver out of its Cellophane cover. The kitchen was in darkness, but Ramirez saw the gun. He blinked at it blearily as if his eyes could hardly focus.

This wasn't booze that was giving him this sickly pallor, it was something stronger. Matthew thought about the little girl who mimed sticking a needle into her arm.

'Are you OK?' Matthew hissed. Ramirez shrugged and walked out of the kitchen.

Out on the beach there was pale phosphorescent light coming from the foaming of the waves. The sight of the ocean and the black boat tugging at the end of its mooring rope made Matthew recoil. Something inside his body was telling him that the sea was where death lived and it had to be avoided at all costs. He took some deep breaths and followed Ramirez across the sand. Ramirez walked slowly and stumbled occasionally. He was either blitzed out of his mind or he was half-unconscious with heroin. Either way, this plan was insanity.

For the first time in a long time, Matthew felt a cold chill all over his body as the cool Atlantic wind blew. The hairs stood up on his arms. The café behind him was deserted, and Ramirez's boat was the only one visible. To his left, the monstrous face of the Rock of Gibraltar stared down on him, its ugly escarpment lit by yellow lights that shone upwards towards the summit, picking out cracks and creases. All along the face of the rock there were deep pock-marks, the entrances to tunnels which led deep inside the solid granite. Matthew had read somewhere that Gibraltar had once been one of Western Europe's most important tracking stations and that the belly of the rock was filled with corridors, cables, radar screens, the calm, secret activity of whole nations, burrowing into the earth like mindless insects.

Matthew felt the cold splash of water around his feet as Ramirez eased himself wearily into his black, rubber boat. Ramirez seemed to move in slow motion, as if he were already underwater. Matthew laid the knapsack in the boat and then climbed aboard. The presence of the Rock was like a silver face peering at him, demanding his attention.

Ramirez scratched his temple and sighed, a picture of a sleepy drunk trying to remember his own name. Finally, something clicked and he pressed a button on the outboard motor.

The motor was three times the size of the engine on Lot's fishing skip, even though this boat was only a fifth of the size. Matthew remembered beating Lot's engine with his fists as he desperately tried to get it to come back to life. Ramirez's engine ticked softly and effortlessly and Ramirez nodded his head from side to side with the rhythm of it as they set off slowly towards the blackness of the open sea.

Beyond the lee of the rock the wind was blowing hard and cold, and Matthew had to burrow down into the boat to keep from shivering. The wind didn't seem to affect Ramirez, and he kept the engine ticking softly, with occasional strokes of the throttle. For a moment, Matthew was sure that Ramirez had fallen to sleep, but then he scratched his head and sighed and looked up at the sliver of moon. It had fattened over three days, but its light was still hazy.

After he had checked the moon, Ramirez reluctantly got to his feet and peered out across the water towards the rock. His expression didn't change as he scanned the water and he finally sat back down again and stroked the throttle. Their progress was even slower than Matthew's drift at the mercy of the current.

'Don't we go any faster?' Matthew hissed and Ramirez flinched as if he'd just been struck across the face with a whip. He put his finger to his lips and glared at Matthew, then he settled back into his dreamy silence.

After ten minutes of idling through the water, the lights of Gibraltar itself became visible around a shoulder of rock. There was the blue strip of lights that marked out the civilian and military airport, and other lights climbing almost to the summit of the Rock. Headlights climbed the rock on a spiralling mountain road and the town seemed to have been wrapped around the granite structure like fairy lights around a tree.

The Skiathos mountain had always filled Matthew with a feeling of anticipation, a feeling of life shining out from within. This Pillar of Hercules filled him with dread.

The flat shore of the town was blazing with the lights of newly built office blocks. Beyond, a huge power station was billowing crimson smoke into the night air. There was an ocean liner docked in the vast naval harbour, and everywhere there seemed to be small vessels cutting through the choppy waters. Suddenly, it seemed impossible to enter this theatre of light without being detected. In the lee of the Rock, in the darkness of La Linea, it had seemed possible, even simple to sneak undetected across an imaginary frontier. Now with the town revealed, Matthew felt as if every light were shining directly on his face, and that detection wasn't only possible, it was inevitable. He could pick out at least two naval vessels among the heavy traffic entering and leaving the harbour dock.

Ramirez peeked up at the moon again. He began to whistle softly into the Atlantic wind.

Then there was a deep thudding sound from above and Ramirez cut the engine completely. Matthew looked up to scan the sky, but Ramirez hissed through clenched teeth to get his attention and signalled to him that he should keep his head down. The thudding grew louder and Matthew angled his head to peek up at the sky to see the lights of a helicopter flying low, a quarter of a mile to the south. The helicopter circled in a tight arc and then headed back towards the rock. This place, it seemed to Matthew, was teeming with life, on land, sea and air.

When the thud of the helicopter had passed, Ramirez carefully refired the engine and the maddening, dry ticking resumed.

Matthew thought that if they didn't accelerate soon, he would explode. Ramirez shifted in his seat and Matthew knew instinctively that this was a signal that something was about to happen. Ramirez turned to Matthew and gave him a huge, lopsided grin.

'*Frontera, veinte metros* . . .' he whispered and then tried a clumsily pronounced translation. 'Frontier . . . twenty metres.'

Ramirez was pointing out a line he was apparently drawing at random in the blackness of the water, a little way ahead of the boat. They chugged on a little further and Ramirez said, 'Ten metres.'

A few moments later he said, 'Six . . . five . . . four . . . three . . . two . . .'

After that the ocean was torn into pieces and Matthew was thrown bodily to the back of the boat. For a moment he was sure that the boat had flipped over on its stern but the nose crashed down on to a wave and then reared up again like a bolting stallion. Matthew could hardly see for the spray and the frantic bouncing of the boat but he could just make out Ramirez's head and shoulders, riding the waves like a cowboy.

The speed they were doing seemed impossible and the terrifying buzz-saw rasp of the engine was deafening. Matthew assumed that the whole of the Rock, the whole of southern Spain, would suddenly be aware of their presence and sure enough, a siren began to wail. Ramirez banked the boat sharply to the left and then to the right. He stroked the throttle and the speed they'd reached before was doubled. The boat was now almost flying across the surface of the water and Matthew wouldn't have been surprised if they had taken off and flown all the way over the mountain.

Now that the boat was at full speed, the travelling was

smooth. They headed for the lights of a distant beach with the directness of a bullet. As they crossed the opening of the naval harbour, Matthew saw a coastal patrol boat flashing frantically in their direction, the vessel labouring to turn about. Matthew yelled at the top of his voice, as if the power in the engine had entered his stomach and torn open his bowels.

More sirens began to blare and another patrol boat began to hoot its disgust. Ramirez looked neither left nor right, and Matthew realized why the rest of the time this guy looked so terminally bored. After this, everything else was just passing the time of day.

They left the second patrol boat dead in the water and a search light swept the water in front of them. Then Matthew and Ramirez were caught momentarily in its blinding light, like the flashing of a mighty camera. The snapshot of Ramirez's hair trailing in the hurricane of speed was burnt on to the insides of Matthew's eyelids. Ramirez seemed to take the search light personally and banked the boat out of its range.

They hit a calm stretch of water and Ramirez throttled down. Matthew wanted him to keep on at that frantic speed, to blow all the pain clean out of his head, and all the memories too. It would have been OK to hit dry land at that same speed and not care about the consequences. Instead, Ramirez eased off the throttle through smoothly hit gears until they were cruising. Matthew suddenly realized that he was soaked to the skin, even though he hadn't felt a drop of water hit him.

Then they were idling again and the world was slowly putting itself back together. They were ten yards from a deserted sandy beach when Ramirez turned the boat around.

'Fun?' he said with a smile.

'Yeah,' Matthew said, 'fun.'

Ramirez climbed to the front of the boat and began to paddle with his arms, heaving the boat the last ten yards on to the beach in silence. When the boat hit the sand, Ramirez handed Matthew his knapsack.

'*Adioos*,' he said.

'Where am I?'

'Gib.'

'Which part?'

Ramirez shrugged. Matthew climbed out of the boat and felt the dull solidity of hard ground. When he turned around, the black speedboat was already disappearing into the darkness and within seconds it had vanished altogether. Matthew was left alone on Catalan beach, within sight of a deserted café and a large white hotel carved out of the rock. A Union Jack flew on the roof of the hotel, snapping in the stiff Atlantic breeze blowing in from the west.

Matthew found a sheltered place beneath the lump of rock that supported the hotel and settled down to rest. The sand was cold to the touch, but he was warm enough to doze. And his skin fizzed with a feeling of well-being too. He decided, as he drifted in and out of dreams, that the finest cure for sun stroke, fatigue, dehydration, was a fast spin around the Rock in a black speedboat.

2

When he woke up, a girl of six or seven was standing a few yards away from him, peering down at him with a half-smile.

'Who are you?' she said.

'That's a good question,' Matthew said and the girl backed off, as Matthew stirred from his painful, curled position on the sand. He sat up and hooked his arms around his knees, tasting the salt and sore skin in his mouth.

'Are you a tramp?' the little girl said.

'No, as a matter of fact I'm a multi-millionaire.'

The little girl carried on staring at him as Matthew stretched his arms and legs. He was still in shade, but the rest of the beach was now bathed in bright sunlight. A little way above his head there was a café serving breakfast and the smell of fresh bacon wafted on the sea breeze. The café was filled with unmistakably British holidaymakers, their tans sudden and painful, their summer clothes a riot of flowers and swirls.

It wasn't until the little girl's mother came to take her hand and looked down on Matthew with undisguised horror that he realized that he couldn't hope to pass himself off as one of them. He was still wearing the enormous khaki trousers which Lot had lent him, and the bottle-green T-shirt, which had soaked up salt, sweat, despair and vomit. His hair was stiff with sea air and from the feeling of it, his face was burnt to hell. Matthew gave the horrified mother a decent English smile anyway.

'Fell asleep on the beach,' he said, with as much middle-class bashfulness as he could manage.

Matthew's other problem was that he was barefoot. Shoes were the first things he bought in the small tourist shop that backed on to the restaurant where breakfast was being served. He bought a pair of white shorts with a crease in them, a flowery-patterned shirt and a sun-hat to cover his matted hair. He also bought sunglasses which made him look like a strange, red-faced wasp when he peered at himself in the tiny sunglass mirror.

The English shop assistant seemed relieved when Matthew reached into his sodden knapsack and paid in English cash. He took his old clothes to the litter bin (*Please* keep Gibraltar tidy) and then set off in search of a telephone.

He knew Sarah's number off by heart; he called her and she shrieked when he told her that he was in Gibraltar. Matthew said he thought it was something of a miracle he'd made it too.

CHAPTER TWENTY-TWO

I

Matthew waited for over an hour in the Trafalgar cemetery, in the heart of Gibraltar town. The little patch of grass and shrubbery is filled with military graves, including the graves of British sailors killed at the Battle of Trafalgar. Nelson himself was pickled in rum and shipped home. His men were buried beneath sun-bleached slabs of marble and stone, in this tiny corner of Britannia, to be mused over by bored tourists. Matthew had seen the place marked on a tourist map, and he had decided that this would be as good a place as any for his reunion with Sarah. He had a little speech prepared about burying the past.

Matthew found a bench in the shade and drank carton after carton of milk to soothe his sore, dry mouth. Sarah had said that she had a hair appointment and so she would be a little late, and since Matthew hadn't told her the story of what had happened to him, the miracle of his deliverance on the Rock, she had no particular reason to hurry to him. Matthew told her that he had flown in that morning from Athens. He knew that if he told her everything he knew, the truth might possibly kill her.

When she arrived among the dappled shadows of the graveyard, her hair was cut short and she looked slimmer than she had for years, in a light-cotton, white dress that made her skin look the colour of wet sand. Matthew took off his sunglasses and kissed her softly on both cheeks. He clasped her hand as tight as he dared, but not enough to show that this was a moment he had been dreaming about, in ordinary dreams and in boiling delirium. Her skin felt cool on his lips and she smelt of sun oil and hair dye.

'You've overdone the sun a little, haven't you, Matty?' she said, with a wrinkle to her nose.

'It was very hot in Skiathos.'

'How have you been?'

'Fine. You?'

'OK.'

Matthew's speech about burying the past suddenly seemed hopelessly out of place and he decided against it. He had somehow expected the reunion to reflect the nature of the journey, but he knew there was no real reason why it should. This soldiers' graveyard seemed to have the breath of disappointment in its very soil. Matthew stretched his arms across the back of the wooden bench where they were sitting and his hand brushed Sarah's bare shoulder. She didn't move and Matthew left his hand there to establish some kind of communication between their old selves.

'I've found out some pretty interesting stuff,' Matthew said casually. 'About what happened I mean . . .'

'I know, I spoke to . . . Joyce, is it? An inspector.'

Matthew hid his urgency to find out how much Sarah knew by pushing back his head and breathing deeply the scented air of the graveyard. Orange blossom and hyacinth.

'And what did Joyce have to say?'

'He said that they wanted to investigate the cassette you told them about.'

'When was this?'

'Almost two weeks ago.'

Matthew made a fast calculation. Sarah obviously hadn't spoken to Joyce since Matthew had fled Skiathos. As far as she was concerned, this was still a regular investigation.

'I told them all along that I was right,' Matthew said. 'And you.'

'And I told you that I didn't want to know.'

'And you still don't want to know?'

Sarah shook her head.

'If some creature out there in this world had really meant to kill her . . . Then I wouldn't want to be in the same world.'

'That's OK. Because I'm going to destroy him for you.'

'Who?'

'I don't know yet. But I'm close. I can tell.'

This wasn't the time to talk about deliverance or premonitions or the westward flow of fate, and Matthew dropped the subject. There was a long and polite silence. Matthew knew what Sarah must have gone through since Tanya's death, and he wanted to let her know what he had been through too. Instead, he let the silence do its work, stroked her shoulder with his hand, felt the warmth of her body beside his own.

'But you know that her death was deliberate,' Matthew said.

'Joyce said only that it was one avenue of inquiry.'

'One avenue of inquiry.'

'That's how he put it.'

Another silence. Two elderly ladies in holiday shorts mooched past the bench where Matthew and Sarah were sitting and nodded a polite greeting. Matthew and Sarah nodded back. After their shadows had passed Matthew said, 'Sarah, I am in desperate, desperate trouble.'

2

For the second time, Matthew spilled out the whole story. Each time Sarah tried to speak, Matthew grabbed her arm and told her that she needed to hear everything. Other tourists drifted by, but Matthew carried on talking anyway. The heat of the day was beginning to penetrate the shadows. Matthew ended his garbled account by asking for the name of the journalist Sarah had known in London. He said he had to make a public statement because only in the spotlight of publicity could he be truly safe.

Finally, Sarah laid her head on her hands and stared down at the ground. Matthew let her take everything on board. She turned to him.

'This is your version of the truth,' she said defiantly.

'This *is* the truth.'

'So who would want to cover up what your mother did so badly that they would kill Tanya . . .'

Sarah seemed to be converting her grief into anger aimed at Matthew. Matthew took her arm and she shook him off.

'I don't know who, I only know that they killed Tanya and Callow and they have tried to kill me. I'm ahead of them, but they'll try again. That's why I need to speak to the press. I need to open this thing out. It's my only chance. And I need you to believe me. Not for any reason, just because I do.'

Sarah resumed her contemplation of the ground in front of her. Her anger seemed to have a will of its own.

'How dare you do this to me,' she hissed.

'Do what to you?'

'Make me listen to this fantasy . . .'

'Ah, Jesus . . .'

Sarah stood up and Matthew grabbed her arm and pulled her back down on to the bench. He held her tightly and stared into her eyes.

'Which part is the fantasy? The boat ride? Lot? The photographs? Here, take a look for yourself . . .'

Matthew snatched up his knapsack where he'd kept the black and white shots of his father's confidential papers. When he opened the knapsack, Sarah peered in and saw the butt of the revolver. This time she twisted out of Matthew's grip and got to her feet. Matthew had to run after her and he grabbed her as she reached the entrance to the garden of remembrance. A taxi driver leaning against his cab began to stare as Matthew swivelled Sarah around and pushed her against a white tombstone.

'Look! Look at these!'

He held the photographs up in her face. Sarah had begun to sob and she turned away.

'Well, look at the photos you stupid fucking . . .'

Matthew felt a hand on his shoulder. He turned around to see the stumpy, chocolate-faced taxi driver glaring at him.

'What's wrong here?'

'Nothing's wrong . . .'

Sarah took the opportunity to break out of Matthew's grip. Matthew ran after her again and overtook her. They were both in the middle of the busy main road that led away from the cemetery towards the land border with Spain. A car swerved and blew its horn. Another braked hard and two more cars began to hoot. Matthew grabbed Sarah around the shoulders and then held her tightly. She sobbed in his arms as the traffic hooted and the drivers yelled for them to get out of the road or they would both be killed.

3

In the cool of an English pub, Matthew and Sarah sat in silence as they sipped their warm beer. In Gibraltar, it seemed, everything had to be more English than it was in England, to make the point that geography and climate meant nothing. The pub reminded Matthew of the places he'd taken Sarah when they first met, grubby, soulless English bars, where the only entertainment was getting drunk quickly.

Sarah had looked at the photographs of the submarine sketches and agreed that she would reserve judgement. Matthew had offered to go back to her apartment and call Konstantinou in Skiathos, put him on conference if necessary. Sarah was unsure about letting Matthew come back.

'I'll have to speak to Paul,' Sarah said at last.

'Paul? Who the fuck is Paul?'

'Saul. He's changed his name to Paul.'

Matthew stared at Sarah incredulously and she chose not to meet his gaze. She shifted uncomfortably in her seat.

'Wait a minute,' Matthew said, 'run that past me again. He's changed his name?'

Sarah shrugged and sipped her beer. She glanced at Matthew trying hard to appear casual.

'That's right. He said he didn't like the name Saul any more. So he decided to change it.'

It was obvious that Sarah wanted to close this topic of

conversation down as quickly and painlessly as possible. She had the profound loyalty of new love. Matthew's look of disbelief was now cruel and theatrical.

'People change their names,' Sarah said, as if it were the most commonplace thing in the world. 'Why not?'

Matthew chuckled in triumph and said, 'I see.'

'What do you see?'

'Nothing. Nothing at all. Nothing odd about that . . . what, you mean, one morning he just woke up and said, "Call me Paul"?'

Sarah picked up an English beer mat and began to turn it on its corners, looking away into the distance. Matthew could see that Sarah thought it just as weird as Matthew that Saul had changed his name and he also began to see that maybe this was a symptom of the fact that things weren't going so well with her new lover. Matthew felt a spark of delight inside, which he hid with increasing bafflement.

'So, is it official this name-change? I mean, has he got himself re-registered?'

'He's applied for a new passport.'

Matthew took a long sip of beer and Sarah hissed, 'look it's a spiritual thing.'

'What is?'

'He's been working on a church. Working on a renovation. He said he'd realized that Saul was a pagan name and he wanted to change it to the Christian version.'

'Jesus Christ, so he's discovered God, has he?'

'Oh, shut up.'

'And you, Sarah, the evangelical atheist.'

'It isn't like that. It was sort of a gesture of respect . . .'

'A conversion on the road to Damascus. A blinding light. That is ironic.'

'What's ironic?'

'While your lover-boy Paul has converted to Christianity, I've been doing the reverse. I've become a pagan. I saw Poseidon with my own eyes.'

Sarah gave Matthew a worried glance, and he decided that

he'd better change the subject quickly. More than ever he needed to maintain Sarah's faith in his sanity.

'Anyway,' Matthew said, stretching and yawning, 'how is the wife-stealing bastard anyway?'

Sarah was about to get angry, but then she laughed and Matthew smiled too. For years jealousy had been taboo between them. Now that taboo could be broken easily and with impunity. Matthew knew that by displaying jealousy, he was saying more about his feelings for Sarah than if he had spoken them out loud.

'He's fine,' Sarah said. 'It's funny, he reminds me of you. His face I mean . . .'

'So, what . . . does he pray at night? Does he say grace . . .'

Matthew caught a tiny glimpse into Sarah's soul and his heart leapt. He hadn't been able to see through her like this in years and suddenly, in just that one tiny gesture, he caught a whole mood.

'He's American,' she said at last and glanced in Matthew's direction to see if that explanation might work on Matthew, when it hadn't worked on her.

'So he's American, so what?'

'Americans believe in things. Not like us. He hasn't got religion exactly, but he says that whole experience of working on the church has moved him. He's changed . . .'

Matthew felt that a trap had been sprung. Sarah was trying her hardest to rationalize her unease and disappointment. Living with a guy wasn't the same as snatching the odd evening or afternoon together. Matthew was sure that Sarah now felt that she had made a mistake.

Sarah gave Matthew another glimpse into her turmoil. She looked all around the bar and sighed.

'I don't know. Maybe it's me. I haven't been very good company. I've been thinking about Tanya . . .'

Matthew dared to put his hand on Sarah's hand. Tanya was still the thread that held them together, even though she was dead.

'I've been thinking about her too,' Matthew said. 'It feels like I've swallowed a screwdriver.'

'It's always there,' Sarah said quickly, relieved that she was with the only other person on earth who understood how this felt.

'Always there,' Matthew said. There was a long pause, filled with the choking thud of a fruit machine paying out cash somewhere in a dark corner of the bar.

'We really fucked up, didn't we, Sarah,' Matthew said.

'But not with her,' Sarah said. 'I've been thinking. We were always OK with her. She would have survived us. I mean, she would have been a normal human being, don't you think?'

'She would have been fine. She would have been just fine . . .'

Matthew wondered if maybe this might be the time to let the feeling rip. The great weight of his grief, staunched and dammed for weeks, was exhausting. But some voice inside told him that it wasn't time yet. Some instinct for danger, which he had developed since his trip to Skiathos, was making him feel uneasy. But the danger was coming from some direction he couldn't locate.

'But he's a weird shit, isn't he?' Matthew said at last.

'Who?'

'Saul. Paul.'

'Leave it, Matty.'

'I want to know how you feel about him. I have a right to know.'

Sarah looked uneasy. Step by step she was showing Matthew how difficult these past days had been for her.

'I don't know . . .' she said and looked at her lap. 'He seems to be obsessed.'

'Obsessed by what?'

'Obsessed by you.'

Matthew felt the beating of a huge drum inside, the marching of a gigantic triumphant procession. In the past two weeks Matthew had hardly had time to worry about this guy who had so sneakily offered his shoulder to cry on, while Matthew was risking his life. Jealousy hadn't been an issue.

'Good,' Matthew said. 'I'm glad. I ought to kick the little shit's teeth down his throat.'

'He's six four.'

'I've got a gun.'

Sarah had to swallow hard to stop herself from spitting her drink into her glass. She shrieked with outrage and laughter.

'Jesus, Matthew!'

'I've changed, Sarah. I've changed back. I know you hate this weird stuff about curses and fate and retribution, but I don't give a shit about the inheritance any more. I know what money is for now. I know it isn't worth a thing.'

'That's what you always said.'

'Before I was being a socialist. Now I'm being existentialist. And now, I mean it. Admit it. This guy Paul or Saul or Janet or whatever the fuck his name is gives you the creeps. I can see it. Finish your drink and we'll go back to your place and use your phone. I need to speak to Konstantinou. He's an existentialist too.'

4

Sarah and Matthew drove in Sarah's hire car through the Ragged Staff gates, past the Queen's Hotel and up the winding road that led up towards the casino. The view over the harbour was breathtaking, but Matthew didn't care for views any more. He looked straight ahead, smoking and telling Sarah that he'd smoke if he wanted to smoke because he was a grown man.

The apartment was a newly built three-storey villa that looked west, towards the naval dockyard and the new town, where a whole society of homes and office blocks was being built on land reclaimed from the sea. Sarah said that Paul would be working until after six.

Matthew called international directory inquiries and asked for the number of Skiathos police station. Sarah mixed two large gin and tonics in the kitchen.

'Are you sure they have a phone on a little island like that?'

Matthew laughed, while holding one finger in his ear.

'They've got a phone, a fax, you name it . . . hello . . . hello, I need to speak to Inspector Konstantinou. Yeah, now . . . tell him this is *Europe* calling.'

CHAPTER TWENTY-THREE

I

'What do you mean "holiday"? Why would someone who lives on Skiathos go on holiday?'

The line was bad and the guy on the other end of the line spoke poor English, but Matthew could just make out that Tony Konstantinou had taken a week's leave and had left the island.

'So where has he gone?' Matthew said, finishing his gin and holding out his glass for another. Sarah took it. The voice on the other end of the line said, 'Away.'

'Away where?'

Matthew had his finger pushed into his ear, but the line was dying. Beyond Sarah's silhouette, there was the Rock, bristling with antennae, all attached to the earth by a vast network of cables and wires that were only visible in daylight.

'I said, *away where*?'

'Don't know . . . away . . . '

Matthew hissed 'shit' under his breath and replaced the receiver.

'Sarah, he's not there, but you have to believe me . . .' Matthew said.

Before Sarah could answer, a key turned in the door somewhere downstairs on the ground floor. Sarah looked startled and an American voice boomed up two flights of stairs.

'He's home early,' Sarah said.

Matthew lounged back in his armchair and nursed his drink.

'So why are you looking so guilty? I'm your husband, remember?'

Dinner that night was an uneasy affair, not least because Matthew insisted on calling Paul Saul and then correcting himself. Paul was even bigger than Matthew remembered, with the same military haircut and heavy, blunt features, like a face flattened with a shovel. When Sarah introduced Matthew to him, his square-jawed mouth fell open and his face drained of colour.

'Surprise?' Matthew said, tinkling the ice in his glass of gin and tonic.

For a long time Paul seemed unable to find the appropriate words, then something clicked in his head and he began the business of pretending to be pleased that Matthew had dropped by.

'So, how come?' he said, helping himself to a glass of mineral water, his face turning scarlet.

'How come what?'

'How come you're in Gibraltar?'

'I was delivered here by Poseidon himself. I'm sorry, I understand you're a Christian.'

'Hey, let me say right off that I'm just so sad about your daughter . . .'

'Me too,' Matthew said.

Matthew had Paul down as a vague annoyance who could be brushed aside easily. The current which had carried him gently to safety hadn't saved his life just so that he could leave the woman he loved in the vice-like grip of this big, over-eager American who blinked with sincerity every time Sarah asked him a question. Matthew was disgusted by his attentiveness.

'This wine,' Paul said over dinner, pulling a cork with his big, meaty hands just as effortlessly as a children's christmas cracker, 'is a Rioja.'

Matthew waited for him to continue.

'Yeah. So?'

'It's the wine of the region.'

Paul sniffed the neck of the bottle and closed his eyes.

'You can smell Spain,' he said with reverence.

'Really,' Matthew said. 'In my experience Spain smells like an open drain.'

Sarah had set the table in silence. There were candles burning and beyond the reflections of the candles, there were the lights of the Rock and the harbour. Matthew thought that Paul was immune to his rampant wit and began to enjoy himself. The meal was salad and cold meats, and Matthew commented that Sarah had never been much of a cook, narrowing his eyes at her as he said it. Matthew also said that it must be difficult for a big guy like Paul, who obviously enjoyed his food, to be with a woman who only ate to prevent death.

'We get along fine,' Paul said. Matthew hadn't drunk for a long time and the wine had gone to his head quickly. The view of the harbour made him think about his wild boat-trip with Ramirez, and some of that same spirit of recklessness was released by the wine.

'Is that right? You get along fine. Sarah? Is that right? You two get along fine?'

Sarah glared at Matthew, as Paul shovelled another forkful of cold meat into his mouth. They ate in silence for a while, then the topic drifted on to Paul's work.

'You should see the roof, Matthew,' Paul was saying. 'The roof on this church is just something else. Sometimes I just can't figure out how those guys made it so *tight*. I mean the lattice. Clever guys, the Moors.'

Matthew choked on wine and supressed laughter.

'Clever guys, the Moors,' he repeated, mocking Paul's eager delivery, and he raised his glass to Sarah and winked at her. She looked down at her lap.

'They built it as a mosque,' Paul said, 'but I guess holy is holy is holy.'

'Yep, holy is holy. Do you feel better now you've changed your name, Paul?'

Paul stopped chewing and his eyes turned to frozen glass. For a few moments he was terrifying, then he snapped back into his breezy earnestness.

'I guess it was a spiritual decision. Pass the pâté, baby,' he said.

Matthew had decided that he and Paul were direct opposites, and that was probably why Sarah had been attracted to him. Paul's down-home straightforwardness was making Matthew's head spin with anger.

'Do you want my wife to change her name too,' Matthew said. Paul cut away half the slab of pâté and laid it on his plate. 'I mean, are you thinking of making all this official? It's a sin isn't it, living together like this? Are you thinking of maybe marrying her?'

'I guess so. Good pâté, baby.'

Sarah clattered her fork on the table. Matthew only had eyes for Paul.

'She's worth a hell of a lot of money, Paul, but then you know that already. The settlement would be for around . . . let me see, twelve million. Except it isn't ever going to happen. You do realize that, don't you?'

'That the way you see it, Mat?'

'Don't call me that.'

Paul had eaten the slab of pâté in three swallows. He scraped the remains on to his knife and licked it off. Matthew wanted to grab Sarah there and then and drag her away from this monster.

'She made the first move on me you know, Mat. Down in your cellar. She said she wanted a man . . .'

Matthew and Sarah got to their feet at the same time. Sarah had tears in her eyes and she stared down at Paul's head.

'Paul, Jesus Christ, why are you being like this?'

Maybe somewhere two hundred feet below in the harbour, Ramirez was counting down from ten to one, waiting to hit the throttle. Matthew felt the same, waiting to let his engine rip.

'I guess I'm just teaching this guy the facts of life,' Paul said, apparently unconcerned. He finally put his fork down on the table and suppressed a polite burp.

'But for now I guess, Mat, that it would be best if you cooled off and sobered up a little. Maybe I should call you a taxi.'

Matthew realized he had stood up with a knife in his hand. If he could dispose of Rook then maybe he could dispose of Paul too. The insane notion of ending Paul's life there and then flashed by like a runaway express train.

'I'll use the phone in the bedroom, baby,' Paul said. 'Maybe you can cool this guy off a little.'

Paul stood up and stumped out of the room, wiping his mouth with a napkin. Matthew had wanted reaction, rage, jealousy. Sarah had said that Paul had been obsessed, but Matthew couldn't see how this guy could be obsessed by anything at all. There was something not right about Paul altogether and Matthew wondered how the hell Sarah could ever have got mixed up with him.

'Well stop him!' Matthew yelled at Sarah.

'No.'

'So you want me to leave?'

Matthew could hear Paul's dull voice vibrating upstairs in the room above on the telephone. The bedroom. Matthew felt the stroke of the throttle.

'Just for tonight,' Sarah said. 'Go to a hotel just for tonight.'

'Come with me.'

'I can't.'

'He's a fucking animal.'

'You made him like that. This isn't how he is. He's kind to me.'

Matthew grabbed Sarah's arms and stared into her eyes.

'What happened to you? You can see through this guy. Do you think he hasn't thought about the twelve million?'

'He isn't like that.'

'You used to be hard, Sarah. You used to swat guys like that like flies. OK, so you fucked him but that's over now. I fucked people too, but it was always you and me. Remember the cave? That cave at Koukounaries. I went back there. It wasn't until I saw that cave again that I realized that it was Rook who came between us. Before Rook we were OK. But Rook is dead now. I killed him for you . . .'

Sarah's eyes opened wide with wonder. Matthew knew there was no going back.

'He was dying anyway, but I paid someone to finish him. I saw his body afterwards. You look at me as if I were insane, but it was the only way. I wanted to cut off his ears and bring them to you. You're mine, Sarah, just like Tanya was mine, but no one is going to take you away from me . . .'

Sarah's mouth had fallen open. Matthew wouldn't allow her to break away from his grasp.

'You killed him?'

'Tell me you're not happy. Tell me it isn't what you've been wanting to hear for ten years. It's over, Sarah. That part of our lives is over. I should have killed him on the night it happened, but I didn't, because then I believed there were rules. Now I know there aren't any rules. I've found out that the world is a wild place. All you need is money and a gun.'

Paul came back into the room and slapped his huge hands together with a grin on his face. Sarah struggled out of Matthew's grasp quickly and began to dry her eyes. Matthew was already beginning to regret what he'd said, but another part of him knew that he had done the right thing. Given time, Sarah would see it his way.

'Hey, hey, let's not get excited in here,' Paul said, trying to take Sarah's arm. She pulled away from him too.

'Cab's on its way,' Paul said. 'He'll take you to a hotel I know. The bar will be open, maybe you can get a little more drunk than you already are.'

Matthew took a swing at Paul's Neanderthal head, but Paul grabbed his fist and twisted his arm up his back. It was a professional manoeuvre and Matthew felt a bolt of pain. There was no point trying to fight against a guy like Paul, but there was always the knapsack. A gun was power, just like cash. Sarah screamed at Paul to let Matthew go, and Paul grinned.

'Sure, honey,' he said and he shoved Matthew against a wall. There was a bluebird tattoo on his upper arm that flashed as he pushed Matthew away. Matthew grabbed the knapsack that was still lying beside the telephone. Sarah put her hands to her cheeks with horror. Matthew felt the engine inside kick into gear and a calmness came over him. The weight of the revolver brought him back to his senses. Paul was still smiling that big, unconcerned smile, with his huge hands on his hips. Matthew smiled back at him.

'How much do you earn a year, Paul?' Matthew said, and Sarah yelled, 'Oh, Matthew, for Christ's sake!'

'How much do you want to leave her alone?'

Paul had stopped grinning. Sarah was shaking her head at the floor.

'Think about it Paul,' Matthew said as he headed for the door. 'A million dollars? Two? Two and a half?'

3

That night, Matthew lay with the air-conditioning running at full speed, not to keep cool but to hear the sound of its whirring engine. After all that time aboard the boat, the sound of machinery soothed him, made him feel that progress was being made.

Every time he closed his eyes he saw Paul's face staring at him with its dull, mean expression. It could only be fatigue and insanity that kept on transposing Rook's face on to his. Matthew paced the room and then found a perch on the window-ledge, staring out at the darkness of the ocean, the twinkling lights of the harbour and of the naval patrol boats. Matthew's turmoil was ripping up his bowels and his heart seemed to know that there was danger out there somewhere.

In the hotel mini bar he found some relief. He drained six miniatures and the alcohol dampened the flames inside. After the eighth he discovered that he was talking out loud to himself, just as he had on board *Europe*.

'That shit. That fucking little shit. OK, OK, so he's a big little shit. You know what I mean . . .'

At 4 a.m. Matthew turned the TV on and began to flick through the channels, from language to language, nation to nation. There was German, French, Spanish, English, Arabic from across the bay and some languages that just made him laugh. Some channels had sober men in suits discussing world affairs, others had Italian women taking off their clothes for money. Matthew was lying on the bed, the TV light flickering on his face, reaching out occasionally to feel the plumpness of his knapsack, the potent weight of a loaded revolver.

'Maybe I'll just shoot the little shit . . . maybe I'll pay Ramirez . . .'

There was a knock at the door. Matthew flicked the TV off and the room was filled with the sound of gulls shrieking. The sky outside had already begun to turn grey. Dawn was breaking over the mountain.

4

'Who is it?' Matthew said, his revolver cocked in his hand.

'It's me, Tony.'

'Tony?'

'Tony Konstantinou, for Christ's sake.'

Instinctively, Matthew raised the revolver to head height and swung the door open. When Konstantinou saw the revolver he ducked back into the corridor, but Matthew grabbed his jacket lapel and dragged him inside. Then he locked the door and hooked on the chain.

'For fuck's sake,' Konstantinou said, his hand on his heart. 'Look, look, you haven't even got the catch on.'

Konstantinou tried to grab the revolver, but Matthew held it away from him. They stared at each other petulantly and then both began to laugh. Matthew looked Konstantinou up and down. The same immaculate suit, the blazing white shirt, but a fuzz of growth on his chin.

'What the hell are you doing here?' Matthew said and he sat down on the bed. Konstantinou had already spotted the parade of empty brandy and whisky miniatures on the bedside table.

'It isn't good to drink alone, Mr King.'

'Yeah, well, I've had a stressful few days.'

Konstantinou picked one of the miniatures up and sniffed it like a true detective.

'Got any more?' he said at last.

'Two whisky, two brandies.'

'Give me a brandy.'

Matthew knelt at the mini bar and tossed Konstantinou a brandy.

He twisted it open and swigged from the bottle.

'You're not an easy man to find,' Konstantinou said, leaning on the window-ledge.

'That's sort of deliberate,' Matthew said.

'It's lucky you used my name on the hotel register, otherwise I'd never have found you.'

Matthew had decided it wouldn't be a good idea to use his own name when he checked into the hotel. The name Konstantinou had seemed suitably exotic.

'This hotel was the last one I tried,' Konstantinou said.

'OK, look, I'm sorry I put you to so much trouble. You still haven't answered my question. What the fuck are you doing here?'

After a few moments they smiled at each other and shook hands. Matthew put the revolver back in his knapsack and they talked until the sun was high enough to fill Matthew's hotel room with golden sunshine.

5

'I've got another friend who works at the forensic laboratory in Athens,' Konstantinou said. 'He's a communist, so he did a little digging for me. It turns out that the hand that went missing really was a mistake. Some old guy in dispatch got the hand mixed up with a hand from a motorcycle accident. I mean it, Mr King, my country sometimes makes me ashamed . . .'

'Will you get to the point.'

'The day after you left, I sent the foot.'

'The foot?'

'Callow's foot. And I asked them to match that up with your blood sample. Two days later they faxed me the result . . .'

Konstantinou smiled triumphantly and flicked his cigarette out of the open window down fifty feet to the ground below.

'They said it's 99.9 per cent certain that whoever that guy was, he wasn't your half-brother. Not even a cousin. You know, it makes me think sometimes . . .'

Konstantinou had finished his second brandy and was starting on the first of the whiskies.

'. . . It makes me think sometimes about the world. About how they can know these things. I take a little drop of your blood and they can say for sure who you are.'

Matthew had leapt to his feet. He had been lying on the bed, listening to Konstantinou's story with his eyes half closed. The revelation that the body that washed up in Skiathos wasn't Matthew's half-brother after all had hit him like 2,000 volts.

'Wait a minute,' Matthew said. 'What are you saying?'

'I'm saying that the body wasn't Callow.'

Konstantinou took a swig of whisky. He was being casual and off-hand just to be perverse.

'Are you serious?' Matthew yelled.

Konstantinou shrugged his shoulders and turned to look out at the Rock of Gibraltar which was now bleached with early-morning sunlight.

'Yeah, I'm serious.'

Matthew began to work through the implications. There was another knock at the door and they both froze.

'Bedlinen,' said a fluting female voice.

'Later,' Matthew said to the floor and resumed his furious speculation.

Konstantinou left his perch on the window-ledge and went into the bathroom. He started to piss with the door open, the sound of his piss making him raise his voice.

'That's what I mean about the world. It makes me think that everything is connected. I read a story in the papers about that earthquake in Japan. There was an earthquake in Japan and it broke up the production lines of silicon chips. So, suddenly, there's a shortage of silicon chips for computers. And straight away there are guys in London and Chicago making a living from stealing the things. There are gangs of guys with guns in cities all over the world breaking into warehouses stealing these things . . .'

The stream of Konstantinou's piss stopped and then started again in a dribble.

'A security guard gets shot in the head in Prague. Why? Because there was an earthquake in Japan.'

He emerged from the bathroom, drying his hands on a fluffy white bath towel. His mouth fell open when he saw Matthew pointing his revolver at him.

'If you don't stop talking shit, I'll shoot you.'

Konstantinou smiled.

'OK.'

Matthew put the gun on the bedside table. He could tell that Konstantinou was bursting with pride at the work he had carried out, but nothing on earth would make him admit it.

'So, from the top . . .' Matthew said.

'I've told you. It wasn't Callow.'

'Who was it then?'

Konstantinou shrugged nonchalantly.

'I faxed the genetic fingerprint from the foot to Interpol in Paris. No record.'

'So why was he carrying Peter Callow's passport?'

Konstantinou sat down on the bed. He began to leaf through the hotel house magazine.

'How could some fish-gut eating islander ever work something like that out for himself?'

Konstantinou closed the magazine and turned to Matthew with a smile.

'Does the name Saul Hoffman mean anything to you?'

Matthew swallowed a mouthful of whisky too fast and he choked. Konstantinou stood up and patted him on the back gently.

'Hey, hey, you should be careful with that stuff. Drinking on an empty stomach . . .'

Matthew took a huge gulp of air.

'Did you say Saul . . .'

'Hoffman. Do you know him?'

Finally, Konstantinou's cool broke into a triumphant giggle.

'I haven't even started yet, Mr King . . .'

He punched his hand with his fist and declared, 'It's like I just said, the whole world is connected.'

6

In the days after Matthew had left Skiathos, Konstantinou had been busy. He'd been talking to the whole world. After the genetic profile from the foot drew a blank with Interpol, a boat fishing for mullet out of Koukounaries bay hauled up a badly decomposed head. Konstantinou took the head personally to the laboratory in Athens and established that it belonged to the same man.

He took a room in Piraeus, took some leave and set to work. He had a friend in the lab make up a dental profile, which Konstantinou faxed to police departments all around the world, asking for an ID on a murder victim. Two days later, the FBI ('the FB fucking I, Matthew!') gave him the name Saul Hoffman, along with an address.

Konstantinou got a phone number from the address in Nantucket and called it. A woman called Teale said the Hoffmans had moved out two months ago, just before their divorce became final and gave Konstantinou the number of Hoffman's ex-wife.

Saul Hoffman's ex-wife said that her husband had disappeared the day after they'd both appeared in court to settle his alimony payments. She hadn't heard from him since or received any money. She cried for half an hour on the phone, saying that the bastard had left her with almost half a million dollars' worth of debts and big guys in suits were measuring up her house. Konstantinou then asked her if she knew a man called Callow.

'She said that Callow and Hoffman were friends. They both

worked as designers in the same naval yard. She said they attended life classes together. Painting. I asked her if she knew where Callow was now and she said she didn't know. After that I told her that her husband was dead.'

Konstantinou paused in his explanation, as if this were a painful memory. Then he smiled.

'She tried hard to sound upset. I think it was the best news she'd had for months. I suppose he was insured.'

Matthew listened to Konstantinou's explanation and then picked up the phone and asked the hotel reception to give him an outside line.

'Well?' Konstantinou said, his eyes alight with triumph.

'Well what?' Matthew said, waiting for the line.

'Tell me I'm a fucking genius.'

'You are without doubt the most able and well-connected detective in the western world. Do you have Maria Callow's number?'

Konstantinou's look of delight turned into disbelief and then weary disgust.

'At least you could thank me.'

'I'll thank you when it's over. It won't be over until I speak to Maria Callow. Do you have her number?'

Matthew got a line and Konstantinou handed him a small leather notebook the size of a cigarette packet. Matthew flicked through the pages and then realized that it was laid out according to the Greek alphabet. Konstantinou snatched the book off him and found Maria Callow's number. Matthew began to dial.

'So why do you need to speak to Maria Callow?' Konstantinou said, not wanting to sound as if he'd been left behind.

'Work it out for yourself,' Matthew said, peering out at the harbour. Konstantinou sneered as if he knew the answer already and Matthew took pity on him.

'I think they did a swop,' Matthew said at last.

'Who did?'

'The real Peter Callow and the real Saul Hoffman.'

The connection was taking a while. Matthew could hear what

sounded like electronic gears shifting, wires fusing. All that military hardware in the belly of the mountain made Gibraltar's phone connections a little delicate.

'They did a swop of identities. It's the only thing that makes sense. Hoffman has an alimony obligation he can't meet. Maybe he wants to make a clean break. His friend Peter Callow has an idea . . . hello . . . hello Maria . . .'

Konstantinou was about to speak, but Matthew shushed him with his hand.

'Hello Maria, it's Matthew King. Listen, this is a bad line, so I'll have to be brief. I have Inspector Konstantinou with me and he needs some information about your brother to complete the identification of the body. Just hold the line a second.'

Matthew covered the mouthpiece and Konstantinou hissed.

'What the fuck are you talking about?'

'Ask her if her brother had a tattoo. Ask her if he had a bluebird tattoo on his upper arm . . . left arm . . . here.'

Matthew pointed to his upper arm. Konstantinou hesitated.

'Just do it,' Matthew said. 'A bluebird tattoo on his left upper arm.'

Konstantinou took the phone, still baffled.

'Why am I asking?'

'Because if Callow had a bluebird tattoo, he's here on the Rock, he's calling himself Paul Hoffman and he's sleeping with my wife.'

CHAPTER TWENTY-FOUR

I

At 9 a.m., the phone rang. It was Sarah and she was in tears.

'You're a fucking fool, Matthew,' were her first words.

'Oh, thank you. Good morning to you too.'

'I can't believe you offered him money.'

'I was angry.'

Matthew took the phone to the window and stared at the Rock. The entrances to the secret tunnels were more visible in daylight. Konstantinou had taken all of the bullets out of Matthew's revolver and was polishing them with a tissue. He'd said that there was so much sea salt on them that the gun would have blown up in Matthew's face if he'd tried to use it.

'But I told him you'd been through a lot,' Sarah said. 'He forgives you.'

Matthew shrieked incredulously. He unlocked the mini bar and took out a bottle of mineral water which he opened with the phone crooked between his chin and shoulder. He was shaking with fatigue and nervousness and the cold water froze his insides.

'He forgives me. Well then that makes me feel so much better.'

'And he wants to help you,' Sarah said.

Matthew sat down on the bed and Konstantinou gathered up the newly polished bullets. He began to push them into the empty chambers.

'Help me, how?' Matthew said.

'You said you wanted to speak to a journalist. Paul said he has friends on the *Herald Tribune* in New York. And in Paris.'

'Go on.'

He wants to talk to you, Matthew. He's upset, for God's sake.

Last night . . . after you'd gone . . . he cried.'

Matthew couldn't help himself and he let out a huge shriek of laughter. The idea of tears forming on that dull, expressionless face was just too ludicrous. Matthew's laughter was half hysteria, half burning anger.

'You see you're just so fucking sure of yourself, aren't you,' Sarah said as Matthew hooted with laughter. 'You think you know someone . . .'

'Sarah, I'm sorry.'

'He wants to talk so that you two can sort things out . . .'

'When?'

'He's been so kind to me, Matthew.'

'When?'

'Now. This morning. He's up at Lookout Point. He's sketching . . . He draws. He's an artist.'

There was a long pause.

'OK, Sarah, I'll go and talk to him,' Matthew said at last.

'You will?'

'Yeah. We need to clear the air . . .'

Matthew reached out a hand and Konstantinou handed him the loaded revolver.

'Where did you say he'd be?'

'Lookout Point. It's almost at the top of the mountain. You can see the whole world from up there.'

2

The centre of Gibraltar town looked like a recreation of England in the late fifties, except hot. The same shop fronts, the same English faces, but here and there the black cloak of a North African to relieve the drabness, and in a side street the incongruous image of an Oriental Jew sitting at a shoe-shine operated by a Moroccan street beggar, right there in the doorway of Boots the Chemist. The whole town had an uneasy, fortress feel to it, with the tension that frontiers create hanging in the air like ancient battle smoke.

Matthew shook Konstantinou's hand in the shade of an awning over a tobacco shop that sold cut-price cigarettes.

'I want to thank you, Tony, for everything you've done . . .'

Konstantinou rolled his eyes and stamped on a half-smoked cigarette.

'How many times do I have to say this. I'm coming with you.'

Matthew shook his head.

'You've done enough.'

'Here, here's a cab. Hey taxi!'

'You stay here, Tony. I'm serious. I already owe you . . .'

'If you offer me money, Mr King, I swear I'll kick you in the balls. This is my investigation and I want to see it to the end.'

The green and white taxi had pulled up at Konstantinou's feet. Konstantinou opened the door but Matthew didn't budge.

'Get in the cab.'

Matthew stretched his neck and wiped sweat from his face. It was almost ten and the sun on the Rock was murderous. Naturally, Konstantinou didn't feel it. Matthew spoke to the driver direct.

'Drive on.'

'No, no, wait.'

Matthew leant in to the taxi driver's window and waved his finger at his own temple.

'I'm sorry, my friend isn't used to the heat.'

'Get in the cab, Mr King.'

'I don't want to be responsible for you getting killed, Tony!'

The cab driver slumped into his seat, his yellow eyes moist with boredom.

'You want the cab or not?' he growled.

'Yes.'

'No.'

The cab driver shrugged and shifted gear. At that second, Matthew pushed Konstantinou back into the doorway of the tobacco shop and leapt into the cab. He slammed the door and locked it.

'Lookout Point,' Matthew said, and the cab pulled away, with Konstantinou still struggling to get to his feet.

The taxi driver was a native Gibraltan, short and dark, and as he drove past the huge Moorish castle at the foot of the mountain, he explained that this town had been besieged more times than any other square mile of territory in the world. And it had changed hands more often too. He listed all the nations who had held it: Phoenicians, Romans, Africans, Semites, Greeks, Carthaginians, British. All of them left a little piece of themselves here. Matthew guessed that he gave his little guided tour in the hope of getting a bigger tip, but he couldn't be sure. Sometimes, Matthew decided, people did things just for the sake of doing them.

'You know Lookout Point?' the driver said, as they began to climb the steep mountain road that curled around the Rock.

'No. This is my first time here.'

'You're in for a treat. You can see Africa, you can see Spain, you can see Gibraltar. It's the only place in the world where you can see three countries, two continents and two seas . . .'

As they climbed higher, the nations and continents and oceans began to come into view. To the south, the black shoulders of the Atlas Mountains, the second Pillar of Hercules. Directly below, the hot, white strip of the airport, and beyond that, the jumble of high rises and shanties of La Linea.

Higher still and the southern plain of Spain appeared, like a vivid green and brown map under a heat haze. The wild Atlantic to the west, the Mediterranean to the south . . .

The driver pointed out all the landmarks along the way. Matthew had his head against the window of the car, thinking hard about Peter Callow.

Some time, maybe years ago, Peter Callow had found out about the inheritance. He found out that he had a half-brother who had done rather better out of his mother's will than he had. His half-brother received £25 million, while he just inherited a pile of stones on some island in the Aegean. It was bad enough that his mother had given him away when he was a baby. Now there was this monstrous injustice, and so Callow had set about finding a way of getting his hands on what he thought was rightfully his.

Maybe to begin with it was just curiosity that sent him to visit Matthew's home. Naturally he couldn't have used his real name when he came to call, so he borrowed the name of his best friend, Saul Hoffman.

While he was staying at Matthew's house, he witnessed for himself the vastness of his half-brother's wealth, the despicable idleness, the bickering between Matthew and Sarah, the whole inglorious ugliness of their lives.

To begin with, he simply decided to seduce Matthew's wife and settle for half the inheritance. But that wouldn't have satisfied his aggravated sense of injustice. To get hold of all the money he would need to get rid of Matthew altogether, and the natural heir to the fortune, Tanya.

What Matthew didn't know for sure, he could fill in with intuition. After all, Callow was his half-brother, and it was their mother's tainted blood which they shared. Matthew remembered seeing the man he thought was an architect, sitting at his easel on their vast sweeping lawn, peering intently at every window of the house. It was then that the beauty and the completeness of the plot came to him, as elegant as the façade he was drawing.

Before he could dispose of Tanya and Matthew, he had to shed his old identity or risk being the prime suspect for the murders. That was when the idea of a swop came to him. Maybe Saul Hoffman was already close to the edge with debts, and when Hoffman's divorce became final, Callow made his offer, giving Hoffman the chance to start a new life and flee to Skiathos. If Hoffman and Callow were friends, and if they looked even remotely similar to each other, then the swop would have seemed plausible. After the exchange of ID and passports, Peter Callow couldn't allow the man who had taken his identity to carry on living. He'd hired someone in Greece to murder him on the hydrofoil, knowing that the body would be so badly cut up by the engine he'd be impossible to identify. Matthew surmised that the killer had also been hired to kill him. The fat guy in the bar in Athens. All along, Matthew's half-brother had been second-guessing Matthew's moves. Callow had sent Matthew

the cassette, knowing that the postmark would lure him to Skiathos. Once in Skiathos, Matthew would be an easy target for the
Greek hit man. If it hadn't been for Konstantinou, the plan
would have worked.

Matthew's theory also explained the mysterious name-
change from Saul to Paul. Now that Callow had his new identity, he could muddy the waters further by changing his name
and getting a new passport. The swop, the murders, the se-
duction of Sarah had all been so carefully worked out that
Matthew couldn't help but marvel at his half-brother's in-
genuity. But Matthew had been pretty ingenious too. And
lucky.

'Sometimes we come up here and we look out for the smuggler boats,' the driver was saying, curling the car around another
tight bend. 'That's why we call it Lookout Point. We radio the
coastguard to warn them and we get a reward.'

'That's very public-spirited of you,' Matthew said.

'Sure it is. Thirty pounds we get each time we call.'

At last, the driver pulled up in a parking space which had been
carved out of the sheer face of the rock. Beyond here, the road
was open to military personnel only. When Matthew got out of
the car, he could hear the stiff Atlantic breeze humming in the
communication wires that led down from the top of the Rock. A
few yards above his head, there was the opening to one of the
tunnels that led into the solid granite.

Matthew reached into his knapsack and gave the driver
double fare, saying he'd appreciated the guided tour. The driver
looked embarrassed and drove away quickly. Matthew guessed
he had just under £6,000 in cash left from the money he'd taken
with him to Skiathos. Along the way he'd spent around a million. If it was going to cost more, he'd pay it, but Matthew had
the feeling inside that at the end, this thing wouldn't be about
money.

On the other side of the road, there was a viewing area which
bowed out over the drop of the mountain, with a three-foot-high
wall around it. There were two coin-operated telescopes, pointing at the clear blue sky. In between them sitting at a flimsy

wooden easel, was Peter Callow, busy with his sketch of the world.

'Glad you could make it,' Callow said, not looking away from his drawing for more than a second. So far, he had filled in the Atlas Mountains and had just begun to sketch the coastline of La Linea.

'Do you draw yourself, Matthew?'

'No. My mother did.'

'You should try it. It kind of relaxes you.'

The wind blew cold. Somewhere down below, a helicopter scanned the sea for black boats, like a clumsy bird of prey. Callow angled his dark charcoal pencil against the grain of the paper on his easel and began to sketch a fringe of ocean. He then used his thumb to smudge the lines.

'You know, I'm curious,' Matthew said. 'About your name. You used to call yourself Saul. Now you call yourself Paul.'

'I guess you can call me whatever the hell you like,' he said with a chuckle.

'Then how about Peter. Peter Callow. That's your real name, isn't it?'

Callow kept on smudging the lines with his thumb, which he wiped on his black jeans. He was so big that the easel looked as if it might blow over if he breathed on it. Matthew was sitting on the wall with his back to the drop, holding on tightly to his knapsack.

'So you know,' Callow said, apparently deep in concentration with his drawing.

'I've worked most of it out. There are some parts I don't understand, but those parts I can fill in for myself.'

Callow angled his head around his easel to catch the outline of the power station which was still billowing crimson smoke into the air. He began to fill in the smoke with short stabs of the pencil.

'But I suppose what I really don't understand is why. Why someone with your intelligence should work so hard to get something that you could have had if you'd only asked. That was all you had to do. You could have knocked on my door that first day when you were pretending to be so impressed with my house and you could have told me who you were. You could have just come out and asked for your share of the money. I would have given it to you. I would have given the whole fucking thing to you. I would have run from that house as if it were on fire and screamed with joy.'

Callow laughed, still preoccupied. He bent down and picked up a rag from under his canvas chair. He wiped the charcoal off his fingers. Matthew slipped his hand into the knapsack and felt the butt of the revolver.

'Sure you would, Matthew,' he said and he wiped his nose vigorously, like a man who has just been swimming in the sea. 'But the money wasn't the whole thing.'

'What then?'

The wind moaned in the communication wires above their heads and Matthew thought he heard a voice from the mountain saying, 'He's all yours.' Callow got to his feet.

Matthew clutched the revolver.

'You killed my daughter,' Matthew said. 'You killed my sweet, innocent baby.'

Callow reached into the pocket of his black jeans and pulled out a crumpled sheet of paper. He smoothed it out and picked up a piece of rock. He rested the piece of paper on the ledge overlooking the sheer drop down to the ocean, and then laid the rock on top of it. The paper fluttered in the wind.

'That's your suicide note, Matty,' he said softly. 'It's a strange thing, but my handwriting is almost identical to yours. Maybe it's not so strange. I wrote some stuff about Sarah, about your daughter, about how you can't stand to go on alone. So now all you have to do is jump.'

Callow jerked his head towards the sheer drop as if Matthew would obey.

'No?' Callow said.

'No,' Matthew said and he reached into his knapsack. The sight of the butt of the revolver took Callow by surprise. At that moment Callow leapt from behind his easel and within seconds he had Matthew around the throat, pushing his head back over the sheer drop of the rock. Matthew had the revolver half in and half out of the knapsack. Matthew could feel himself being lifted off the ground and could feel the swirling air below him, nothing but gulls and wind and then hard rock.

Callow's face was close to Matthew's and he could smell the sweat and gum. Now Matthew could see the twin demons in his eyes, his mother and Rook combined in one ghastly look of determination. He managed to pull the barrel of the revolver clear of the knapsack but it was still pointing at the ground, pinned against Matthew's leg by the weight of Callow's body.

Matthew was almost clear of the wall. One more shove and he would be over. He felt for the safety catch with his thumb but he couldn't be sure if the bullet would hit Callow or go into his own leg. He had no choice but to find out.

A car pulled up in the lay-by opposite just as Matthew pulled the trigger. Over Callow's shoulder, Matthew caught a glimpse of the green and white taxi sign on the roof. There was a deep thud somewhere below Matthew's waist and an echo that rang around the mountain. But there was no pain. Matthew had fired but he felt no pain. Callow fell back against the wall and ground his teeth together in a silent exclamation of agony.

Matthew felt a dreadful calmness come over him. Konstantinou came and stood between Matthew and Callow.

'I'm going to arrest him, Matthew,' Konstantinou said.

Matthew was breathing hard, his neck sprained from the iron grip of Callow's huge arms.

'Get out of the way, Tony,' Matthew said.

'There are procedures,' Konstantinou said. 'There are procedures that have to be followed.'

'Get out of the fucking way.'

Matthew raised the revolver. Callow was bent almost double with his back against the wall. He was grinding his teeth again but taking deep breaths. He straightened up.

'The guy's insane,' Callow groaned. 'He tried to kill me.'

The wind blew and the wires moaned. Somewhere far below a patrol boat hit its siren and a speed boat reached an impossible speed. Maybe Ramirez, maybe not.

Konstantinou turned his back on Matthew and addressed

Callow in a voice loud enough to be heard above the moaning of the wind.

'Peter Callow, I am arresting you on behalf of the Hellenic Department of the Interior on suspicion of involvement in the murder of . . .'

Matthew pulled the trigger as the sirens down below were switched off. A helicopter thudded. Konstantinou was frozen to the spot as Matthew grabbed his half-brother's lifeless body and lifted it effortlessly over the wall, then watched as it dropped all the way down to hell.

Then he picked up his knapsack and emptied the money into the void as well. The gentle updraughts of warm air around the mountain kept the bills floating and swirling around the Rock for a long time before they all finally fell into the ocean.

POSTSCRIPT

Matthew had no idea how long he'd spent leaning over the precipice, watching the money float down into the crashing breakers. The body hung on a jagged outcrop for a few seconds and was then sucked into the ocean by a huge wave which looked to Matthew like a white crested emissary of Poseidon, snatching the carrion to drag it down into some sunless cavern, deep beneath the Continental Shelf.

When he straightened, Konstantinou was wiping his eyes and Matthew looked at him for a long time, while the wind moaned in the communication wires. Suddenly, from nowhere, a Barbary ape the size of a small child skipped on to one of the upturned telescopes and twitched into the wind. Then, in one lightning manoeuvre, it jumped on to the wall, grabbed the suicide note which Callow had written and disappeared on to the rock face below.

'I've never seen anyone shot before,' Konstantinou said.

'I'm going to see my wife now,' Matthew said. 'She's down there somewhere.'

They both looked down on Gibraltar town, a scruffy pink and white mirage beneath the heat haze.

'What will you tell her?' Konstantinou said.

'The truth. You can be my witness. She'll believe you.'

Matthew realized that he was still clutching the revolver. He tossed it into the abyss and they both set off walking down the winding mountain road.